Til Death
Do Us Party

**The Liv and Di in Dixie Mystery Series
by Vickie Fee**

Death Crashes the Party

It's Your Party, Die If You Want To

One Fete in the Grave

Til Death Do Us Party

Til Death Do Us Party

Vickie Fee

KENSINGTON BOOKS
KENSINGTON PUBLISHING CORP.
http://www.kensingtonbooks.com

KENSINGTON BOOKS are published by

Kensington Publishing Corp.
119 West 40th Street
New York, NY 10018

All Kensington titles, imprints, and distributed lines are available at special quantity discounts for bulk purchases for sales promotion, premiums, fund-raising, educational, or institutional use.

Special book excerpts or customized printings can also be created to fit specific needs. For details, write or phone the office of the Kensington Sales Manager: Attn.: Sales Department. Kensington Publishing Corp., 119 West 40th Street, New York, NY 10018. Phone: 1-800-221-2647.

Kensington and the K logo Reg. U.S. Pat. & TM Off.

First Printing: April 2018
ISBN-13: 978-1-4967-1598-2
ISBN-10: 1-4967-1598-5

eISBN-13: 978-1-4967-1599-9
eISBN-10: 1-4967-1599-3

10 9 8 7 6 5 4 3 2 1

Printed in the United States of America

For my sensational siblings,
Pam and Chris

ACKNOWLEDGMENTS

Thanks to the kind bus drivers and bartenders in Las Vegas for answering nosy questions. Thanks to the team at Kensington for their support. Thanks to my editor, Martin Biro, for his enthusiasm and insight. Gratitude to my agent, Jessica Faust, for her patience and advice—and the killer title on this one. Thanks to my blogmates at Chicks on the Case—Cynthia, Ellen, Lisa, Kellye, and Marla—for sharing wisdom and always making me laugh. Thanks to my sister Pam and her neighbors, Lisa, Shelley, and Delta, for being my fan club and East Coast marketing team. And much love to my husband, John, for his indulgence and encouragement.

Chapter One

Landing in Las Vegas was somewhat akin to touching down in Oz. We'd barely left the tarmac before being greeted by the flashing lights and ringing music of the airport slot machines. It was all we could do to drag our menfolk away from the siren call of the one-arm bandits. Mama, my mother-in-law Miss Betty, my best friend Di, and I took our respective partners by the hand and pulled them away. I elbowed my husband Larry Joe in the ribs and caught my mother-in-law giving her husband Daddy Wayne a you'd-better-behave look.

"Really," Mama said, admonishing her fiancé, Earl. "Can't y'all wait until we get to a real casino? I think there are more exciting things to see in Las Vegas than the inside of an airport."

Being in a not-married, still tentative relationship, Dave was the only man who got let off the hook. Di brushed her hand against his and he interlaced his fingers with hers. I shot Larry Joe a knowing look, which he returned with a smirk. As close friends of the couple, we'd had a ringside seat for their on-again, off-again romance, which certainly looked on-again at the moment.

We'd journeyed to Las Vegas for Mama and Earl's wedding. Her original plans for the nuptials had included a gondola ride out to a small island in the man-made pond on Earl's farm. And swans. And a guest list nearly as large as the population of Dixie, Tennessee, the small town we all call home.

As a professional party planner by trade, I could have accommodated a gondola of sorts, and probably the other items on her wish list, as well. But now Mama had moved on to a whole new wedding vision. She and her congenial groom were to be married in a classic Vegas chapel with a minister dressed as Elvis. Dixie's proximity to Memphis meant I could have found an Elvis impersonator without much difficulty. But the chapel where Mama and Earl's wedding was booked had three Elvis-style ministers on-site every day until midnight, which is definitely convenient.

We headed to the baggage carousel to collect our checked luggage. In addition to a small carry-on Earl was toting for her, Mama had checked a large suitcase, cosmetic bag, and the equivalent of a steamer trunk—the kind of case on rollers traveling salesmen use to transport their samples. To say she has a lot of baggage would be an understatement fraught with emotional connotations. She never travels light, but Mama was especially overpacked this trip because she and Earl planned to rent—or buy, at the right price—a Winnebago and set off on their honeymoon from Las Vegas for a tour of the Southwest.

The rest of us retrieved our average-sized luggage,

while Dave and Larry Joe helped Earl with Mama's belongings. Mama and Miss Betty had to swat at Daddy Wayne's arm when he attempted to help the other men with the load. My father-in-law had had a heart attack about a year ago and all of us, especially my mother-in-law, now keep a close watch on his health.

We hauled our gear to the curb out front and waited along with other travelers for the shuttle to arrive and deposit us at our hotel. The shuttle driver put up a fuss over the size of Mama's largest case, but Mama gave him one of her mean, squinty looks. He sized her up, with her face set like flint, and apparently decided she wasn't someone he wanted to tangle with. He acquiesced and used bungee cords to strap the case behind the driver's seat.

Before we even pulled away from the curb, Mama had struck up a conversation with a woman from Georgia, who had made the trip to see her new grandchild. She was not happy that her daughter had chosen to live in Sin City, and even less thrilled with her "no-account, deadbeat son-in-law."

Mama cut off the chatty Georgian with the not so peachy attitude, saying she had to phone her nephew to let him know we'd made it in. My first cousin, Little Junior, is the only son of Mama's only sibling, Uncle Junior. My uncle lives in Phoenix, but his son currently lives in Las Vegas. Everyone on the shuttle could hear my mama's side of the conversation.

"Little Junior, this is your Aunt Virginia. We've made it in and are on the way to the hotel now. . . . Your cousin Liv, her husband Larry Joe, and her in-laws Wayne and Betty McKay, and a couple of friends of ours. Oh, and my fiancé Earl, of course. No, no. We're on the complimentary shuttle. Is he? Well . . . Can you come to the hotel tonight or will we see you tomorrow . . . ? Okay, that sounds wonderful. Just give me a buzz. Love you, too, darlin'."

Mama put her cell phone back in her purse and announced, "Little Junior is going to come to the hotel this evening. I can't wait to see him. Said his daddy is going to try to drive up from Phoenix for the wedding. I'll believe it when I see it."

It was the first time in Las Vegas for all eight of us. On the ride from the airport, we gawked like the tourists we were as we passed palm trees, the Statue of Liberty, the Eiffel Tower, and some of the biggest hotels I'd ever seen. In addition to Mama's loud southern accent, I overheard snippets of conversations among other passengers speaking Spanish, and what I guessed to be Japanese.

The shuttle stopped at the front entrance under the large portico of our big, but not too big, nice but moderately priced hotel-casino. I'd like to be able to take credit for booking it. Since I'm a professional planner, a task like this one would normally get dumped into my lap. But Mama and Earl had enlisted a travel agent to handle all the arrangements, saying they didn't want to impose, especially after my assistant Holly and I had already put a lot of work into planning the wedding in Dixie that they had decided to cancel. It was true I had taken some time away from my business, Liv 4 Fun, to work on Mama's eccentric wedding ideas. But I had put even more time into tracking down a killer after

Earl had been arrested for a murder he didn't commit.

I had given up the wedding-planning portion of my business a couple of years ago—too much drama—but still occasionally got roped into planning a wedding for family. However, I'd rather plan a wedding any day, even for my high maintenance mama, than to look for a murderer, especially when the accused is someone I care about. With Earl's name cleared and the real killer behind bars, I was determined to enjoy our trip to Las Vegas, despite my mother and all her baggage.

A porter loaded our luggage onto a large cart. Earl, who was picking up the tab for the travel and accommodations for the whole entourage, checked us in and handed us our key cards. We followed the porter up to our block of rooms on the sixth floor to drop off our bags. The guys were itching to get down to the casino. But Daddy Wayne wanted to hit the early bird special at the hotel buffet, and Mama was hungry, so the casino would have to wait. I wanted to stretch out on the bed for a bit after the long flight, but clearly I was not in charge of the schedule.

"Everybody freshen up a bit and we'll meet by the elevators in fifteen minutes," Mama said, disappearing into her room without waiting for a response. I knew that Mama's room had a connecting door to Earl's room—for after the wedding. She felt it was important to explain that to me for some reason. I also knew that Di had a connecting room with Dave because Mama told me when she booked the hotel she didn't know what arrangements would be convenient for them. Frankly, I didn't know either, but felt certain they could figure that out for themselves. But Mama being so accommodating to that arrangement seemed a bit out of character for her. She'd been full of surprises lately—from announcing her engagement without warning a little over a month ago to deciding to get married in Las Vegas instead of having a more traditional wedding in Dixie.

After a quick stop in the bathroom to use the facilities and apply some fresh lipstick, I decided to allow myself the luxury of stretching out on the bed with my feet up for five whole minutes. My head had just hit the pillow when my phone dinged that I had a text. I was sorely tempted to ignore it, but couldn't resist checking to see who it was. It was from Holly, my invaluable assistant at Liv 4 Fun.

> I hate to interrupt your vacation, but please call when you have a moment.

Holly's not the needy sort, so I knew she wouldn't ask me to call if it wasn't important.

"Hi, Holly, what's up?"

"How's glorious Las Vegas?"

"We just arrived. We're going down for an early dinner in a few minutes."

"I'm sorry to bother you. . . ."

"Don't be silly. It wasn't really fair of me to leave town when we have a big event scheduled this week. So, what's going on?"

"I'm afraid we've hit a huge snag with the banquet and sock hop," Holly said.

"What's wrong?"

"We've lost our venue."

This was huge. Having the band cancel, or a vendor not come through with decorations, or transportation issues was a headache, but there were work-arounds for those problems. Losing the space where an event was to be held at the last minute, especially for a large group—in this case a high school class reunion—was a major setback.

"How could that happen? Did Sindhu and Ravi have a fire?"

Sindhu and Ravi Patel owned and managed the only hotel in Dixie. They were professional, dependable, and they were also personal friends. I couldn't imagine a scenario, other than fire or flood, in which they would cancel an event booking.

"No fire, thankfully, but just as catastrophic for us, I'm afraid. The health department has shut down the restaurant and there's no possibility of it reopening before next week," Holly said, exhaling a mournful sigh.

"No way? Not even if we offer to pitch in with repairs?"

"I'm afraid not. I already offered to bring in reinforcements. Floor and drain repairs to address 'imminently dangerous backflow' require ordering materials, two days' worth of work, and at least a full day for the concrete to set and dry. That's in addition to a full day of moving out appliances and doing a steam cleaning of the walls to address a 'serious accumulation of grease' behind the appliances. Then the health department will have to do a new inspection before they can get approval to reopen."

"That sucks," I said, summing up our situation as eloquently as I could manage.

"Ravi apologized profusely and offered to give an additional discount to the Class of 'Sixty-Eight members who would be staying at the hotel, on top of the good room rate he had already provided. I told him that wouldn't be necessary. He and Sindhu will be taking a financial hit with the restaurant's closure, plus plenty of disgruntled guests who won't be getting the breakfast special. I guess I should have checked with you about that. . . ."

"No, no, Holly, you made the right call. We just have to figure out what to do now."

"Well, we know the country club is already booked, since that was our first choice. I checked with the hotels in Hartville and their dining and meeting rooms are already booked."

"Since they're having the sock hop at the high school immediately afterward, we can't hold the banquet in Memphis or Jackson, even though that would open up a lot more possibilities," I said.

"Not on our budget."

"That's true," I said, recalling how the reunion committee had wanted to hold a tight line on expenses so as many classmates as possible could afford to attend.

"And we can't move the dinner to the school gym," she noted.

The gym was out for a variety of reasons: no kitchen, lack of space, and most germane, it had taken a major campaign just to get the school board to agree to the sock hop, and that included several caveats.

Larry Joe walked over and tapped on his watch to remind me it was feeding time for Mama and his dad. I got up, slipped my shoes back on, and grabbed my purse. I trailed behind my husband into the hallway, still talking to Holly.

"Do you think Earl would let us use his tractor barn?" Holly said, obviously feeling desperate.

"We'll save that as a last resort," I said. "In the middle of August, I think we want to stick with an indoor, air-conditioned venue."

"I know. Plus, we need a space with a kitchen. George is still willing to prepare the dinner, if we can provide a space for him to work in."

I thought for a long moment.

"Try the VFW, the Elks Lodge, and the Moose Lodge—and any of the churches with larger parish halls that would allow us to serve alcohol on church property."

"Gotcha, darlin'."

Between dealing with my high maintenance mama and troubleshooting event difficulties back home, I had a sinking feeling this might turn out to be the most stressful vacation ever.

Chapter Two

Daddy Wayne was impatiently holding the elevator door open for me as I ended my call with Holly.

"Liv, your cousin is going to meet us in the lobby beside the grand staircase," Mama said as our whole group piled into the elevator. Everybody was there right on time. I think we all were being solicitous of Mama, since we were here for her wedding. And in general, it's easier to just humor her.

We stepped out of the elevator and everyone fell in line behind Mama, who made a beeline toward the lobby staircase. She can move with remarkable speed when she wants to, for someone of her age and girth.

The last time I remembered seeing Little Junior he was a pimple-faced teenager who stood about five-foot-three. He looked about the same height now, but the acne on the sides of his face had been replaced with muttonchop sideburns. Jet black hair lapped his collar and heavy gold aviator glasses completed his pint-sized Elvis wannabe appearance.

Mama, who's nearly six feet tall, squealed and scooped her nephew into a bear hug, then released him, took a step back, and cupped his face in her hands. "You are a sight for sore eyes," she said, before planting a big kiss on his forehead. "It's been too long."

"You too, Aunt Virginia," he said, gazing up at her. "I'm so happy about your upcoming marriage. I wish you both every happiness. Where's the lucky groom?"

Earl stepped up and offered a handshake to my diminutive cousin. "Pleased to make your acquaintance, Little Junior. Call me Earl or Uncle Earl, if you're so inclined."

I had the distinct impression he'd prefer to be called just Earl.

"Congratulations, Uncle Earl. You're getting a real treasure in my aunt Virginia. She's as sweet as pun'kin pie."

"You remember Larry Joe and his parents, Wayne and Betty McKay. And these are our dear friends, Di Souther and Sheriff Dave Davidson, who were a big help during Earl's recent troubles."

After hugs and handshakes all around, Earl said, "Virginia and I are taking everyone to supper." Turning to Little Junior, he continued, "Son, this is your town. Where should we go to eat?"

Little Junior said it would be hard to beat the buffet right here in the hotel. This obviously pleased Daddy Wayne, who was pacing back and forth impatiently. "And, if you don't mind, I'll ask my girlfriend, Crystal, to join us for dessert when her shift ends."

"That sounds like a plan. We'd love to meet her," Mama said.

Little Junior texted Crystal as we walked toward the restaurant. My father-in-law was sprinting toward the buffet, but just before he reached the finish line, Earl edged past him and told the cashier to put all nine of us on his credit card.

"I don't feel right letting Earl pay for everything, including meals," Larry Joe said to me in a hushed tone.

"I know, me too," I said. "But Earl has a heart of gold, and he's almost as stubborn as my mama. I don't think there's any point in trying to argue with him. We'll just have to think of something extra nice to do for Mama and Earl—we'll call it a wedding gift."

My husband nodded approvingly.

Daddy Wayne headed for the feeding trough before all of our party had even made it through the turnstiles.

"I swear you'd think Wayne hadn't eaten for days, the way he's behaving," my mother-in-law said, looking embarrassed. "Son, you need to help me rein in your dad a bit. I know he's on vacation and it's okay for him to splurge a little. But I don't want him clogging his arteries after having those stents put in."

"Mama, we're only going to be here for a few days, so don't worry yourself," Larry Joe said. "Even if he goes completely off the rails with his diet, I don't think he can do too much damage in such a short time. But we'll try to pick some healthier places to eat and avoid the all-you-can-eat buffets after tonight."

The waiter pushed together two tables to accommodate our group. The large restaurant was a little noisy for conversation, but we didn't have any trouble hearing Mama or Little Junior over the din. As his Elvis appearance suggested, Little Junior was a bit of a performer. He regaled us with his plans for a career in show business. Mama listened with rapt attention and said very little, which is unusual for her. But she's always doted on her only nephew. I'd always assumed it was because she had two daughters, so he was like the son she never had.

Except for his diminutive stature, Little Junior was the spitting image of his daddy, from the slant of his forehead to his tendency to self-aggrandizement.

"I took voice lessons for over a year to refine my natural singing talent. And I worked with a choreographer who specializes in routines for Elvis tribute artists. We don't like to be called impersonators, because we each bring our own Elvis style to the stage. I placed second overall in one Elvis tribute competition and I took first place in my height category," he said.

"Height category?" Di whispered to me. I gave her ankle a gentle kick.

"That's wonderful," Mama said, beaming with pride.

"I've been in the chorus of a couple of shows with multiple tribute artists. And I've had some big ovations at Elvis tribute nights at various clubs. I'm just waiting for my big break. In the meantime, I'm driving a cab to pay the bills."

Little Junior's phone buzzed. "Excuse me for a moment," he said, holding up his hand and turning sideways in his chair to take the call.

I had lost count of how many trips my father-in-law had made to the buffet, although I'm sure Miss Betty was keeping track. Yet, as he cleaned what had to be at least his second plateful of desserts, he still groused when Little Junior suggested we move to the casual food court area.

"Crystal just finished her shift in the casino and says she'll meet us at the ice-cream parlor."

"What's her job in the casino?" I asked.

"She's a cocktail waitress. She makes pretty good tips, especially when someone's on a winning streak."

Feeling stuffed, I decided to pass on dessert. In fact, feeling the need to burn off a few calories after a big meal, I wished it were a longer walk to the food court—like a couple of miles.

Despite having already had sweets at the buffet, Daddy Wayne and Earl went straight to the counter at the ice-cream parlor. Mama called out to Earl, "Get me a scoop of chocolate ice cream, will you, hon?"

Di and I exchanged a look of disbelief.

In a moment, we were approached by a bleached blonde in a short-skirted black uniform with a keyhole neckline that showed off her ample cleavage. My cousin slipped his arm around Crystal's waist and she slung her arm around his shoulders as he introduced her. She stood about half a head taller than my petite cousin. I'm not a good judge of age, but she looked about twenty years older than Little Junior to me.

"Everybody, this is my sweetheart, Crystal Pryor."

I was surprised when Mama jumped up and gave

Crystal a big welcome-to-the-family hug, but I felt obliged to follow suit. Larry Joe and Dave stood up and exchanged polite handshakes with her.

Earl and Daddy Wayne returned from the ice-cream counter. After placing their sundaes on the table and handing Mama her single scoop on a sugar cone, both men nodded and exchanged hellos with Crystal.

"Sit down, sweetie, you've been on your feet all day," Little Junior said, pulling a chair out from the table for her, and giving her the seat of honor next to Mama, the matriarch of our little clan.

I had expected Crystal to have a husky voice, but instead she spoke in a sweet, singsong tone. Goes to show you can't judge by appearances.

As during dinner, when Mama had fallen quiet and let Little Junior do all the talking, she listened to Crystal with keen interest, interrupting only to prompt her for details, and occasionally to mention what a catch my cousin was.

Crystal explained that she had worked as a waitress most of her life, and at this particular casino for the past six years. She was divorced, with no kids. She actually grew up in Las Vegas and her mother still lived in town. She stopped short of saying she and Little Junior were living together, wisely assessing that information might meet with my mama's disapproval. But I got the distinct impression they were sharing living quarters.

Crystal stood up and patted Little Junior on the shoulder. "I'm going home to soak in a hot bath."

He stood and gave Crystal a sweet peck on the cheek. "I'll call you later. I'm going out in the cab for a few hours to make some cash."

Crystal sashayed away.

"Little Junior, if you've got the meter running, us women can be your first fare," Mama said, glancing around the table.

"And just where are you women off to?" Earl asked, eyebrows raised.

"I want to go run over to the wedding chapel and take a quick look around. We've only seen pictures on the computer. I want to see for myself where we'll be getting married."

"Maybe I should come with you. I don't know if y'all should be wandering around a strange city by yourselves," Earl said.

"It's still daylight, for Pete's sake. And we won't be by ourselves. Little Junior is going to be our driver. Aren't you, hon?" she said.

"Yes, ma'am. Don't you worry, Uncle Earl."

Earl's right eye twitched and I suspected he was still adjusting to a pint-sized Elvis calling him "uncle."

"What am I supposed to do while you're gone?"

This proved Earl was in love. I believe most men could find plenty to do in Las Vegas out of the sight line of their significant other. *Maybe he would be able to rest comfortably under my mama's thumb after they're married*, I thought.

"My guess is all of you men will make a beeline to the casino as soon as we're gone," Mama said.

"We can leave whenever you're ready, Aunt Virginia," Little Junior said.

"Liv, Betty, Di, are we ready to roll?"

"Virginia, I hate to beg off, but please excuse

me," my mother-in-law said. "I have a headache. I think I need to go upstairs and lie down for a bit."

My instincts told me Miss Betty's headache was named Wayne McKay, and she wanted to be close enough to check on him if he stayed in the casino longer than she thought he should.

"What about you two?" she said, her eyes darting between Di and me.

"I'm game," Di said.

"Let's go," I added.

We all stood up and Mama took a step toward Earl. He picked up on his cue, leaned over, and gave her a little kiss.

Daddy Wayne and Earl were given strict instructions on how much they were allowed to gamble before calling it a night. I shot Larry Joe an admonishing glance that I hoped was discreet.

"If you feel the need to just flush money down the toilet, go to the bar and drink a few of the high-priced beers," Mama said, before turning about face and marching toward the front door. Di and I fell in step behind her and Little Junior scurried ahead to open the door for her, although a doorman beat him to it. We waited under the portico while Little Junior went to fetch the cab.

Once my cousin was out of earshot, I had to ask, "Mama, you seemed to take a real shine to Crystal, which kind of surprises me. She's a little old for him, don't you think?"

"Well, you know Little Junior's mama died when he was only thirteen. And his first stepmom was no prize," she said, before turning to Di and adding,

"My brother has been married twice more since then, and is currently divorced."

Turning back to me, she continued, "I think a more mature woman, a mother figure if you will, might be just what Little Junior needs. Besides, Crystal seems reasonable and at least she can hold down a job."

Little Junior pulled up to the curb and the doorman opened the door to the backseat for us. Mama walked around him, opened the front door, and slid onto the front passenger seat.

"Darlin', do you know where the Burning Love Wedding Chapel is?" Mama asked.

"Sure do. In fact, I've been meaning to stop by. I put in an application there and want to check and see if I'll be getting an interview."

"What kind of job are you applying for?" she asked.

"Performing weddings as one of the Elvis ministers."

"Don't you actually have to be a minister to do that?"

"I am a licensed minister, Aunt Virginia," he said earnestly. "I've been ordained by a religious organization recognized by the county clerk's office. And the county issued me a certificate that gives me authority to officiate at weddings."

"Didn't you at least take a few seminary classes before you got ordained?" Mama asked.

"No, ma'am. I'm just performing weddings, not preaching or proselytizing. People who want a religious ceremony generally go to a church, not a chapel in Vegas."

"That sounds reasonable," she said. "Have you performed a wedding yet?"

"Yes, ma'am. I officiated at a friend's wedding on a hilltop overlooking Lake Mead. It was a really beautiful occasion. There's something special about launching a couple on their lifelong journey of love."

"That's poetic, Little Junior. I think you're a romantic at heart," Mama said.

"That's what Crystal says."

He looked over at Mama and I thought I could detect a blush to his cheek. I turned to Di, who just rolled her eyes.

We pulled up in front of the Burning Love Wedding Chapel on the Strip. My cousin hopped out and hurried around to open Mama's door. Di and I had already climbed out by the time he helped Mama to her feet. His taxi was a midsize sedan, not as roomy or as easy to exit as my mother's Cadillac.

The chapel was sweet—a whitewashed building, topped with a steeple. The sign out front said OPEN TIL MIDNIGHT SEVEN DAYS.

We entered through a door in the center of the building. To one side was the steeple-topped wing, with a chapel that seated fifty. To the other side were two other chapels, one able to accommodate a good-sized crowd and the other a very cozy space for about fifteen guests, according to the information Mama had been given by the travel agent.

The center of the building had a reception area, with a love seat that looked like a backseat framed by a bumper and vintage Cadillac tail fins. There was also a desk and a couple of tables and chairs, where prospective customers could peruse wedding photos and pricing information.

The woman at the reception desk was wearing a trim business suit and a corsage. As we approached, with my cousin leading the way, she said, "Junior, we haven't had time to process your application. As I told you, we'll call if we want to schedule an interview and audition."

"I know, I know," Little Junior said. "This is my aunt from Tennessee. She and her fiancé have a wedding booked here day after tomorrow. She just got into town and wants to take a quick look around."

"Oh, well, welcome to the Burning Love Wedding Chapel. I'd be glad to show you around. My name is Taylor and I'm the wedding coordinator," she said, extending her hand to Mama.

"I'm Virginia Walford. My fiancé, Earl Daniels, and I are scheduled to get married at six p.m. on the twelfth."

Taylor scanned through the register and said, "Ah, yes. You're booked in the It's Now or Never Chapel for a deluxe wedding package. Very nice."

She tapped a few keys on the computer and the copier shot out a printed sheet of paper.

The It's Now or Never Chapel was the smallest one on-site, since there would only be seven of us, other than the bride and groom. Or eight, if Little Junior's girlfriend accompanied him. I supposed it was within the realm of possibility that Uncle Junior could even show up.

"Ms. Walford, if you and your friends will come with me, I'll give you a tour of the facility," Taylor said. She grabbed a clipboard, put the paper she had retrieved from the printer on it, and waved for us to follow. She walked at a brisk pace, her snug skirt showing off her assets.

"If you'd like to take a peek, we have a wedding in progress in the Blue Hawaii Chapel."

We looked through the heart-shaped glass windows in the double doors leading into the medium-sized chapel. The floor was covered in royal blue plush carpeting, and arrangements of tropical flowers flanked a stained-glass window depicting a sunset.

An Elvis tribute artist cum minister, or maybe it was vice versa, was singing "Love Me Tender," accompanied by the strains of a synthesizer. The bride and groom were standing in front of him with their backs to us. She had on a short, mostly white sundress and a wreath of flowers crowning her head. He was wearing khaki shorts and a Hawaiian shirt.

There were a few scattered guests seated on padded pews. When Elvis finished his number, a man and woman sitting on the front pew got up and stood to either side of the happy couple. The minister said a few words in a passable southern accent—although it wouldn't impress the home crowd in Memphis—his mouth sporting the trademark Presley lip curl. The attendants handed him the rings, which the couple then exchanged after turning to face each other. Reverend Elvis sang a short medley of Elvis tunes before pronouncing them husband and wife.

While the resident Elvis was crooning, I couldn't help but smile as I caught a glimpse, out of the corner of my eye, of my cousin thrusting his chest forward and arching his upper lip in a lopsided sneer.

The minister lunged into an Elvis karate pose with his hand outstretched dramatically and said, "You may kiss the bride."

The guests broke out in applause as the newlyweds locked lips in a passionate kiss.

"Right this way," Taylor said, putting her hand on Mama's shoulder, prompting us to move along.

"That Elvis did a nice job and sounded pretty good on 'Love Me Tender,'" Di said.

"I know *he* thinks so," Little Junior muttered quietly.

"We set a high standard for all of our performing ministers," Taylor said.

There was no one in the small chapel, which was booked for Mama and Earl's nuptials. It was all white, with white cushioned seats on the chairs, a white wall, and white flower arrangements.

"This is the It's Now or Never Chapel," Taylor said, walking down the aisle to the front as we followed. She looked down at her clipboard.

"I see you have ordered live pink and white rose arrangements, which will replace the standard arrangement of carnations and daisies here. Very nice. The floor is white, but you may opt to add an aisle runner in your choice of colors."

Looking to Di and me, Mama asked, "What do you two think? Should I add a pink runner to match the flowers?"

"I don't think you need anything to compete with your purple dress," I said, thinking about how a minister dressed as Elvis would attract enough attention.

"I think you're right," Mama said.

"You've booked a short rehearsal time the afternoon before the wedding, which is unusual, but provided on request," Taylor said. "Of course, the live floral arrangements won't be brought in until the day of the wedding—to ensure they're fresh.

"You can have the minister escort the bride in, if you choose. He'll go over all that with you at the rehearsal. But I thought I'd mention it in case you were still undecided about that aspect. The bride may choose to walk down the aisle unescorted if she prefers. Any questions?"

"Is there a dressing room here? It may sound silly for a mature bride, but I'd prefer it if Earl didn't see me in my dress before the ceremony."

Thinking about my mama as a bride made my eyes go all misty. Earl already seemed like part of the family—to me and Larry Joe and my in-laws, at least. My younger sister, Emma, was being a horse's patoot about Mama getting remarried, even though it had been almost five years since our daddy passed away.

Taylor told us there were dressing rooms for the bridal parties, then led the way for us to check them out. They were tucked behind the main reception area in the center of the building, along with the restrooms. Little Junior remained in the reception area while Di and I followed Mama and Taylor to the dressing rooms.

Taylor was busy telling us all the things Mama could add to her wedding package—for a price, of course. Suddenly we heard some raised voices and scuffling noises coming from out front. We rushed down the little hallway leading to the reception desk and found my cousin and the Elvis minister we'd seen performing the wedding up in each other's faces, exchanging angry words and chest thumps.

". . . you should try putting in an application at one of those sad, little chapels downtown, where the standards are low. Even with your shoe lifts, you're too much of a shrimp to perform here. Not to mention, your singing sucks."

The idea that my cousin might be so short even with shoe elevators caught me by surprise. But a more pressing concern was that it looked like he was about to throw a punch at a guy who stood a good half foot taller than him. Before I could take it all in, Mama had marched over and stepped between the two men and given her nephew a sharp shove to the middle of his chest.

"Little Junior, you stop this nonsense and behave yourself, right now," she said, giving him one of her mean, squinty looks.

Taylor had grabbed the other man by the arm and said firmly, "That's enough, Steve."

Taylor jerked her head sideways, indicating Steve should beat it, and he pouted as he shuffled away.

"I apologize for my nephew's behavior. Acting like a blamed schoolboy," Mama said, shooting Little Junior a withering glare.

"No need to apologize. Steve was completely out of line. But, you know, boys will be boys," Taylor said with a weak laugh.

I jumped in, "Mama, have you seen everything you need for now?"

She nodded.

"Thank you for the tour, Taylor. We'll be back tomorrow for the rehearsal," Mama said.

"Of course. It was so nice to meet you," she said, extending her hand for shakes all around, and handing me a business card emblazoned with her name and the chapel's contact information.

Little Junior retrieved the taxi and pulled up to the front door. Di and I climbed into the back while he ran around to open the front passenger door for Mama.

Once we were en route back to the hotel, Mama said, "Little Junior, what in the world came over you, getting into a tussle? You're a grown man, for Pete's sake."

"I'm sorry, Aunt Virginia. Steve Warrick just gets under my skin. He's so full of . . . himself."

Junior explained that Steve got some pretty good club gigs performing as Elvis, both solo and in revues, including a run he'd recently finished at our hotel.

"Before he got on as a regular at the wedding chapel, he drove a cab part-time, too. Now he acts like he's all high and mighty. Too good to talk to the likes of me. But what galls me the most about him is the way he treated Crystal. She went out with him a few times—back before she met me. Fortunately, she saw through his phony act pretty quickly."

That Steve had dated his girlfriend was clearly what upset Little Junior the most. In just the short time I'd seen him with Crystal in front of the ice-cream parlor, it was obvious he was crazy about her.

"It's okay, sugar," Mama said, reaching over and patting him on the arm. "But you can't let guys like him goad you into a fight. You're too good for that."

"Yes, ma'am," he said, shooting Mama a boyish smile that almost made me want to tweak his cheeks. "You ladies want me to take you on a little tour and point out some of the highlights of Vegas? The meter's off. It's my treat."

"That's sweet, hon, but it's been a long day. I think I'd better get back to the hotel before Earl starts to worry. My, the way that man fusses over me," Mama said, feigning annoyance when anyone could see she was pleased as punch with her attentive fiancé.

Little Junior pulled up in front of our hotel.

"'Night, ladies."

Mama reached in her purse and pulled out her wallet.

"Put that away, Aunt Virginia. Your money's no good here."

"That's not right, Little Junior. You hauling us around kept you from taking paying customers. Let me at least give you a few dollars," she said.

My cousin waved her off. "Earl already bought me supper. And besides, y'all are family."

He ran around the car to help Mama out of the front seat. She leaned down and gave him a kiss on the cheek.

"Thanks for the ride, Little Junior," I said. "Will we see you tomorrow?"

"You can count on it."

Inside the hotel lobby, Di and I parted ways with Mama, who was anxious to go upstairs and check on my mother-in-law and make it an early night.

"Good night, Mama," I said, giving her a little hug.

"'Night, darlin'. I'll see you in the morning."

"Good night, Mrs. Walford. And thanks again for including me in your wedding trip," Di said, reaching over and giving Mama a pat on the arm. Di's typically not much of a hugger.

"You're very welcome, hon. You two should probably round up your men in the casino before they lose their shirts."

Mama headed toward the elevators, moving slowly. I could tell she was worn out.

"I can't imagine Dave parting with too much of his cash," Di said. "Does Larry Joe have a weakness for gambling?"

"Not that I know of. We've only been to the casinos down in Tunica a few times, and honestly he seemed more interested in the all-you-can-eat buffet."

Di and I started wending our way through the huge casino. Dave and Larry Joe were nowhere to be seen, but as we passed the blackjack tables, Di suddenly froze in place.

"You look like you just saw a ghost," I said.

"You could say that. The guy in the red shirt there," she said, nodding toward the table directly in front of us. "That's my ex, Jimmy."

"I thought he was still serving time in a Texas prison."

"So did I," she said.

Jimmy spotted Di, gathered up his winnings, and started walking toward us.

He extended his arms and shared an awkward hug with Di in which both of them seemed to be trying to embrace without actually touching.

"I didn't know where you landed when you

left Texas," he said. "Can't believe you ended up in Vegas, too."

"Actually, I'm just here for a few days with friends," she said. "This is my best friend, Liv McKay. Liv, this is Jimmy Souther, my ex-husband."

We shook hands tentatively.

"Nice to meet you," he said. I just nodded.

Di hadn't taken her eyes off Jimmy since he approached us. I felt uncomfortable, unsure if I should stay or go. But when Jimmy offered to buy Di a drink and she accepted, I made my exit.

"I should really find my husband before he loses too much money," I said, making an excuse. It seemed to barely register with Di when I started walking away.

I scanned the room looking for Larry Joe, but had an uneasy feeling about leaving Di with a man I'd never heard her say a nice word about.

I walked a short way and slid behind a slot machine where I could discreetly keep an eye on her. I assumed they'd just have a drink for old time's sake and a short, awkward conversation. But they seemed to be having an amiable and lengthy chat.

I texted Larry Joe, describing my whereabouts, telling him I was ready to call it a night, and ready for him to call it a night, too. He ambled over with Dave in tow—a possibility I should have anticipated.

"Hey, Liv. Where's Di?" Dave asked.

I didn't know quite how to respond, but absently glanced toward the bar. Dave, a sheriff and detective by trade, followed my gaze. He spotted Di sitting at the bar, sharing a drink and a laugh with another man.

"Who's he?" Dave asked with an angry glare. I was familiar with that glare. It was the same one he'd laid on me and Di whenever he felt we were meddling in a murder investigation.

"She just ran into someone she used to know."

"Then maybe she'd like to introduce me to her friend."

I doubted it, but Dave charged toward the bar before I could say anything.

I grabbed Larry Joe by the arm and started leading him in the direction of the elevators.

"What's your hurry?" he asked.

"I don't want us to be witnesses if something should happen that we might be called upon to testify in court about."

"Whaaa?"

"I'll tell you after we're out of the casino."

I briefly filled him in once we were in the elevator.

"I only got a glimpse, but he looked like a normal guy to me," Larry Joe said. "From what little you'd told me about her ex, I expected him to have horns and a tail."

"The devil takes on many disguises," I said.

Chapter Three

Larry Joe was snoring by the time his head hit the pillow, and I wasn't far behind him.

I woke up about 8:00 a.m. as he emerged from the bathroom, freshly showered and running an electric razor across his face.

"Hey, honey, you been up long?" I said, stretching my arms over my head before walking over to give him a kiss.

"Probably only fifteen or twenty minutes."

That qualified as sleeping in for Larry Joe, who by seven is generally at the office of the trucking company he co-owns and operates with his dad. I usually arrive at my office between eight-thirty and nine o'clock. But since my work as a party planner includes plenty of evening and weekend work, including some late nights, my schedule varies much more than his.

We had gone to bed earlier than usual for us, but a full day of travel and near-constant togetherness with my mama and Larry Joe's parents had been exhausting, so we both had slept soundly and slept in.

Before getting in the shower, I checked my cell phone and saw I had a voice mail from Mama time stamped 5:45 a.m. Thank goodness I had put it on silent.

"Liv, this is Mama." As if I couldn't see the caller ID or wouldn't recognize her booming voice. "Earl and I are going with Betty and Wayne to the early bird breakfast buffet downstairs. It starts at six-thirty."

"So what's the word from your mama?" Larry Joe asked.

"The lovebirds and your folks hit the breakfast buffet at six-thirty this morning."

"I'm surprised Dad waited on that late. He usually has breakfast at five-thirty."

"If he was able to slip away from your mom, I bet he sneaked down to the doughnut shop while he was waiting for the buffet to open. Which reminds me—we should try to encourage lunch and dinner options at someplace other than an all-you-can-eat buffet. Your mother is worried sick about your dad eating himself into another heart attack, and wants to encourage moderation."

"I know," Larry Joe said. "I don't understand how somebody can be married to a man for forty years and still believe she can change him."

"We cling to hope."

Larry Joe snapped a towel at my backside before giving me one of his trademark lopsided grins, which showed off his left dimple. He had to put on a broad, toothy smile to show off both dimples. I think he's kind of cute either way.

"If you still have to shower and put on your

makeup, I think I'm going to wander downstairs and get some coffee and a doughnut myself. I'll call Dad and see what the plan for the day is. I'll text you when I know. So what're your plans for this morning?"

"Until Mama tells me differently, I'm going to go roam around the meeting rooms area of the hotel and see if I can find the American Association of Event Planners conference."

"I thought you said you didn't register for that."

"I didn't. I'm not going to go into the sessions. But it never hurts to network, exchange business cards, and chat informally with other planners. I might even run into someone I know from Memphis or a previous conference."

"If you do that, can we write this trip off as a business expense on our taxes?"

"I doubt it. Besides, we're not paying for it; Earl is."

"Oh, yeah. Well, I better get moving. Dad and Earl have been up for hours already."

"Okay, honey, I'll see you later. Don't forget your room key," I said. He gave me a quick kiss before leaving.

I put the DO NOT DISTURB sign on the door so housekeeping wouldn't walk in while I was in the shower. I showered, dressed, and put on my makeup. Just as I was about to leave the room, Larry Joe texted: We're off to do man stuff. I'll call later.

Some wives would have been concerned about the exact nature of the "man stuff" their husband was getting up to in Sin City. But I trust Larry Joe. And I trust Daddy Wayne and Earl even more. I knew if Earl was wandering from Mama's side, she most likely had given him a to-do list.

I called my mother's cell phone, which went straight to voice mail. So, I texted Di to see if she wanted to join me for coffee. No reply. Di is an early riser, typically arriving at the post office every day by 7:00 a.m. to start her job as a mail carrier. I assumed she had a late night and was sleeping in. I was dying to know how things went after Dave and Jimmy were introduced.

I took the elevator down to the lobby level. Since I appeared to be on my own, I decided to turn right and explore the hotel in the direction opposite the casino. I assumed the meeting facilities were in that direction, since I saw a sign with an arrow that said MEETING FACILITIES. I wandered down a corridor that appeared to be designated for meeting rooms, but saw only a few people chatting in tight circles. I turned to leave, but as I did I heard someone call out, "Liv. Liv McKay!"

Unfortunately, I recognized the shrill voice, but it was too late to hide. I mustered a faint smile as she hurried toward me with tiny steps.

"Jana."

I leaned into her outstretched arms to share a limp shoulder hug. "It's so good to see you," I lied.

"I didn't think you ever attended event planners conferences, what with your little business still standing on shaky start-up legs," Jana Hively said, with her usual charm. I knew her only well enough to dislike her. She had been a member of the American Association of Event Planners in Memphis and I'd had the displeasure of once serving on a committee with her.

"Honestly, I'd forgotten all about the conference

until we were on the airplane. I'm here for a family wedding."

"Oh, my. Who's getting married?"

"My mother."

"Good heavens, I can't imagine my own mother, or anybody really, wanting to get married in Las Vegas. Is your mother not a churchgoer then?"

I took a deep breath, trying to keep good thoughts rather than murderous ones. *Be kind. Reap heavenly rewards. Gather stars in my crown . . .*

"Actually, she is a churchgoer. But Mama and Earl are both widowed and had the big church wedding the first time around. They decided to do something different, something fun this time. So, they're getting married at the Burning Love Wedding Chapel with an Elvis-impersonator minister. After the wedding, the two of them are taking off in a Winnebago across the Southwest for their honeymoon. And I couldn't be happier for them."

"Well, good for them—going against convention. I wish them the best."

"Thank you, Jana."

I was planning to say my good-byes and make a hasty retreat, but Jana cut me off.

"I know you didn't register for the conference, but I can slip you into one of the sessions. The next one is on Web sites for small businesses."

I didn't relish the idea of hanging out with Jana, but I was at loose ends at the moment and a presentation on Web sites could be useful, since I needed to update mine.

"Well, if you're sure it's okay for me to crash, maybe I could sit in for part of the session. If my mother texts me, I may need to slip out. We still need to do some shopping and such."

"Oh, I completely understand. It's fine. People are coming in and out all during the sessions."

Still feeling a bit hesitant, I said, "And I haven't had any breakfast or even coffee yet. . . ."

"Oh, there's still plenty of doughnuts and muffins, and even rice cakes and fruit cups for people who are into that," Jana said, deflecting my last real excuse.

We filled paper cups with coffee and I grabbed a couple of mini muffins. Jana introduced me to a couple of people as we made our way to our seats. Since it was a presentation, at least I wouldn't have to chat with Jana.

I sat through the whole session without a word from Mama, or Di or Larry Joe. But it was inform-ative and I scribbled down notes on the back of business cards I dug out of my purse. Naturally, this caused Jana to look at me askance, but she didn't offer me any paper. After the session I was determined to get away from her before she asked me to lunch.

"Jana, it was so nice running into you. Thanks so much for slipping me in for the Web site presenta-tion. I better go tend to my mama."

At this point I had a huge lapse in judgment and asked Jana for advice.

"By the way, I'd like to take my mother and a couple of other ladies in the wedding party out for an elegant little dinner tonight—a kind of bache-lorette party, if you will. But very low key. I think the men are taking the groom-to-be out for drinks. Could you recommend a restaurant? Something a bit more intimate than the big ones here in the hotel. Have you encountered anything like that since you arrived for the conference?"

"Oh, hon, didn't you know? I'm not just in Vegas for the conference. I live here now. I'm the event planner here for the hotel. You go shopping with your mom, get a manicure. I'll arrange everything—gratis, of course."

"Oh, no, Jana, that's much too generous. I couldn't possibly accept. . . ."

"I won't take no for an answer. What are friends for? It'll be my wedding gift to your mother, from one Tennessee gal to another. Besides, it's no trouble. All I have to do is make a couple of phone calls. I can reserve a small, private dining room at another hotel—I have a friend there. The food is wonderful."

I started to speak, but she raised her hand, anticipating my question.

"And it's very affordable. I'll book it with my it's-all-in-who-you-know discount and you can dine on beef tenderloin for less than sixty dollars a head, including a bottle of house wine, and use of a very private dining room."

I could hardly argue with the price. And, as an outsider, I didn't have the connections to book a private dining room on such short notice.

"Jana, are you sure? I mean, you have the conference going on, as well as your own job."

"No trouble. Give me your cell number and I'll text you with the particulars. Would you like me to arrange a limo to pick y'all up at the hotel?"

"No, thanks. I have a cousin in town who is taking care of transportation for us."

I decided not to mention he was an aspiring Elvis tribute artist, who drove an old taxi to make ends meet.

Jana may not be my favorite person, but I felt pretty good about having a nice evening in store for Mama. And I wouldn't have to do anything except hand a waiter my credit card. I glanced at my watch. It was only a little after 11:00 a.m. Not a bad day's work.

I paused in front of the elevators to check my messages. There was a voice mail from Mama. I must have missed it when I switched the phone to silent during the Web site session.

"Liv, this is Mama. Betty and I went to the beauty shop to get our hair done. Little Junior picked us up and drove us to the hairdresser Crystal goes to. I thought her hair was cute, didn't you?"

Mama asking a question in a voice mail that you have no opportunity to answer is pretty much also the way she carries on conversations in person.

"Anyway, Randi—that's spelled with an *i*—has invited us to have lunch with her and the manicurist at the Chinese buffet next to the salon. They say it's really good. After lunch Betty and I are going to have our nails done. There are two nail techs here, so if you and Di want to join us, we can all go ahead and get manicures before the wedding tomorrow. If you want to come, call Little Junior to pick you up at the hotel and drive you over."

I still had no reply from my earlier text to Di, which worried me a little. So I called her.

"Hi, what's going on?" she said, before I had a chance to speak.

"That's what I was going to ask you. Earl and

Larry Joe and his dad are off doing man stuff of some sort. Mama and Miss Betty are at the hairdresser and invited us to join them after lunch for a manicure, if you're game. Do you want to do lunch and then get our nails done?"

"I'm meeting Jimmy for lunch at eleven-thirty, but I can meet you in the lobby at twelve-thirty to go to the salon, if that's not too late for you?"

"Sounds like a plan."

"I'll see you in a bit," Di said, ending the call quickly, before I could ask questions about her lunch date.

I had a whole list of questions I planned to ask her.

I strolled toward the food court, feeling a little sorry for myself that I had traveled to Vegas in a party of eight and was having lunch as a party of one. I consoled myself with a large slice of pizza, followed by an ice-cream cone.

Chapter Four

During lunch, Larry Joe called and told me he, his dad, and Earl were out shopping for campers.

"No offense, honey, but I can't believe Mama would leave something as important as picking out her honeymoon camper up to you three."

"She's not. We're just reconnaissance shopping. Once we narrow it down to a few good prospects, she and Earl will make the final decision together. Although I doubt Earl will have much to say about it."

"That sounds more like my mama. By the way, you didn't mention Dave. Is he not with you?"

"No. I talked to him briefly, but he said he has a buddy on the Vegas police force he was hoping to catch up with today. Yeah, I'm coming," Larry Joe yelled away from the phone. "Look, hon, I gotta go. We're moving on to the next camper lot."

"Good luck."

I couldn't help wondering if Dave catching up with a police buddy included him checking up on Jimmy Souther's criminal record.

As I left the food court area to meet Di, I got a text from Jana, saying everything was arranged. Dinner was at seven-thirty. The concierge at the hotel would direct us to the private dining room. Perfect. I texted Jana with a thank-you, and asked her to add a moderately priced bottle of champagne to my dinner order.

Di was already standing near the entrance staring out the front doors when I got to the lobby area, about twelve-twenty. At least she hadn't had a long lunch with Jimmy. She turned my way as I approached and waved in recognition.

"Sorry I didn't reply to your text earlier. I didn't sleep much and was slow to get moving this morning."

"No problem. Where did you and Jimmy have lunch?"

"We just grabbed a quick bite at the bar and grill on the second level. So, where are we going to get our nails done?"

Clearly, she was trying to change the subject, but I wasn't about to let her get away with it.

"What difference does it make where we're getting our nails done? I want to hear what happened last night when your current beau and your ex-husband met. Or is it too painful to talk about?"

"It's too stupid," Di said. "Why do men puff out their chests and lock horns like something on *Wild Kingdom* when they think another male is infringing on their territory? And, as unlikely as it sounds, Jimmy Souther was actually acting more mature than Dave Davidson."

"Did they get into a scuffle?"

"No, nothing physical. After introductions and

hellos, Jimmy tried to get back to his drink and our conversation—which Dave had interrupted. Dave leaned between us, telling me he was calling it a night on gambling and suggested I should come with him and join up with you and Larry Joe.

"I gave him a drop dead look and said, 'Tell Liv and Larry Joe good night for me. I'll see all of you in the morning.' But instead of leaving, like a gentleman, he said he thought he'd stick around and join Jimmy and me for a drink. Then he started getting all up in Jimmy's face like he was interrogating a suspect. I honestly believe Dave was trying to find out if Jimmy had violated his parole or trying to goad him into doing something to violate his parole."

"What did you do?" I said.

"There wasn't much I could say without making it worse. You know how bullheaded Dave can be. When he gets like that, he shall not be moved. Jimmy had given me a business card for the place he works. So I finally just told Jimmy I'd talk to him later when the law wasn't around. I grabbed my purse and left. Fortunately, the elevator door closed just in time to shut Dave out. He makes me so mad sometimes," Di said, shaking her head.

"How did you end up hooking up with Jimmy for lunch today?"

"Oh, I told you he gave me his card. He works as a bartender, and while we were talking last night he told me he was fixing to head out to work the late shift. Bars are open twenty-four hours in Vegas, you know. So after I got back to my room, I waited an hour and called the bar. They were busy and he could only talk a minute, so we arranged to meet here for lunch. He couldn't stay long because he had a meeting about a business venture he and a friend are trying to get going."

I wanted to ask Di more about Jimmy and his new "business venture," but I spotted Little Junior standing beside his cab under the portico, waving his arms wildly to attract my attention.

"Oh, here's our ride," I said.

"Don't bring up Jimmy in front of your cousin," Di said, touching me on the sleeve as we walked out the front door. "I don't think he keeps many secrets from your mama."

I realized I hadn't told Di about Larry Joe saying Dave had gone to catch up with an old buddy. But seeing how upset she was with Dave already, I decided maybe it was best not to mention it.

"Ladies, your carriage awaits," Little Junior said, opening the car door for us.

He pulled away from the curb, down the driveway, and expertly merged into traffic on the busy Strip. He was actually a good taxi driver.

"Thanks for hooking Mama up with Crystal's hairdresser. Mama sounded pleased when I talked to her."

"No problem. I didn't want your mama getting gouged by the prices at the hotel salon. Plus, I know Randi's good—Crystal's been going to her for years. And I want Aunt Virginia to look her best for the wedding. I know that's important to a woman."

My cousin had grown up to be a sensitive and considerate man, who absolutely doted on my mother. It was hard for me to believe this was the same kid who had tried to flush my little sister's Barbie down the toilet.

"Little Junior, a friend of mine has arranged for a private dining room at another hotel tonight. It's kind of a little bachelorette dinner for Mama with just us women. Would you be able to drive us over this evening? We have a reservation at seven-thirty."

"Of course. I'll pick y'all up at about five after."

"Thank you. But, Little Junior, I insist on paying you something. We keep taking you away from paying fares and that's not right."

"No, Liv. I won't accept a dime. You hurt my feelings. I mean, y'all are family. You wouldn't charge your mama for planning a party, would you?"

I've been tempted, I thought.

"No, probably not."

"Well, then."

"Thanks, cuz. You've been more than generous, and I know it means a lot to Mama, getting to spend some time with you."

"Don't know if she told you, but she invited me and Crystal to the wedding."

"Well, of course. Like you said, you're family."

I was glad for him to be at the wedding, but I just hoped he wouldn't get into another altercation with his rival Elvis impersonator.

The beauty salon was in a nondescript shopping center away from the glamour and neon of the Las Vegas Strip. This wasn't the part of the city where tourists usually ventured. This was where the locals shopped and ate and had their hair done.

Little Junior dropped us at the door.

"Aunt Virginia's supposed to call me when you gals are finished. See ya later."

When we entered the Touch of Beauty Salon, Mama and my mother-in-law were sitting side by side at the manicurists' tables, their fingertips soaking in small bowls of warm, sudsy water.

"Hey, girls," Mama said as we walked in. "Randi, this is my daughter, Liv, and her friend, Di."

We exchanged hellos, then Mama nodded to each of the manicurists. "This is Noki and Liz."

"We only have two manicure stations, so I'm afraid you'll have to wait for them to finish with your mom and mother-in-law," Randi said. She was tall and brunette with a cute, short hairstyle that framed her round face.

"Oh, that's fine," Di and I said, nearly in unison.

"Can I offer you two a Coke or a bottled water?" Randi said. We declined, explaining we'd just finished lunch.

There was only one other customer in the place, getting her hair cut by another hairdresser. Randi picked up two straight-back chairs from the waiting area and set them opposite Mama and Miss Betty.

After we sat down I told them about the beef tenderloin dinner in the private dining room scheduled for tonight. Mama seemed pleased—and impressed, so I didn't mention that Jana had arranged everything. It's not often I have an opportunity to impress my mother by just keeping my mouth shut.

"That sounds wonderful, Liv. And if we have definite plans, that'll get Earl out the door. He was all wishy-washy about going out for a drink with the guys. But I think that's what he should do the night before his wedding—as long as they practice moderation."

Wouldn't want him to have too much fun.

"Liv, you don't think they'll go to some nudie bar, do you?" Mama asked.

Di burst into laughter, but fortunately so did my mother-in-law.

"Can you imagine Wayne McKay walking into a strip club?" Miss Betty said, still trying to get her giggles under control. "His face would turn bright red."

"So would Earl's ears," Mama said, starting to chuckle at the thought.

They apparently didn't think the sight of strippers would cause Larry Joe to blush, but I tried not to take offense.

Mama got her nails painted a pale lavender shade to go with her wedding dress, which was a rich purple color. The rest of us decided to go with various shades of pink.

We learned that Randi and Crystal were chums, going way back. Unfortunately, that was about all we learned.

Mama plied her southern charm, trying to get Randi to dish any dirt she might have on Crystal. But, while hairdressers generally may not mind sharing a tidbit of juicy gossip, the smart ones know when to keep their mouths shut. Randi was smart.

As we were paying the bill, Mama called Little Junior to come fetch us.

"Mama, do you want to go shopping now, or do you want to go back to the hotel and rest a bit first?"

"I don't have much time to shop before Earl and I go to the chapel for our wedding rehearsal. But, Little Junior, is there a budget shoe store in this area? I'd like to buy another pair of sensible walking shoes for our trip, but I don't want to pay a fortune for them at one of the fancy shoe stores at the hotels."

"Yes, ma'am. There's an outlet shopping center not far from here. I think they have a couple of shoe stores."

"Mama, I don't think I had a chance to tell you last night. Holly called to tell me the restaurant at the hotel has been closed down temporarily by the health department."

"I always thought George's Country Kitchen looked like a clean place. Why did it get shut down?"

"Sounded like it was mostly some drain issues, but it will take some time to make repairs and get a re-inspection. It's a headache for Sindhu and Ravi—and George of course. But it's a headache for us, too, since it's where we were scheduled to hold a dinner for a high school reunion this weekend. Holly's having to scout another location today."

"I ran into Belinda Mays at the beauty shop a few weeks back and she was telling me some of the things you and Holly were planning for their fiftieth class reunion. I think it's so clever calling it the Dixie High 'Sixty-Eight Comeback Special and doing it with an Elvis theme during Death Week," Mama said.

The week of August 16, commemorating Elvis's death, is called Elvis Week by the organizers, but commonly referred to as Death Week by locals. Hordes of tourists from across the globe descend on Memphis for this annual event, which culminates with the Candlelight Vigil at Graceland.

"When the reunion committee told us the dates they were looking at for the gathering, an Elvis theme immediately sprang to mind," I said. "And since they *are* the Class of 1968, it was such a perfect tie-in with Elvis's television comeback special the year they graduated," I said.

"I was kind of surprised when she told me they were having a pool party on one of the days. I was three years behind Belinda in school and I can't imagine our class having a pool party. I wouldn't put that much of my skin on public display—and who wants to see a bunch of saggy old folks in bathing suits?"

"Nobody *has* to wear a swimsuit unless they want to, Mama. On Friday night, there will be an outdoor luau—well, not an authentic luau. I couldn't imagine this group eating raw fish or tarot roots. But they will be digging a pit for a whole hog barbecue and we'll throw in some side dishes with pineapple and coconut to support the theme. Anyway, Malcolm Tate volunteered to host it at his place—"

"Is he that guy with the Spock ears?" Mama interrupted.

"Spock ears," Little Junior said, breaking out in giggles.

"I guess his ears are kinda pointy, now that you mention it. Didn't you know him in school?" I asked, although I knew I shouldn't encourage her.

"He didn't go to Dixie High. He married Marilyn Danvers, Class of 'Sixty-Eight. She passed away a couple of years ago, but after fifty years I guess he's an adopted classmate," Mama explained.

"Anyway, he has a huge shady yard and a swimming pool near the house. And it *is* August and hotter than blazes, so we decided to serve fruity cocktails with little umbrellas poolside. People can swim if they like. But by including swimwear as an option, it means everyone can feel free to dress as casual as they like. I doubt many people will actually get in the pool, but some of them may want to sit on the edge and dangle their legs in the water to cool off."

"That sounds reasonable," Mama said, nodding approvingly.

"And after dark, we'll have an outdoor viewing of *Blue Hawaii* on a big screen."

"Ooh, that'll be just like going to the drive-in pictures," Mama said.

"That's what we hope."

"And who knows, Spock Ears may find himself a new wife—or at least a girlfriend among Marilyn's old classmates. That big place with a swimming pool is bound to make him attractive to some of the ladies in that group, pointy ears or not," Mama said.

It was hard to argue with that logic, so I didn't.

Chapter Five

Little Junior pulled into a driveway with strip shopping centers on either side. He pointed out the shoe store options and Mama directed him to the one she thought looked most promising. He dropped us at the curb.

I knew from experience that shoe shopping with Mama would inevitably lead to a discussion of bunions and ingrown toenails. I left Miss Betty to enjoy that chat and told them Di and I would be browsing in the discount party store next door.

"Do we need to pick up any supplies here for your mom's bachelorette party tonight?" Di asked, picking up a coconut bra and waving it in front of her chest.

"No, we're good. I'm always looking for party and decoration ideas, though. So . . . you never had a chance to tell me about your lunch with Jimmy and his new business enterprise."

"He and his high-school best friend's cousin, who's been living in Vegas for a few years now, are saving up money to start a party photo-booth rental business. They'll start with one or two for parties, and eventually he'd like to have some in malls or entertainment districts in town. In the meantime, he's working a lot of hours at the bar and it sounds like he's making good tips."

"That sounds promising," I said. "I'm curious about how Jimmy ended up in Vegas. If he's recently out of prison wouldn't he have to stay in the state of Texas for a certain amount of time to check in with a parole officer?"

"Yeah, he had to get permission to leave the state and show that he had a job lined up and a place to live. It helped that he has an aunt who lives near Vegas. Not that he sees her much, but having family in the area looks good on paper. And he has to check in with a probation officer here."

"So what was it like seeing your ex-husband out of the blue, like this?"

"I was kind of rattled at first. Honestly, seeing Jimmy cleaned up and shaved reminded me a little of how he looked when we first met. We were just dumb kids. I don't know . . . it kind of took me back to a simpler time, you know? And I guess I'm glad to see he's out of prison. Not that I let him off the hook for too many bad choices to count. And I certainly don't let him off the hook for taking part in an armed robbery. But he was just the driver—he never pulled a gun on anybody. And he insisted that he didn't know the other guys were going to pull guns. Nobody believed him. But I know him well enough to believe he's actually dumb enough to have gotten roped into that kind of situation. I'm glad he's served his time. Glad for him, and glad for his mama. She's a sweet woman and it broke her heart when Jimmy got sent away.

"I may be wrong—I've been wrong about Jimmy Souther plenty of times. But I'm hopeful that he's actually grown up and gotten his act together this time."

Hearing Di talk about her ex with a forgiving tone was a change. Not that she ever talked about him all that much.

"Do you plan to see him again?"

"If you mean 'see' in a romantic sense, don't be ridiculous. I've worked too hard to build a life for myself apart from Jimmy. But I probably will see him again before we leave town. I just want to be encouraging. He messed things up for himself, but he also had some rough breaks. And that concludes everything I have to say about my ex-husband. And don't even ask me about Dave."

I already knew better than to ask about Dave when the two of them were on the outs.

"Let's check on the Golden Girls," I said.

We left the party store and peered through the window of the shoe store. Mama and Miss Betty were at the checkout counter. We loitered on the sidewalk waiting for them to come out. I waved to Little Junior, signaling it looked like we were ready to leave.

Little Junior pulled up to the front of the hotel to drop us off. "Aunt Virginia, when do you want me to pick up you and Uncle Earl for the wedding rehearsal?"

"We should probably leave in forty-five minutes or so. Are you sure you shouldn't go get some paying fares? Earl and I can catch a taxi."

Completely ignoring her remark, he said, "I'll pick you up here in forty-five minutes. And, Liv, I'll be back to pick you ladies up at just after seven."

He drove away and we ambled into the hotel lobby.

"Mama, have you and Earl gotten your marriage license yet?"

"We're going to do it after the rehearsal tonight."

"It's a government office. Are you sure they'll still be open?"

"Yep. I called. The marriage license bureau is open until midnight seven days a week. Things work a little different here in Las Vegas."

"Apparently so," I said.

"Liv, how dressed up should I get for this fancy dinner tonight?" Mama asked.

"I was wondering that, as well," Miss Betty said.

"Mama, you can get as dressed up or dressed down as you like. It's your night. And since it's a private room, we don't really have to worry about what other people are wearing."

"Then I'll wear a dress, but no panty hose," Mama announced.

"That sounds good to me," Miss Betty said.

We all headed up to our hotel rooms and I called to double check our reservation, just to make sure Jana was true to her word. Everything was confirmed and we were good to go. I decided a nap was in order.

My head had just hit the pillow when I realized I hadn't heard an update today from Holly about a new venue for the reunion dinner, so I called her.

"Hi, Holly, where do we stand on the banquet venue?"

"We're sitting pretty. We're booked at the Moose Lodge. The space is almost as large as the dining room at the hotel restaurant—and they upgraded the kitchen just a couple of years ago. Plus, I believe the woodsy ambience of the lodge will actually make a nicer space for the banquet than the nondescript restaurant."

"Wonderful," I said. "Describe the change of venue to the reunion committee chairman the same way you just did for me."

"Don't worry, darlin'. I can handle him. Now, when do you get your mama married off?"

"Tomorrow night. Tonight I'm taking her, along with Miss Betty and Di, to an elegant little bachelorette dinner in a private dining room at a nice hotel. Impressed?"

"I am. How did you score that?"

"There's actually a planners conference at our hotel. I'd gotten an e-mail for it, but had forgotten all about it until we were getting ready to leave for Las Vegas. Anyway, you'll never guess who I ran into."

"Do tell."

"Jana Hively. You remember—from the association of event planners in Memphis? Turns out she's the events coordinator at the hotel here, and she offered to set everything up. Made a couple of phone calls and we're good to go."

"I didn't know you two were close. In fact, I thought you had a less than fond relationship with Miss Jana."

"I thought so, too. Maybe she's just feeling homesick and wanted to do a good turn for a fellow southerner. Regardless, I'm not one to look a gift horse in the mouth."

"If you do look, be careful. You might find fangs," Holly said.

"What makes you say that?"

"Well, this is gossip, mind you. But I heard that Jana's husband requested a transfer with his company to Las Vegas so Jana could take the job at some big hotel there. He took what was essentially a demotion to accommodate her career. Then shortly after they moved to Vegas, she dumped him for some singer she had booked for a show at the hotel. Just watch your back, darlin'."

"Since I'm not close to her in that way, I should be okay. But thanks for the warning."

I hung up with Holly, feeling relieved we had a venue for the reunion dinner—and intrigued by the juicy bit of gossip about Jana.

I set the alarm on my phone for a thirty-minute nap. I had just dozed off when Larry Joe came in.

"Sorry, hon. Did I wake you?"

"No. I was just resting my eyes," I lied.

He lay down next to me and I put my head on his shoulder.

"Did you guys complete your mission of scouting suitable honeymoon campers?"

"I think we did. Mind you, your mama may think differently. Although, I believe I know which one she'll pick."

"How's that?"

"It's basically Buckingham Palace on wheels. Comes with everything except a butler."

"Let me guess. It's also the most expensive option."

"Yep. By tens of thousands of dollars."

"You think Earl will actually show her that one?"

"If he's smart, and if she shows the least bit of interest in any of the others, he won't. But I have a feeling that camping with your mama is going to cost him more than a world tour would have. What about you? Did you get anything done today?"

"My nails," I said, holding my hand up so he could admire my manicure.

"That's a pretty color pink," he said, taking my hand and giving it a kiss.

"We're leaving the hotel about seven for a girls' night out. It's really just a nice dinner. I ran into an event planner I knew from Memphis. She works in Vegas now and set everything up for me. Have you guys made any plans for Earl's last night as a single man?"

"Nope. Party planning is women's work," he said, knowing the remark would earn him a slap on the thigh. "We'll just take him out for some drinks. Actually, Dave was supposed to ask his cop friend for the names of a couple of places we might want to go."

"You fellas behave. Nothing too wild. Mama distinctly said 'no nudie bars.'"

"No worries there. Even if I were inclined to go to a nudie bar, I wouldn't want to go with Earl and my daddy."

"Good to know you have chaperones."

"Honey, Dave asked his cop buddy to look up

Di's ex-husband. Did you know he has a rap sheet as long as my arm?"

"No, Di never gave me a list of his crimes. But I gathered that he'd been in trouble with the law, even before he landed in prison for armed robbery."

"Why was she hanging around with him last night? Do you think she still has feelings for the guy?" he asked.

"No, not like you mean. She told me today that while Jimmy had made more than his share of mistakes, he'd had some bad breaks, too. And he was just the driver in that armed robbery charge. He never pulled a gun on anyone. I think she's just happy to see him finally getting his life together. She's known him since they were just teenagers.

"I really don't think Dave needs to look at Jimmy as competition. But I also don't think Di would be happy if she thought Dave was trying to stir up trouble for Jimmy with his parole officer."

"I'll try to mention that to Dave if the subject comes up. Aren't you glad you married someone wonderful, like me?" he said, giving my shoulder a squeeze and kissing me on the forehead.

"I am. Most days," I said. "I'd love to stay here and snuggle. And I'd really love to take a nap. But I have a bachelorette party to go to."

"I bet you and Di will be having more fun than Dave and I will."

"Really? We'll have our own set of chaperones along for the ride, too, you know."

Little Junior pulled up to the front door just after 7:00 p.m., as he'd promised. We took what had become our assigned seats, with Mama in the front, and me perched on the backseat between Di and Miss Betty.

"Liv, it's pretty sweet you being able to snag a private dining room at one of the big hotels. I guess you know some tricks of the trade, having your own party planning business," Little Junior said.

"Something like that," I said sheepishly, before quickly changing the subject. "So, Mama, I haven't talked to you since the wedding rehearsal. How'd things go?"

"We asked the minister to change a couple of small things, but I was real pleased. I think it's going to be fun, but still appropriate. One thing is worrying me, though. Earl said he had a little surprise for me. I told him, 'Earl, you know I don't much like surprises, especially when it comes to something important like our wedding.' He told me not to worry, that he was sure I'd like this surprise."

"I wouldn't worry, Virginia," Miss Betty said. "I think Earl knows you pretty well."

"He'll probably know you a whole lot better after traveling for two weeks together in a camper," Di chimed in.

"I know y'all think it's a crazy idea, but I think it'll be romantic—and an adventure. Neither of us has traveled in this part of the country, so now we'll get to see it for the first time together."

"Mama, I think it's sweet, how the two of you will be riding into the sunset in a Winnebago for parts unknown."

I did think it was a little crazy, but I didn't say so. Being trapped in a small space with my mama for two weeks certainly qualified as an adventure. Not one I'd sign on for. But if Earl loved her enough to marry her, I hoped it turned out to be a dream honeymoon—whatever a dream honeymoon meant to them.

Little Junior dropped us off with instructions to call him later with a time for him to pick us up. He told us not to rush.

"Y'all have a wonderful time. Aunt Virginia, this time tomorrow you'll be a married lady," he said, with a smile and a wave.

I knew we came to Las Vegas for a wedding. But hearing someone say out loud that in less than twenty-four hours my mother would be married—and married to someone other than my daddy—left me feeling a bit dazed.

I'm truly fond of Earl. He treats my mother like a queen, and I think they're good for each other. But since I knew she planned to take Earl's name after they married, it suddenly struck me like lightning that Mama was going to have a last name different from my maiden name, my family name.

"Earth to Liv," Di said, waving her hand in front of my face. "We don't know where to go."

I snapped back to the present moment.

"Sorry," I said blankly. "Wait here while I ask the concierge for directions."

After conferring for a moment, I rejoined the group. "Follow me," I said.

After taking the elevator up to one of the top floors, we snaked down two hallways as I'd been directed. The sign on the door said RESERVED.

It was truly lovely, and looked more like an elegant dining room in someone's home than a hotel. Brocade drapes framed a city view and a Victorian fainting couch sat beneath the window. Beside the fireplace, a candlelit table featured finely polished silver and a centerpiece of fresh flowers. In a moment, a tuxedoed waiter entered from a side door.

"McKay, party of four?" he asked.

"Yes," I replied.

"And which of you is the bride-to-be?"

We all pointed to Mama.

"Ah, very good. Welcome."

He pulled out a chair and motioned for Mama to take a seat. Then seated each of us in turn. He picked up a slender pitcher of ice water from the table and filled our glasses.

"Your waiters will be out to greet you in just a moment. I wish you all a lovely evening."

Before exiting, he stopped at a sideboard topped by a small stereo and turned on some quiet music.

"Oh, Liv, this is so classy," Mama said. "And I wouldn't mind having this wallpaper in my own dining room."

"It is beautiful," Miss Betty said.

While my mother and mother-in-law were discussing the furnishings, Di leaned over and whispered, "Who did you have to sleep with to pull this off on such short notice?"

"I told you there's an event planners conference at the hotel. I ran into somebody I knew from Memphis and it turned out she lives in Las Vegas now. That's one of the tricks of the trade Little Junior mentioned," I said, giving Di a sly wink.

"I know we had a big lunch, but I'm starving," Mama said.

"Me too. You know they say Chinese food doesn't

stick with you. I'm a bit hungry, but I'm absolutely parched," Miss Betty said, picking up her water glass.

A moment later, four beefy waiters marched in single file, wearing tuxedo pants, bow ties—and no shirts. My mother-in-law sprayed water out her nose.

I'm going to kill Jana, I thought.

A shirtless waiter stood behind each of our chairs, and they all introduced themselves—Tom, Rudy, and Hank. Mine's name was Todd.

Rudy, Mama's attendant, spoke up. "We're here to serve you. Please let us know if there's anything you need. Anything at all."

Then they each took an elegantly folded napkin from the place setting in front of us, unfurled it with a snap of the wrist, and laid it across our laps, leaning in with their faces very close to ours.

I could feel Todd's breath on my cheek, but my eyes were glued to Rudy, who was standing directly across from me flexing his pectoral muscles, undulating from one side of his chest to the other. Miss Betty's face was beet red, but her eyes were fixed on Todd, making me wonder if his chest was performing a similar feat.

Di's waiter, Hank, took the bottle of champagne I'd authorized Jana to order—for an extra fee of course—from the ice bucket, and expertly popped the cork. He filled Di's glass, then handed the bottle to Todd, who filled my glass and passed it on.

The fab four retreated, saying the first course would be served in just a few minutes.

As soon as the men had left the room, Mama started waving her napkin in front of her face in a fanning motion.

"Whew, mercy, Liv. Are you trying to give Betty and me a heart attack?"

I opened my mouth, prepared to apologize and explain how it wasn't my idea, but before I could speak Mama continued.

"Not that I'm complaining, mind you," she said with a school girl giggle.

"I know," Miss Betty chimed in. "I guess it's just a little bit naughty. But, what is it they say? What happens in Vegas stays in Vegas?"

"That's right. Your secret's safe with me," Di said. "I see all kinds of things during the course of my mail route that I never breathe a word about. What happens in the privacy of one's home—or on their vacation—is nobody's business but their own."

"I'll drink to that," I said, raising my glass and breathing a sigh of relief.

We all *chinked* our crystal stemware, which produced a pleasant ring.

"To Virginia and Earl. May their wedding night be as exciting as our dinner," Miss Betty said.

Hearing those words come out of my very straight-laced mother-in-law's mouth elicited surprised looks, followed by laughter. I think she even surprised herself.

They brought our dinner out in courses, describing each dish before setting the plates before us. Each one was served with a flourish, showing off a bulging bicep or firm bottom.

They filled our wineglasses with the house red just before dinner. The fish course was scallops with prosciutto and asparagus, followed by mushroom and leek soup, and a mixed greens salad. Then they served a watermelon sorbet to cleanse our palates—and cool us off. Mama kept fanning herself every time they disappeared through the dining room door.

The main course was beef tenderloin with carrot medallions and haricot verts.

"'Harry-co-vair' is just French speak for green beans, isn't it, Liv?" Miss Betty asked.

"Yes, ma'am."

"They're a bit undercooked for my taste," Mama said, spearing a bright green bean that hadn't been cooked down southern-style to a dull sage color.

Our hunky servers cleared the plates after the main course. Rudy—the one with the dancing chest muscles—paused at the head of the table.

"We'll be back in just a few minutes to serve up a special sweet treat for you ladies," he said, giving us a wink before marching out behind his fellow waiters.

"They're such polite young men, aren't they?" Miss Betty said with a hiccup, causing me to worry that she'd had more alcohol than she could handle.

"Yeah, I'm sure their mothers are very proud," Di said with a smirk.

"I really hope their 'sweet surprise' is something chocolate," Mama said.

Three of the guys walked in, one carrying a coffeepot, one carrying a tray with a bowl of sugar cubes and a pitcher of cream, and one balancing a tray with four bowls of vanilla ice cream. They busied themselves serving the coffee and ice cream.

Rudy, Mama's assigned hunk, followed them rolling out a serving cart, equipped with a propane burner on one side and a variety of ingredients, including bananas, on the other. He set about preparing Bananas Foster for us, tableside.

He expertly peeled the banana with a knife as he twirled it with a fork. He then seductively sautéed the bananas in butter and added some banana liqueur. He removed the pan from the heat and added a splash of rum before tipping the pan toward the burner to ignite the dessert. Flames engulfed the bananas and leapt in the pan.

All four of us gasped and burst into applause. We thought that was the showstopper of the dessert course. Little did we know . . .

Rudy circled the table spooning flaming bananas on top of our ice cream. After they'd finished serving the coffee and dessert, Todd gathered the trays and pan, put them on the cart, and pushed it through the door. He reemerged in just a moment.

Todd went to the sideboard and changed the stereo to some upbeat dance tune and joined the others, who had lined up at the head of the table.

"Welcome to Vegas, ladies!" Rudy said. All four men grasped the front of their waistbands and ripped off their break-away pants. Clad in black Speedos with a tuxedo shirt and red bow tie design on the front, our waiters began to gyrate their pelvic regions to the beat of the music.

I managed to avert my eyes from the spectacle to check the response of my dinner companions. Miss Betty had her hands over her eyes, but was peeking out through her fingers. Mama had dispensed with using her napkin as a fan and was mopping her brow with it.

Di was digging around in her purse. When she pulled out a couple of five-dollar bills, I slapped her hand and shot her a scolding glare. She thought better of it and dropped the cash back into her bag.

The good news was neither Mama nor Miss Betty was looking at me. The bad news was I felt certain they'd both have plenty to say after we left. One of the dancers had retrieved some red boas from the sideboard drawer. They circled the table, draping a boa around each of our shoulders. Di jumped up, snaked her boa around Hank's waist, and used it as reins to pull him closer as they danced.

Out of the corner of my eye I could see Todd's washboard abs rippling up and down just inches from my face. But I was more interested in the performance across the table. Rudy was standing beside Mama, his hips slowly swaying. He offered one hand to Mama and motioned with the other for her to join him. When my mama, who likes to sing hymns as she washes dishes, got up and started shaking what God gave her, I decided, why not?

I stood and leaned across the table toward my mother-in-law, who appeared to be contemplating Tom's navel. Or, at least, I think it was his navel.

"Miss Betty, what happens in Vegas stays in Vegas!"

She giggled as she leapt out of her chair and flung her arms around Tom's neck. I grabbed Todd's outstretched hand and he twirled me around a couple of times. I looked up to see Mama doing the hand jive, and Di had gone back into her purse for those five-dollar bills.

By the time the music stopped, our coffee was cold and our Bananas Foster had melted into a lumpy puddle. I handed Todd my credit card and signed the check, leaving a generous tip.

The elder members of our bachelorette party

were still red faced and laughing loudly as we left the private dining room.

My last name had been McKay for twelve years and this was the first time I'd seen my mother-in-law get a snootful. She was a bit unsteady on her feet, so I thought I should make sure she was good and sober before my husband or father-in-law got a good look at her.

As we made our way to the main entrance, I spotted a Starbucks and suggested we stop there.

Mama and Miss Betty stopped at the restroom, while Di and I went in and ordered coffees for all of us.

"Liv, I never imagined I'd have such a good time with your mama and mother-in-law. Who knew they were such party girls?"

"As far as I know, only you and I know. And let's keep it that way. I'm going to kill Jana."

"Why? Everybody had a good time. You should thank her."

"Fortunately, it turned out that way. But Jana totally set me up, trying to sabotage my mother's wedding eve dinner."

I phoned Little Junior, asking if he could pick us up in thirty minutes. I hoped everyone would be acting respectable by then. Miss Betty's eyes were a bit bloodshot, but hopefully Daddy Wayne would assume she'd been crying.

Mama and Miss Betty finished powdering their noses and joined us in the coffee shop, where Mama struggled to hoist herself onto a bar stool at a pub-height table.

"Oh, Liv, you calling Little Junior to pick us up reminds me," Mama said. "When you asked me about the rehearsal on the way here, I didn't want to say anything in front of him, but—now you all know I'm not one to gossip. . . ."

This was news to me.

"But, I think there's some hanky-panky going on between that wedding coordinator and Steve, the Elvis that got into it with Little Junior. I know she was all firm with him at the time, telling him to knock it off. But this afternoon Earl and I arrived a bit early for the rehearsal. There was nobody at the front desk, so we walked through to the chapel. I thought I'd go ahead and let Earl take a peek at where we'd be getting married.

"Taylor and Steve were standing in the aisle of the It's Now or Never Chapel arguing in loud whispers at each other. I couldn't understand all of what they were saying, but Taylor said something about 'We can't let him find out,' and Steve said, 'She thinks she owns me, but she doesn't.' The two of them calmed down a bit. He put his hands to her waist and pulled her to him, rubbing his face against hers. And she didn't seem to mind any.

"At that point, Earl cleared his throat, apparently feeling conscience pangs about spying on them. I swear he's such a Boy Scout. Not that I don't appreciate Earl being virtuous, but . . ."

We walked out and stood under the portico, waiting for Little Junior to pick us up.

"You know," Miss Betty said. "I know the weather news said it was something like a hundred and seven today, but it doesn't seem as hot to me as when it gets over one hundred degrees back home."

"You're right, Betty. I've noticed that, too. I mean, it's hot. But you don't feel like a wrung-out dishrag the minute you step outside like you do in the South," Mama said.

"Maybe there is something to that saying, 'It's not the heat, it's the humidity,'" I said.

My cousin arrived at the curb, and as usual, helped Mama into the front seat.

"You ladies are all rosy cheeked. I'm guessing you had a glass or two of wine with your dinner."

"Well, of course we did. What's wrong with that?" Mama said. "It is a special occasion after all."

"Yes, ma'am, it is. There's nothing wrong with that at all."

Mama glanced over the seat and told me to call Larry Joe to see what the guys were up to. I was surprised to learn, and so was she, that they were already back at our hotel.

"Earl and Daddy have been practically pacing the floor, worrying about you all," Larry Joe said after answering my call.

"Why in the world would they be worried? We were just having dinner."

"I told them that. But you know Earl is a man in love. He hardly takes a step without your mama telling him which foot to put forward. And Daddy, for all his complaining about Mama's nagging, can barely stand it when she goes somewhere without him. But y'all *have* been gone kind of a long time just for dinner," Larry Joe said.

It did my heart good to know he was a little bit at loose ends without his sweetie, too.

"Well, dinner started late and it was served in courses," I said, with what I hoped would be enough of an explanation.

"I know this will come as a huge surprise, but Daddy wants some ice cream."

I arranged for us to meet the men at the ice-cream parlor, and told the others about the plan. My mother-in-law predictably complained about Daddy Wayne veering off his diet.

"Miss Betty, don't give him too hard a time. Apparently, he's been pining for you. And Mama, Larry Joe said Earl and Daddy Wayne have practically been pacing the floor waiting for y'all to get back. It's kind of sweet, really."

Little Junior dropped us at our hotel and declined Mama's invitation to join us at the ice-cream parlor.

After we entered the lobby, Di pulled me aside.

"I think I'll part company with you. If Dave happens to be with the men, I'd just as soon not be around him right now," Di said. "Besides, I'm not sure you want me there if the husbands and fiancé start asking questions about our dinner."

"You may be right. I'll see you in the morning," I said. Di said her good nights to Mama and Miss Betty and headed toward the elevators.

Our three men, sans Dave, were sitting on a bench near the ice-cream shop like three sulky bumps on a log. Earl was the first to rise. He walked over and gave Mama a peck on the cheek. Larry Joe and his dad were just behind them. My father-in-law touched Miss Betty on the sleeve and asked what kind of ice-cream treat she wanted. He said they had waited for us before ordering, but the milky spot at the corner of his lips told me this wouldn't be Daddy Wayne's first scoop tonight.

Larry Joe laid his arm across my shoulders and planted a kiss on top of my head.

"How 'bout you, hon? What flavor do you fancy?"

I requested one scoop of orange sherbet, and Larry Joe said he thought he'd have the same.

Mama, Miss Betty, and I sat down in a row at three small bistro tables that had been pushed together. The curlicue design on the bistro chair backs was cute, but uncomfortable. In a few minutes, the men returned, each holding two dishes of ice cream, and sat down across from their respective mates.

"Virginia, why don't y'all tell us about your girls' night dinner?" Earl asked. "Larry Joe said it was the fancy kind, served in courses."

"It was delicious. The main course was beef tenderloin, served with carrots and green beans. And the first course was scallops with that Italian ham—what's it called, Liv?"

"Prosciutto."

"Yeah, that. And we had a salad and some mushroom soup. And they served a watermelon sorbet just before the main course."

"What did you have for dessert?" my father-in-law asked, without looking up from his bowl.

"*Ooh*, that was a highlight," Miss Betty said. "One of the waiters cooked it tableside on a cart. It was one of those flambé things."

"Oh, you mean one of those desserts they set on fire," Earl said.

"Yeah, hon. That's right. It was Bananas Foster, made with butter and rum."

"Betty, did you say one of the waiters? How many waiters did y'all have?"

"We each had our own waiter," she said, looking a bit flustered.

Mama jumped in.

"Yeah, you know, like in those really fancy restaurants, where they bring you something before you know you need it, and clear everything as soon as you've finished. Real classy."

"I guess the waiters were decked out in penguin suits, too," Daddy Wayne said.

"They had on formal wear . . . with bow ties," Miss Betty said, with a coy smile.

"Sounds like a nice evening," Larry Joe said. "I'm proud of you for being able to pull together something special, even being in a strange town and all."

"Yes, sir. She really outdid herself," Mama said, reaching over and patting me on the knee. "I'd ask what you three got up to tonight, but I'm not sure we want to know."

"Nothing we need to apologize for, I assure you," Earl said. "We had some decent but expensive burgers and then went to a bar and had a few drinks."

"I'm guessing the women working at this bar weren't wearing turtlenecks and long skirts," Mama said.

"All the waitresses in Vegas I've seen so far dress skimpy, but these gals were nothing out of the ordinary. You'd have to take out a loan to afford more than a couple of drinks in there, though," Daddy Wayne groused.

"Yeah, it was pricey, even pricier than the hotel

bar. We didn't stay long—which is why we ended up back here so early," Larry Joe said.

I couldn't help wondering if the guys were being as completely honest and forthcoming about their evening as we'd been about ours.

Chapter Six

Since it was her wedding day, I figured I'd better check in with Mama first thing and get my marching orders. I called her before I'd even brushed my teeth.

"Good morning, Mama. How is the bride feeling today?"

"I feel stiffer than a starched collar. This hotel mattress is too firm. But I'm not going to let it get me down—not today."

"That's the spirit. So, what's first on the agenda? What do you need me to take care of?"

"I don't need you to do anything at the moment, hon. Earl and I are going shopping for campers. He and the guys picked out some for me to look at today. Wish us luck. If we come up empty, I guess we'll be sleeping in a pup tent on our honeymoon."

I smiled. Remembering what Larry Joe had told me about the very top of the line camper, I had a strong feeling they wouldn't come up empty on their shopping trip—but Earl's wallet might.

"Okay, Mama, don't overdo it on being out in the

heat. Maybe you should take some bottled water with you. And be sure you make it back in time to rest a bit for the wedding."

"Don't worry. I'll call you later on."

Larry came out of the bathroom already showered and shaved. He had on his pants and grabbed a shirt from the closet.

"Mama doesn't have any chores for me this morning. You want to go sightseeing together?" I asked.

"I'm sorry, Liv. My mama called early. She's got a sick headache. I have a feeling she had a couple of glasses of wine at your girls' night out, am I right? Mama's not much of a drinker. Anyway, she wants to stay in and rest so she'll be feeling well for the wedding this evening. She asked if I'd babysit Daddy and make sure he doesn't spend all day just eating, since he's been acting like a kid in a candy store. You're welcome to come along, but you'd probably have more fun hanging out with Di or hooking up with some of those event planners."

"Yeah, don't worry about me. I'll find some way to occupy myself. Besides, if Mama and Earl make short work of buying a camper, I'm sure she'll think of something she wants me to do. Although I'm hoping I can avoid having to shop for more items for her 'trousseau.' Honestly, if Mama buys much more than she's already packed, there won't be room for Earl in the camper."

Larry Joe filled his pants pockets with change and keys and his wallet off the dresser, then kissed me good-bye.

It was still a little early, so I texted Di. About thirty seconds later she called.

"Hi. Do you want to do something or do you have plans with Dave?" I asked.

"I have plans to avoid Dave. I'm up to anything that involves us getting out of this hotel, so I don't have to run into him."

"Okay, I have a couple of brochures lying on the dresser," I said, paging through the tourist flyers. "What sounds good? There's a five-acre indoor amusement park at Circus Circus. It includes a roller coaster that goes backward with negative g-force."

"I'll pass."

"Here's a place with a 117,000-gallon aquarium."

"Do the fish perform some kind of show?"

"They're fish, not trained seals. Okay, moving on. There's the Fremont Street Experience. That has a little bit of everything—shopping, restaurants, and free entertainment under a giant LED canopy."

"That sounds good. It gives us options and gets us out of here," Di said.

"I think it said in the brochure we can take a bus to the Fremont thing. It might be cheaper," I said.

"Let's just grab a taxi. That'll be faster; I just want to get away from the hotel—now."

We asked the driver to drop us off at the Fremont Street Experience.

"It's really neat to come here after dark," he said.

"I bet," I said, thinking that was probably true of Vegas in general.

He dropped us off near the front of the canopy that covered five or six blocks, creating a pedestrian mall. We walked along without conversation for a bit, just people watching. They say there are all kinds of people—and most of them were here.

"This looks like it would be an ideal location to shoot an episode of that reality show about tragic fashion choices," I said.

There were shops offering every tacky Vegas souvenir you could think of. Naturally we stopped to look at most of them. We contemplated buying strawberry daiquiris, a favorite libation of ours, in these huge Eiffel Tower–shaped drink containers. But when we found out the containers held sixty ounces we thought that might be a bit much, even for us. At least this early in the day.

As we walked there was the constant sound of people screaming over our heads, thanks to a pair of zip lines near the top of the canopy. It was noisy, so I felt like we could talk in relative privacy. Only people talking nearly head to head would be able to hear any conversation.

"You still on the outs with Dave?"

"He's still acting ridiculous. He asked me if I'd seen Jimmy again. 'Again' being after he came over and stood between us while we were having a drink the night we arrived in town. I told him that yes, Jimmy and I grabbed a quick lunch here at the hotel yesterday. And he just said, 'I guess you're grown,' and stormed off. He couldn't have acted more like a gorilla if he had beat his chest and flung poo."

"Are you maybe trying to make him jealous? Just a little?"

"No, I'm not trying to make him jealous, even a

little. But I don't like him acting territorial. I can talk to whomever I please. It's not like I'm romantically involved with Jimmy."

"Does Dave know that?" I asked.

"Of course he knows. I haven't seen Jimmy in more than six years. He knows that."

"He knows you haven't been seeing Jimmy. But maybe he's worried you still have feelings for the guy. You were married to him, after all."

"So are you telling me I shouldn't talk to Jimmy?"

"No. And I'm not saying Dave hasn't behaved badly. I'm just saying, try to see it from Dave's point of view. What if he had an ex-wife he hadn't run into in six years and then started spending time around her as soon as you arrived in Vegas? Would you be a little jealous?"

"No. I wouldn't. We're not married or even engaged. What right does either one of us have to be jealous? Could we please talk about something else?"

I spotted a bistro on the corner and suggested we stop there for an early lunch—and maybe a drink. We had a lunch of deli sandwiches and fries, and some wine.

Di and I chatted about work and friends back home and seasonal vegetables—just about everything except Dave and Jimmy, which was fine by me.

Strolling through the mall after lunch, we passed a photo booth with backgrounds, such as the Eiffel Tower and the New York skyline, and Di said she wondered if Jimmy's plans for his photo booth business included anything like that.

I didn't know what to say, but fortunately I was saved by the buzz of my phone.

"It's Holly, I better take it," I said. "Hi, Holly, what's up?"

"I hope I'm not interrupting."

"No, it's fine. It's just a little noisy here. We're at an outdoor mall," I said, walking a few steps into a void away from the walkway and pressing my fingers over my non-phone ear. "How's it going?"

"Things were going pretty well. I'm working my list, double checking with vendors and the caterer. But, the reunion-goers started arriving in town en masse today and suddenly the reunion committee is acting like I'm their personal tourist information bureau. They're calling me to ask questions about Memphis attractions, including quizzing me on prices and hours of operations—stuff they could easily look up online or pick up the phone and just call the place they're talking about, which is what I've been doing for them. I'm trying to be kind, but the constant interruptions are getting a little annoying."

"I'm sorry, Holly. If it's mainly one or two people who keep calling, don't answer those numbers. Call them back in, say, half an hour when you're at a stopping point with what you're working on. Maybe if they have to wait a bit, they'll actually pick up the phone or Google something themselves. They didn't engage us to plan activities for them today, so you are *not* at their beck and call. Is everything worked out for George to prepare the Saturday night dinner at the Moose Lodge?"

"Yes, I took him by and let him have a look at the kitchen. We're good. I'm sorry to complain. I guess I am a little nervous about handling a biggish, multi-day event without you here. But we really are in good shape. Just slightly annoying clients. So what's new, right?"

"Always."

"So is tonight the big night?"

"Yes, tonight my mama gets married. I think I'm more nervous than she is."

"She's marrying a wonderful man and you're there to share the moment. I'm sure everything will be great. Give Virginia my best."

I walked back over to where Di was standing.

"Problems with the fiftieth reunion?" Di said.

"Not really. Just touching base."

"Have you ever been to a high school reunion?"

"We've only had one, so far. My tenth. And, yeah, Larry Joe and I went. It was mostly people we see fairly often. But there were a few who'd moved away. It was nice to see them."

"I can't imagine going to my fiftieth class reunion. I guess it's nice they still have such a large group of classmates," Di said. "Your mama is only a couple of years behind this class, right?"

"Yeah."

"She seemed pretty impressed with what you and Holly have cooked up for this group. What you wanna bet she'll be calling on you to plan her class's fiftieth reunion in a couple of years?"

"Perish the thought."

I started looking for a bar that gave entry into one of the hotels. We found one, so we began snaking our way through the hotel-casino, where we could catch a taxi at the entrance. I wanted to get back to the room to rest up before the wedding tonight, or at least before Mama came up with some to-do list for me.

Di didn't specifically say so, but I gathered she was meeting up with Jimmy again today. She didn't ask for my advice, so I didn't offer any.

Di had been typing on her phone during my call with Holly. I assumed she was just catching up on social media, but I was wrong. When we got to the front of one of the downtown hotels, I started to wave at one of the cabs parked out front, but Di grabbed my arm.

"Our ride will be here in just a minute," she said.

"Did you call Little Junior?"

"No, Jimmy's picking us up."

Chapter Seven

Di's ex pulled up in a Toyota that looked brand new.

Di got in the front passenger seat and I climbed into the backseat.

Jimmy briefly glanced back at me, nodded, and said, "Hi," before turning his full attention to Di.

"We noticed a photo booth along the promenade under the long canopy, with backgrounds of the New York skyline and the Eiffel Tower. Is that the kind of photo booth you're looking to invest in?" Di asked with keen interest.

"Yeah, eventually. We'll start out with the smaller, portable kinds. But later expand to some larger ones in leased spaces like at the Fremont Experience. They're pretty cool, right? And there's an endless variety in the kind of photo experiences you can create with them. Truly something for everyone."

Hearing Jimmy launch into a sales pitch that sounded like it was lifted from a sales brochure worried me. I hoped he wasn't going to try to hit Di up for money. But that concern wasn't one I planned to share with Di.

As Jimmy pulled up to our hotel, I spotted Larry Joe and his dad getting out of a taxi. Dave was with them. Apparently, he'd hooked up with them at some point—probably for lunch. I was hoping Dave wouldn't see us getting out of Jimmy's car. But Jimmy made absolutely sure that was not the case.

He revved the engine a bit, sped up, and zipped up to the curb, sliding in between two taxis.

Dave's dark glare cast a shadow over us as we got out of the car. I walked briskly over to join Larry Joe and his dad. Di was lagging behind and Dave remained statue-like next to the entrance. After we made it into the lobby, I glanced back to see what was going on with Di and Dave. I couldn't hear what they were saying, but I could tell it wasn't a friendly conversation.

I started asking Larry Joe and Daddy Wayne about their day so far. As expected, it included lunch at some big buffet at a neighboring hotel that Daddy Wayne had seen an advertisement about. He was recounting the highlights of the dessert bar when Di came storming past us toward the elevators.

Dave spoke as he walked slowly past, saying he might try his luck in the casino for a bit.

Daddy Wayne said he thought he should check on my mother-in-law. We were following behind him moving in the direction of the elevators. I told Larry Joe I wanted to rest a bit before Mama returned with a to-do list for me. Larry Joe said he thought maybe he should keep Dave company.

"He seems kind of down," Larry Joe said.

"I think it would be nice of you to spend some time with Dave. I'll try to gently nudge Di in his direction if she gives me the chance."

Upstairs, I stretched out on the bed, but my cell phone buzzed almost the minute I closed my eyes.

"I plan to go downstairs and drink for a while. Care to join me?" Di said.

"I suppose I could join you for an afternoon cocktail."

I wasn't really enthusiastic about drinking, but I was hoping I could encourage Di in the direction of moderation—and in the direction of making nice with Dave.

I met her at the elevators.

There wasn't much conversation as we walked across the lobby, into the casino, and straight to the bar.

We ordered two strawberry daiquiris and sat silently for a few moments before Di said, "He could clearly see that *both* of us were in the car with Jimmy. That would seem to make it obvious there was nothing romantic going on—even for somebody as dense as Dave."

"Maybe he just wonders why you want to spend time with your ex at all, knowing what Jimmy put you through."

"Then why doesn't he ask me instead of making assumptions, stupid assumptions," she said, staring straight ahead.

I wanted to suggest maybe she needed to be the one to start that conversation, but I didn't know how to phrase it in a way that wouldn't make her even madder.

My phone vibrated. I looked down and saw I had a text from Mama about shopping. I decided to ignore it for the moment. In hindsight, that may not have been my best move.

Since Di didn't seem interested in continuing the conversation about Dave and Jimmy, I changed the subject.

"So, what are you planning to wear to the wedding tonight?"

"A cute sundress in a green print. I got it on sale at that place up on the highway, near Rascal's Bar and Grill."

"Green sundress? I can't place it. Have I seen you wear it?"

"No, it's new. Prepare to be wowed," she said with sarcasm, but also with a hint of a smile.

I thought I might broach the subject of Dave again, but then I caught a whiff of Mama's signature perfume, overpowering the fragranced air-conditioning, clouds of cigarette smoke, and the food aromas wafting from the neighboring restaurant buffet. This olfactory assault told me that, as usual, Mama was wearing too much perfume. It also alerted me that she had spotted us.

I swung around on my swivel bar stool. I heard her before I saw her.

"Olivia Louise."

Being called by my first and middle name meant I was in trouble.

"You," she said as she widened her eyes and nodded her head forcefully toward me. "You were supposed to go shopping with me before the wedding to complete my trousseau for the honeymoon."

I'm not sure just how much she thought she could fit in a Winnebago.

"Where's Earl?" I said, trying to deflect attention away from myself.

"All the guys are in the casino. I can't believe you two are bellied up to the bar in the middle of the day," Mama said, half sitting on the bar stool next to me.

"We were just having a little girl talk—about *things*," I said, looking at Mama and nodding sideways toward Di. I hoped the forlorn look on Di's face might elicit a smidge of sympathy.

But no. Mama leaned around me to make eye contact with Di.

"Wayne told me about her tooling around Vegas with her ex-husband. Di, until now I'd always reckoned you to be above average in the smarts department. You need to send your ex packing and fling your arms around Dave's broad shoulders."

Di maintained a stony silence.

"Mama, I really don't think it's our place to tell Di what to do. She has to think things through for herself."

"Hmm, let me see if I can help," Mama said, raising both hands, palm sides up. "Handsome sheriff who's crazy about her. Or fresh-out-of-prison ex-husband who left her in a world of hurt." She raised one palm higher for Dave and dropped the other for the ex.

"Di Souther," Mama said, giving Di a squinty-eyed look. "Pull yourself together. Liv McKay, come with me. I don't have all day."

Mama grabbed my hand and tugged—hard. I acquiesced and waved good-bye to Di, who had drained her daiquiri and was waving the bartender over to order another drink.

I asked Mama if she wanted to look at any of the shops in the hotel.

"Don't be ridiculous. I don't want to pay a fortune for something I could buy at Walmart."

She walked hurriedly toward the door and hailed one of the taxis lined up out front. We got into the back and she asked the driver to take her to the nearest discount department store.

"What specifically are we looking for?" I asked.

"I'd like a housecoat or a lightweight robe and a pair of terrycloth slippers."

"Oh, okay. That shouldn't be too hard to find."

I was relieved beyond words to learn the kind of lingerie Mama had in mind. As happy as I was about her impending nuptials, I didn't relish the idea of shopping with my mother for any barely there sleepwear.

We pulled into the parking lot of a department store I'd never heard of—this particular chain must not have stores in the South.

Our driver dropped us at the door and Mama asked him if he would wait.

"I don't expect we'll be more than fifteen minutes," she said.

"I keep the meter running while you shop," he said without inflection.

"I'd expect nothing different," Mama said as we got out.

"*Hey,*" he called out, this time with inflection. "You have to pay me for the ride thus far. Just in case you don't make it back, for some reason."

Mama started to argue with him, but I took some money out of my purse and handed it to him.

"Thank you. We won't be long."

I tugged on Mama's arm.

"We don't want to stand around arguing with the man while the meter's running."

Inside the store, we asked directions to the plus-size department. The taxi driver had chosen well. The stock, at least in the plus-size department, seemed aimed at a more mature demographic. Mama made short work of completing her trousseau. She held two snap front housecoats up in front of her and eyed them in the three-way mirror before handing one of them to me to hold for her. Then she looked through a bin of slippers that were on clearance. She steadied herself by hanging on to the shelving fixture while she held the bottom of one slipper up to the underside of her shoe.

"These should work," she said, before hot-footing it to the checkout lanes. After paying for the items, Mama walked briskly out the door and waved to the taxi driver, who was parked illegally on an end space, cross-hatched with yellow lines. He pulled over to pick us up.

The taxi ride to and from the store cost considerably more than the eighteen-dollar housecoat and four-dollar clearance slippers. But Mama seemed content. I decided not to ask why she didn't call Little Junior for a ride. But maybe she felt, as I did, that we had already kept him away from paying fares too much.

* * *

I was dressed and helping Larry Joe with his tie when I received a text from Di. She said to go on to the chapel without her; she'd meet us there. I took this to mean she'd left the bar at some point and met up with either Dave or Jimmy. I wanted to believe it was Dave, but I had a sinking feeling it wasn't.

Little Junior wanted to handle the transportation, so shortly after we arrived in Vegas Mama had canceled the limousine she and Earl had hired for the wedding. My cousin had mentioned to Di and me that he had a surprise planned for Mama. He didn't say what it was, and after seeing her less than enthusiastic response to Earl telling her he had a surprise in store for her, I decided not to mention it.

Since Mama didn't want Earl to see her before the ceremony, Little Junior would be taking the women, minus Di, apparently, and plus Crystal, to the chapel first. The men would be traveling to the chapel in the new Winnebago Earl and Mama had bought earlier in the day. I hadn't seen it yet, but Larry Joe said it was a luxury barge on wheels.

Mama, Miss Betty, and I waited at the front entrance for Little Junior. I was holding the garment bag containing Mama's dress, and my mother-in-law was carrying Mama's oversized makeup bag. Mama was holding a hanky and a small handbag.

We didn't have to wait long to discover what Little Junior's surprise was. He pulled up in a 1959 pink Cadillac convertible. His smile was broader and shinier than a car grill as he hopped out of the car and rushed around to open the front door for Mama. Crystal climbed into the backseat and Miss Betty and I joined her.

"Your chariot awaits," he told Mama, motioning for her to step inside. "And don't worry, Aunt Virginia, I'm going to put the top up, so your hair won't get mussed before the wedding."

Mama did look relieved—and pleased.

I had half expected Little Junior to be dressed as Elvis, but he looked normal, or close to normal. He was wearing a blue suit. He still had the mutton-chop sideburns, but his hair was combed in a more contemporary, less greased fashion. My cousin actually cleaned up nicely.

Crystal also looked attractive, wearing a blue knee-length dress instead of her casino uniform.

We drove to the Burning Love Wedding Chapel, with Elvis tunes playing on the stereo. Apparently this car had been retrofitted with a CD player. Little Junior pulled up to the door just as a florist's delivery van was pulling away.

"Oh, good. Hopefully that means Mama's bouquet will be fresh," I said.

"I should hope so," Mama said. "They're charging us a blamed fortune for the flowers."

Mama stepped out of the car, turned to Little Junior, and with a stern look said, "I don't want any foolishness between you and Steve today. You hear me?"

"Don't you worry, Aunt Virginia. I promise not to embarrass you and Uncle Earl on your wedding day."

"You just leave it to me," Crystal said. "I'll make sure the boys behave."

Taylor greeted us and led us back to the dressing

room, with Mama following her and us trailing Mama.

"I'd better go to the little girls' room before I put my dress on," Mama said.

I'm not sure why she needed the big cosmetics bag, since she already had her makeup on. But she did touch up her blush and powder her nose, before putting on a fresh coat of lipstick. Miss Betty and I each pulled out our own lipstick and did a touch-up, as well. Mama slipped behind a privacy screen and peeled off her outer garments before slipping into her dress. I helped Mama with her zipper and Miss Betty fastened her necklace.

Mama turned to face the three-way mirror and all three of us stood there admiring the way she looked in the deep purple floor-length dress. It had sequins, an Egyptian-inspired collar, sheer sleeves, and a short train. It was a bit over the top—and suited Mama's personality perfectly.

"Aw, Mama, you're beautiful," I said, stretching up to give my nearly six-foot-tall mother a kiss on the cheek.

"Liv's right, Virginia. You look lovely."

In a moment, there was a tap on the door. It was Taylor.

"Gordy, your photographer, would like to snap a couple of pictures, if you're ready."

"Sure," I said, opening the door.

He staged an artful photo of Mama in front of the mirror poised to put on her lipstick, while Miss Betty fastened Mama's necklace and I held her bridal bouquet. And a second photo with a mother-daughter moment as I handed Mama her bouquet.

"Beautiful. Thanks," Gordy said, as he took a look

at the pictures he'd just shot on his digital camera. "Everyone's in place in the chapel whenever you're ready to begin."

Gordy walked ahead of us. I felt butterflies in my stomach as we reached the chapel. I gave Mama's hand a squeeze before slipping inside.

Mama had asked Larry Joe to walk her down the aisle. He was waiting for us just outside the chapel doors.

Miss Betty and I hurried to our seats just as the music began to play. She slid into a seat beside Daddy Wayne in the front row. I sat down in the front row on the opposite side, leaving the end chair open for Larry Joe.

I noted that the Elvis-styled minister at the front of the chapel was Steve—the one who had gotten into a tussle with Little Junior. I was glad he was the officiant because I knew he had a lovely voice, but I was a little nervous, too, hoping he and my cousin would behave.

Standing next to the minister, Earl was grinning from one bright red ear to the other. I noted Earl was wearing an Elvis *Blue Hawaii* print tie and blue suede shoes. I smiled, surmising this was the little surprise he had for Mama, since she had only told me he was going to wear his best blue suit. As I looked back to watch Mama's entrance I could see Little Junior and Crystal sitting just behind my in-laws, holding hands. Di came in and sat down, wearing the new sundress she'd mentioned. It was really cute. Dave slipped in a moment later and took a seat on the row behind Di, just as Mama started walking toward the minister. I had hoped the wedding might stir fond romantic feelings between

the two of them, but the appearance of Jimmy
Souther had apparently nixed that.

Gordy was positioned halfway down the aisle. He
snapped a picture of the bride, and then stepped
aside. Steve began singing "Can't Help Falling in
Love" as Mama floated down the aisle like Cleopatra
on the Nile. Despite my best efforts, a tear tumbled
out of the corner of my eye.

When Mama and Larry Joe reached the front,
Larry Joe took his seat. Mama handed me her bouquet of roses, which matched the ones in vases on
pedestals behind Steve. He took Mama's hand,
placed it in Earl's and continued singing, looking
only at Mama and Earl. The photographer had
moved to the front, left-hand side of the chapel and
kept snapping photos unobtrusively.

"Take my hand, take my whole life, too . . ."

Steve wrapped up the song, but his crooning
didn't sound as smooth as it had the first night
when we had watched the wedding ceremony
through the chapel door windows.

"Dearly beloved, I want to thank you all, thank ya
very much for gathering here today. Earl couldn't
help falling in love with Virginia and wants to be
her forever teddy bear."

The minister's intro elicited smiles and chuckles
from our little congregation, but his voice was a bit
shaky. Looking more closely, I could see his face was
bathed in sweat.

"And the two of them have decided it's now or
never for them to be joined in the noble estate of
matrimony," Steve said, looking unsteady on his feet
and gently swaying from side to side. He suddenly
stopped and gasped. His face took on a bluish tinge

and I thought he might be having a heart attack. His body seemed to spasm. With another gasp, he fell to the floor.

Dave rushed to the front and knelt down beside Steve. After checking for a pulse, he began to perform CPR and called out for someone to dial 911, and for someone else to check with the desk to see if they had a defibrillator on the premises. Di dialed 911. Larry Joe rushed out of the chapel. And Mama crumpled onto the chair next to me, sobbing.

Taylor rushed into the chapel after Larry Joe had asked her about the defibrillator. She looked down at Steve as Dave valiantly continued with CPR. She began to sob, her shoulders shuddering, when it seemed apparent he was beyond reviving. Dave continued CPR until the EMTs arrived. He stepped away to let them take charge, then he turned to us and shook his head. I had given my seat to Earl, who had his arm around Mama with her head on his shoulder. Obviously, having the minister drop dead during the ceremony had put a damper on the wedding.

The police had arrived just after the paramedics and had taken a statement from each of us, not that there was much we could tell them. As the cops were taking statements I couldn't help noticing Crystal, who had previously dated Steve, was shedding no tears. Little Junior, who wasn't a fan, was surveying his surroundings as if he was studying the sparse decor. I imagined he was thinking there might be an opening for him now as a minister at the Burning Love Chapel. Looking around, I noted that the photographer had apparently slipped out of the chapel at some point during all the hubbub.

The police officer took our contact information and said that an autopsy would have to be performed. But all indications were that Steve had suffered a heart attack.

The paramedics had rolled the deceased out on a gurney and the cop was standing in the doorway to the chapel chatting with Dave.

Taylor may have broken down in tears when she saw Steve lying on the floor, but she composed herself enough to talk business.

She apologized to Mama and Earl and asked if they would like to reschedule.

"I'm sure this has been upsetting, but I know you're only in town for a limited time. If you want to go ahead with a wedding today, we do have an opening at eleven p.m. tonight in one of the other chapels. Of course, there would be no additional charge for the larger space."

Mama and Earl looked at Taylor in disbelief. For once my mother was speechless. Earl spoke up.

"Thank you, but I don't think Virginia and I are in any frame of mind to continue with the wedding tonight."

"Of course. Just give me a call when you're ready." Taylor started to walk away, but stopped and turned back to face the nearly wedded couple. "Oh, by the way, take the rose arrangements with you, if you like, since you've already paid for them."

I wanted to get up and smack Taylor for her appalling lack of sensitivity. But Little Junior rushed over to Mama and offered to carry the flowers out to the car if she wanted them.

"Sure, hon, if you want to," Mama said blankly.

I assumed my cousin was just eager to do something nice for Mama and toting flower pots was the best he could come up with. He and Crystal walked to the front to retrieve the floral arrangements. When Little Junior picked up the vase from one of the two pedestals, something shiny tumbled to the floor with a metallic thud.

The cop stopped his droning conversation with Dave midsentence and walked to the front of the chapel to have a look. He pulled a handkerchief out of his pocket and picked up a silver-colored flask. He held it up, examining it more closely, then left the chapel without a word.

We assumed we were free to go.

My in-laws got into the Winnebago with Mama and Earl. The rest of us piled into the vintage pink Cadillac. Little Junior got behind the wheel and Crystal sidled up to him. Di climbed in the front seat next to Crystal and Dave got into the backseat. Larry Joe and I exchanged a puzzled look before sliding onto the backseat, with me in the middle. The ride back to the hotel felt like a funeral procession.

Chapter Eight

Despite having gone to bed early, mentally and emotionally exhausted, I didn't sleep well and woke up early the next morning. The wedding chapel had turned into a funeral parlor after our Elvis-impersonating minister dropped dead.

I knew Mama was up by now and I wanted to check to see how she was doing, but I didn't know what to say. Should I encourage her to move forward with wedding plans? I thought about calling and asking Holly's advice, but she wasn't typically an early riser; in fact she usually slept later than I did. So I called someone I knew was already up and going and could be trusted to give me common sense advice. Winette King works at Sweet Deal Realty, located downstairs in the same building as Liv 4 Fun's office on Dixie's town square. She's also a dear friend I could count on to tell me exactly what she thought.

"Hi, Winette, it's Liv."

"I gathered that from the caller ID, but I'm still

surprised to hear from you so early in the morning. Is everybody okay?"

Hearing from me this early in the day caused Winette to jump to the conclusion that someone must have died. And she was right.

"All of us are fine, but we did have a troubling experience last night at the chapel. The upshot is that the minister keeled over dead before Mama and Earl could say their 'I dos.'"

"Oh, my, I would certainly call that troubling."

"I know the man couldn't help dying, but I just wish he had dropped dead before he came in the chapel. Then they probably would have just substituted another Elvis-impersonator minister and continued with the ceremony. As it was, Dave jumped in and performed CPR until the ambulance arrived. And the police came and took statements from all of us. Our wedding celebration turned into a wake. I know that sounds cold. I am truly sorry the minister died. He was too young to die of a heart attack like that. It's just Mama and Earl have been through so much lately. . . ."

"No, Liv, I completely understand. And I do so hate that for your mama—and Earl. *Mmm, mmm*," she said, and I could clearly see Winette in my mind's eye, pursing her lips and shaking her head.

"So what now?" she asked.

"That's what I was hoping you could tell me. Do I encourage Mama to go ahead with the wedding at the chapel, or at a different chapel? Do I offer to arrange a quick wedding at another venue here in Vegas? Do I suggest we go back to Dixie and resume the original plans for a wedding there?"

That last option was the least appealing to me. But seeing how disappointed Mama was last night and the forlorn look on Earl's face just broke my heart. I was willing to wade through swans and conjure up gondolas and gondoliers if it would give them the happiness they deserved.

"Winette, I consider you one of the wisest women I know," I said sincerely. "What do you think I should do?"

"If I'm the wisest woman you know, the first thing you should do is broaden your social circle. But as far as your mama's concerned, I don't think you should talk to her about wedding plans today, unless she brings it up. I think you should get her out doing something fun, something to get her mind off things. If she sits around too much she's just going to be thinking about that dead man in the chapel and her wedding that almost happened."

"You're right. Mama can be emotional at best. She's in no state to make new wedding plans today.

"And speaking of emotions, Holly's got her hands full with that class reunion this week. If you have a chance, could you call and give her some encouragement? I think she's trying not to bother me while we're here in Vegas, so she may need a sympathetic ear," I said.

"Will do. And, good luck with your mama. I'll keep her in my prayers."

Talking to Winette made me feel better. I hoped I could come up with something to make Mama feel better, too.

While I was on the phone, Larry Joe, who had already showered and dressed, whispered to me that he was going downstairs to get us coffee and doughnuts.

Just after I hung up, he came through the door holding two cups of coffee and a white lunch sack. I walked over and took one of the cups and the sack out of his hand, and he kissed my forehead. I grabbed a couple of napkins off the stack lying on top of the doughnuts and used it to extract a chocolate doughnut from the bag.

I sat down on the bed, leaned against the headboard, and bit into my breakfast. Larry Joe sat in the easy chair in the corner of the room.

"So what's the plan for today? Have you talked to your mama yet?"

"No, but Winette gave me some good advice. She said not to propose new wedding plans to Mama and Earl today. But to try to get them out doing something fun."

"Sounds smart to me. The dead body kind of cast a pall over the whole wedding thing. Where do you plan to take them?"

"Di and I went to this kind of outdoor mall yesterday. But it would likely be too much walking for Mama. And I can't really see her or Earl wanting to glide through the air on a zip line."

"Seems unlikely," Larry Joe said, taking another bite of his doughnut and caking his lips with powdered sugar. "They'd probably enjoy something less aerobic."

"Yeah, maybe some kind of tour. That's it," I said.

I started punching in numbers on my cell phone.

"What's *it*?" Larry Joe asked.

"I'm going to see if Little Junior can take them on a tour of Vegas. They can mostly enjoy the view from the car, while Little Junior narrates. But Little Junior could also park and let them take a closer look at attractions where there's not too much walking involved."

"That'll be great for your mama. She worships her nephew. But I think Little Junior may wear on Earl after a while," Larry Joe said.

"Normally, I'd agree. But I think Earl will be willing to put up with Little Junior if Mama's enjoying it."

I explained my idea for the tour to my cousin and how I thought it would be just the thing to cheer Mama up. He was eager to do something nice for her, so it wasn't a hard sell.

I thought Mama might be reluctant to leave the hotel, so I organized my sales pitch in my head before running through it with her.

"Wish me luck. I'm going to talk Mama into having a good time, even if she's dead set against it."

"You do that to people at parties all the time, right?" Larry Joe said, giving me a thumbs-up.

I needed to make this sales pitch in person, so I dropped my phone in my pocket, grabbed my room key card, and walked down the hall. When I tapped on the door, Mama bellowed for me to come in.

Her voice sounded robust enough when she was yelling at me through the door. But as soon as I came in and asked how she was feeling, she answered in a soft, pitiful voice.

"Not too good, hon. I barely slept a wink. Earl and I should have been taking off on our honeymoon today," she said, putting a tissue to her face. The voice may have been an affectation, but the tears were real enough.

"I know, Mama. But that man's death has nothing to do with us, really. We just happened to be the wedding party that was there at the time. Tomorrow we'll start making wedding plans, if you're up to it, but today you and Earl are going on a tour."

"That's very sweet, Liv, but . . ."

I cut her off. "No, hear me out. Little Junior feels so bad about your wedding plans being thwarted. You know he adores you, Mama. And he's determined to do something nice for you. He plans to give you the grand tour."

"I don't know that I'm really up to something like that. . . ."

"Mama, most of the tour will be from the comfort of the taxi. He'll only stop here and there, if you and Earl want, in spots where you won't have to do a lot of walking. It'll give him a chance to do something for you, and also to show off his knowledge of the area. I know you wouldn't want to hurt his feelings. . . ."

"No. And it would be nice to spend some time with him, you know, give him and his Uncle Earl a chance to bond."

I knew bonding time would mean more to Mama and Little Junior than to Earl, but was counting on him being a good sport about it for Mama's sake.

"Little Junior said he could pick you up in front of the hotel in about forty-five minutes," I said, glancing over at the clock on the nightstand. "Can you and Earl be ready to go by then?"

"We've already had breakfast, so I don't see why not. Will you tap on the door, so I can tell Earl about our plans?" Mama said.

I knocked lightly on the connecting door to the next room. Earl opened it almost immediately.

"Hon, Little Junior has come up with the sweetest idea to try to cheer us up."

It wasn't exactly Little Junior's idea, but it was enough for me that Mama seemed pleased. I reminded Mama that they needed to be downstairs in forty minutes and slipped out to let her and Earl talk privately.

I went back to my and Larry Joe's room. He was at the bathroom sink cleaning powdered sugar off his face with a washcloth.

"Mission accomplished," I said, feeling pretty pleased with myself.

"What are your plans for today?" Larry Joe asked.

"With Mama tended to, I was hoping you and I might go out and do something. We've barely gotten to spend any time together. And you did spend quality time with your dad yesterday."

"I spend enough quality time with my dad every day at the office. Do you need to look after Di?"

"Di can look after herself. She's got two men vying for her attention. I've just got the one man, and I'd like to spend some time with him," I said, walking into the bathroom, stepping up behind him at the sink and wrapping my arms around his waist.

"Sounds good to me," he said, his reflection grinning at me in the mirror.

"Where should we go?" I said.

"You think Little Junior would have room for us to tag along on the grand tour?" he said with a smirk.

I smacked his backside.

"We'll ask the concierge for some ideas," he

continued. "No, wait, Liv. I haven't seen you do anything in the casino, except maybe sit at the bar. You haven't so much as pulled the arm on a one-armed bandit since we've been here, have you?"

"I hid behind a slot machine for a few minutes, watching Di and Jimmy."

"That's pretty exciting. How about we leave the Strip and go downtown to one of the old-school casinos."

"I'm sorry, honey, but losing money isn't my idea of fun," I said.

"That's just it. We can experience a little of what Vegas was like back in the day. And we don't have to gamble a lot of money to do it.

"I was reading somewhere online," he said, staring at his smartphone and scrolling with his thumb. "I thought I bookmarked it. . . . Here it is. At some of the downtown casinos, they have minimum wagers of only three to five dollars at the blackjack and craps tables. And, it says at El Cortez you can take a spin on the roulette wheel for just a dollar bid. What do you say?"

What I said was yes, though somewhat reluctantly. But he seemed pumped up about the idea. I've certainly gone along with more outrageous ideas. Like going to an Elvis chapel in Vegas with Mama. I owed it to Larry Joe to humor him once in a while. So we took a taxi and headed downtown.

Walking through the lobby of Golden Gate Casino, we did view a little of that "back in the day" Vegas. There was a row of the original one-armed bandits—just for looks, and the first telephone in Vegas. The phone number was 1.

I'd never played the tables, blackjack and such, back home at the Tunica, Mississippi, casinos because I'd always thought those games were for high rollers. So it was totally worth it to slap down a few dollars just to be able to say stuff like "hit me" and "let it ride."

We tossed one-dollar bills and quarters around with abandon and then hit the bar where rat packers like Dean Martin and Sammy Davis Jr. used to get liquored up. They served us cocktails in coffee mugs, a nod and a wink back to the days of prohibition.

We dined at a classic eatery with very private high-backed booths and ordered a bottle of wine with lunch, which seemed decadent—for us anyway.

"Larry Joe, I'm glad you talked me into the old-school casino tour. This has been fun. And this dressing is really good, definitely homemade," I said, spearing a forkful of salad.

"Yeah, hon, it's been a nice break, getting away from the folks a bit with you—not that I don't love them dearly."

"Always dearly, just not always near me, is that it?"

"Something like that. Speaking of dearly, Dave told me he saw Jimmy drop Di off in front of the chapel last night. Did she tell you she was seeing him again?"

"She didn't, but I had gathered as much when she texted to let me know she wouldn't be riding with us to the chapel. Said she'd meet us there."

"So has her ex become her regular taxi service, or is there more to it?"

"There's nothing romantic, if that's what you mean," I said.

"Are you sure, because Dave was crying in his beer, going on about how Di was wearing this pretty dress he'd never seen her wear before. How she was running around Vegas, buying new clothes to get all dolled up for her ex."

"Okay, I know Dave's feeling jealous, but he's making some assumptions that just aren't true. First off, Di didn't buy that new dress for her ex; she bought it for the wedding. And she didn't buy it when she and I were out shopping in Vegas; she bought it back in Dixie—and on sale at that store next to Rascal's on the highway."

"That's good to know. I just feel bad for Dave. Di is kind of ignoring him. And he's crazy about her, you know," he said.

"I know. But they'll have to work things out for themselves."

It had been a fun day. We caught a taxi back to the hotel for some more private couple time and a nap. I silently resolved that, when we got home, in between planning parties for other people, I was going to plan more date nights for Larry Joe and me.

I was just checking messages when Mama texted. She said they were headed back to the hotel and she'd like all of us to meet in the lobby for dinner at about five-thirty.

We got dressed and steeled ourselves for more family time.

"Honey, I hope Mama's feeling better after the grand tour today," I said.

"How could she not be? She spent the day with her two favorite fellas."

They were running a few minutes late, so the rest of us were already gathered in the lobby waiting when Mama and Earl came in through the front door.

"Little Junior and Crystal will be joining us for dinner," Mama said. "He's just gone to park the car. I'm telling y'all, we had the most wonderful day, didn't we, Earl?"

"You know, I have to admit I really enjoyed it."

Earl sounded sincere, so it seemed my cousin's grand tour was a hit.

While we were all standing in a circle waiting for Little Junior so we could go to dinner, Di and Dave were standing on opposite sides. Something they seemed to be doing a lot of lately. Di spotted a cop from the wedding chapel standing near the door and nudged me.

"Uh-oh, looks like dinner might get delayed by more questions from the cops," she whispered.

Little Junior entered the hotel sporting a big smile and walking with a bounce to his step. But no sooner had he made it through the front door when the cop we recognized from the chapel was joined by two uniformed officers standing on the opposite side of the lobby. The three of them walked briskly over to Little Junior, placed him under arrest, and handcuffed him. He looked shocked and confused as they started to walk him out.

Mama rushed toward him, but Earl and Larry Joe restrained her.

"Don't make a scene, Virginia," Earl said in an intense whisper. "It'll only make things worse for Little Junior. Let Dave find out what's going on."

Dave hurried over to the cop he'd talked with at the chapel, but he didn't seem receptive to a chat just now. Dave walked back over to our group.

"He was being tight-lipped. But I heard one of the officers reading Little Junior his Miranda rights. That indicates he's under arrest."

"For what?" Miss Betty said in disbelief.

"Based on that guy's coloring when I was performing CPR, I'm guessing the flask that was taken into evidence contained some kind of poison as well as whiskey," Dave said.

Mama broke down *boohoo*-ing the way she does at funerals. Earl and Larry Joe took her arm on either side and I followed along behind them to the elevator. People gawked and whispered as we walked by.

Crystal came in from the casino just after they'd taken Little Junior away, thinking she was meeting us all for dinner. Di took her aside to explain things.

Everyone had lost their appetite, except Daddy Wayne, but I heard Miss Betty tell him they could order room service. They joined the procession to the elevators behind my inconsolable mother.

As we stepped off the elevator on our floor, Mama suddenly cried out, "We have to call Junior. I don't know if my brother's heart will be able to handle his only child being arrested for murder."

I told Mama to go lie down and that I'd take care of calling Uncle Junior. She broke down wailing again as Larry Joe and Earl physically kept her on her feet to the hotel room door.

I made the dreaded phone call to my uncle and broke the news as gently as I could. After a moment of silence on the line, he said he'd throw a few things in a suitcase and hit the road in fifteen minutes.

Chapter Nine

Larry Joe and I stayed up and waited for Uncle Junior to make it in. I had promised Mama that we would, and encouraged her to try to get some sleep. She should have been on her honeymoon by now. She and Earl had planned to leave first thing this morning for their honeymoon on wheels across the Southwest. Now our biggest concern was Little Junior.

It was about a five-hour drive from Phoenix to Vegas. Uncle Junior made it in just before midnight. We were able to get him a room on the same floor with the rest of us. After the long drive, he was dead on his feet—and so were we. Larry Joe carried his suitcase. We said our good nights in the hall outside his door.

I slept only in fits and starts, thinking about my cousin sleeping on a jail cot, and even worse, thinking about my mama worrying and crying over him and his daddy. I'd been awake since 5:30 a.m. and decided to go ahead and get up a little after 6:00. Larry Joe was already in the shower. I knew Mama and Earl were generally early risers, but I decided to wait until 6:30 to call, just in case Mama was sleeping in after a difficult night.

"Mama, I hope I didn't wake you."

"Don't be silly, hon. I've been up since before five. Earl and I are having breakfast with your Uncle Junior now, courtesy of room service. I thought we could talk privately about family matters better here. Plus you can't hear thunder down at that buffet with the clatter of dishes and hundreds of people talking at once."

"Oh, good," I said, glad they were eating something. Not that I've ever known my mother to lose her appetite, even in a crisis. "How's Uncle Junior holding up?"

"He's in Earl's room right now on the phone with some man he knows here, trying to track down a good attorney for Little Junior. I'm hoping Dave can help us with the police, or at least to get Junior in to see his son."

"I hope so, too. So, Mama, what do you want to do today? Do you want me to book us for massages at the hotel spa? We can talk about rescheduling the wedding. Whatever you want, just name it."

"I don't want a massage—and I can't think about the wedding until things are straightened out with Little Junior. What I really want is for you and Di to do that thing you do when somebody you know has been falsely accused of murder. I want you to find the real killer."

"Mama, you know I'll do what I can, but this isn't Dixie. We don't really know anybody here and—"

Mama interrupted. "I've gotta let you go, hon. Junior just got off the phone and is trying to tell us something about the lawyer. Check in later to let me know how your investigation is coming along."

Larry Joe emerged from the bathroom, his loins wrapped in a towel. "How are your mama and Uncle Junior this morning?"

"Worried."

"Me too. I can't see Little Junior faring well in prison," Larry Joe said. "I suppose your mama wants you and Di to do some snooping."

"She mentioned it."

"I guess you have to. But stay in well-populated areas. Don't go off into lonely spaces with a potential killer at large. Maybe you should take Crystal with you, since she knows the city well. And keep Dave in the loop, even if he and Di are fussing. Tell her it's not about them right now. And let *me* know what's going on, too. I better check on Mama and Daddy and see if Earl needs to return the Winnebago."

Larry Joe got dressed while I started trying to tame my hair and slap on some makeup. He stuck his head through the bathroom door before he headed out.

"Be careful," he said, with a concerned but resigned look. "I'm serious. Be careful."

"I promise."

He gave me a quick kiss before he left. I texted Di.

Your room or mine?

She replied almost instantly: Come here.

I grabbed my hotel room key card and purse, walked down the hall, and tapped on her door. She opened it, hiding partly behind the door, still in her pajamas.

"I wondered when I'd hear from you this morning. So what's your plan for getting Little Junior out of jail?"

"Unfortunately, I don't have one. But Mama seems to have every confidence that you and I will find the real killer and have Little Junior home by supper time. Any ideas?"

"I know the cops aren't saying so, but since the only evidence they collected at the chapel was that flask hidden behind the flowers, Reverend Elvis must have been poisoned. I think I read somewhere that women are more likely to use poison, while men use guns and knives and such. So, who do we like for killing Elvis in the chapel with the poison?"

"Taylor, the wedding planner," I said. "She and the deceased obviously had something going on. Mama and Earl saw them together, quarreling, then cuddling in the chapel. And she would have known all about Steve's drinking and where he stashed his flask during weddings. I think we should talk to her. But first, let's talk to Crystal. She used to date Steve, so maybe we can dig a bit into his background. Plus, Larry Joe suggested we ask Crystal to go along with us since she's a local and we don't know our way around town."

"How do we get in touch with her unless she's at work? We don't even know her last name, do we?"

"No. But I'm pretty sure she and Little Junior are cohabiting—even though they were careful not to say so in front of Mama. I'll call Uncle Junior and ask for her home number. I don't imagine Little

Junior would have felt the need to hide his living arrangements from his daddy."

"Good idea. But despite how much your mama seems to like her, we can't rule Crystal out as a suspect. She did date Steve before she got together with Little Junior. And, in my experience, being in a relationship with any man usually brings with it grounds for justifiable homicide."

"I won't argue with that. But I can guarantee you that all of Crystal's shine will turn dull for Mama in a minute if throwing her under the bus will get Little Junior off the hook."

I phoned Uncle Junior and, as I suspected, he had a home phone number for Crystal. Crystal's shift didn't start until five and she somewhat grudgingly agreed to drive us to the Burning Love Wedding Chapel. She seemed more enthusiastic about it after I said I'd fill her in on where things stood with getting a lawyer for Little Junior. Although, she might be disappointed with my depth of knowledge on the subject. After talking to my uncle, about all I knew was he had one.

Crystal was supposed to pick us up at the hotel entrance in about thirty minutes. I sat in the desk chair in Di's room, while she stood in front of the bathroom mirror to put on her makeup.

Talking to her without having to make eye contact made it easier for me to ask, "Where do things stand with you and Dave? It seemed a bit chilly between you two at the chapel last night."

"As you know, I'd gone to meet with Jimmy and didn't make it back to the hotel in time to ride to the chapel with you and your mama, so Jimmy dropped me off there. I was prepared to give Dave another chance after he acted like a mule's backside when he met Jimmy. But he was standing at the front door of the chapel and saw me get out of Jimmy's car. When I came in, he just glared at me as I walked past, without saying a word. He makes me so mad I could spit nails. So that's where things stand between me and Dave."

I decided a follow-up question wouldn't be welcome and changed the subject.

Di and I had been waiting for a few minutes when Crystal pulled up in an old Volkswagen Beetle, adorned with flower power stickers and rust. I climbed in and perched my haunches on the narrow back bench, letting Di have the front passenger bucket seat. I had to lean forward to keep from hitting the roof, which positioned my head between the front seats, nearly aligned with Crystal's and Di's heads.

When Crystal pushed the stick shift into gear, the car lurched forward and I almost tumbled onto the console. I grabbed the headrests on the front seats to steady myself. The ride continued herky-jerky as Crystal navigated through traffic. Either the transmission was slipping, or she didn't know how to drive a stick.

"So, tell me about the lawyer for Little Junior," Crystal said.

"His daddy checked around with some folks he knows here and got a really good one. The lawyer was going to meet Uncle Junior at the jail. And, our friend Dave, who you met, is the sheriff back home in Dixie. He's going to help smooth the way with the cops."

I decided to move on to other subjects before she

questioned me further, since I didn't know anything further.

"So, Crystal, do you know anything about Taylor, the wedding planner?"

"Not really. I gathered she was sleeping with Steve. But there's a long list of women in that category. I do know that she's not likely to talk to you two if you just waltz in there trying to interrogate her. Your best bet would be to pretend you want to reschedule your mama's wedding. And, she doesn't care much for me, so I'll wait in the car."

Crystal parked and I climbed over the passenger seat that Di had leaned forward for me, my exit from the vehicle managing somehow to be even less ladylike than when I had climbed in.

"Did you notice Crystal said she doesn't really know Taylor? Yet, Taylor knows her well enough to not like her?" I said.

"Maybe she just assumes Taylor doesn't like her since she dated Steve in the past," Di said, as we walked across the parking lot to the door.

Taylor wasn't at her usual spot when we entered, but I caught a glimpse of Gordy, the photographer, walking by in the side hall leading to the smaller chapels.

"Why don't we go see what we can find out from Gordy, while Taylor's not around?" I said. "Hopefully, he's not shooting a wedding at the moment."

A ceremony was in progress in the chapel where we'd seen Steve performing a wedding our first night in town. We walked quietly down to the chapel where Steve had died and spotted Gordy sitting on the back row of seats sorting through his camera bag.

"Hi, it's Gordy, right?" I said as we stepped into the empty chapel.

"Right," he said, rising to his feet and nodding hello. "You were with the wedding party when Steve collapsed, weren't you?"

"Yes, we were. It was just terrible what happened," I said. "And to make things even worse, the police have arrested my cousin. We know Little Junior could never kill anyone."

"Yeah, Little Junior doesn't seem the type."

"We're looking for any information that could help with my cousin's defense. I'm sure you already talked to the police, but if you could tell us anything . . ."

"The cops were back here first thing this morning and did a thorough search of the building. They carried a few things out in bags, but I don't know what. They also took my camera card to look at shots from during the day. I've got wedding photos on that card that I haven't uploaded yet. They assured me they'd make a copy and get it back to me within a day—or two. All that's on there are pictures I took during ceremonies, so I doubt there's anything that will be helpful anyway."

"Can you tell us anything about Steve?" I said. "Had he acted odd or had a run-in with anybody lately?"

"I heard he had a run-in with Little Junior," he said with a sly smile.

"Was there anything else?" Di interjected quickly, apparently fearing I might lose my temper—and blow our chance for getting any information from Gordy.

"I don't know what it means, but even though

Steve didn't have another performing gig going, he'd been flush with cash lately. He just bought a fancy new car and a TCB ring with real diamonds. And I saw him whip out a wad of cash to pay for drinks when we were at a bar last week with some friends."

"What about you—do you have any other paying gigs besides the chapel weddings?" I asked.

"Quite a few, actually. I do a bit of advertising photography, shoot some events, like charity galas. In fact, tomorrow morning I'm doing a photo shoot at the Venetian with some beauty pageant contestants. Shooting weddings here isn't my biggest paycheck but it's steady work, while the other jobs come and go."

Some people walked into the chapel, presumably guests for the next scheduled wedding, so we took that as our cue to leave. We quietly thanked Gordy as we left the chapel. Just as we entered the lobby, Taylor stepped into the reception area from the back hallway.

"Excuse me. What were you two doing in the chapel area? We have ceremonies scheduled."

"The bride couldn't find her hanky when we got back to the hotel last night," Di lied. "We were just checking the chapel to see if she dropped it there."

"If she did, I'm sure the police collected it as evidence," Taylor said.

"It's monogrammed, so if they found it, hopefully they'll return it," Di said.

"Actually, Taylor, I was hoping to talk to you," I said. She flashed me a fleeting "Oh, no, not you again" expression before she rallied and forced a smile.

"It's Mrs. Walford, isn't it?"

"I'm her daughter, yes. As you can imagine, my mother is still a little shook up, so she's resting. But I wanted to talk to you about rescheduling the wedding."

"Of course. I heard about Little Junior's arrest. I'm sure that hasn't helped his aunt's frame of mind."

I detected some snark in her comment but decided to let it pass.

"Of course, none of us think for a minute that Little Junior had anything to do with Steve's death. You worked with Steve—what do you make of all this?"

"I knew he had a drinking problem and I just assumed he'd had a heart attack, until I heard about the arrest."

"Did Steve have a family? A wife, kids?"

"An ex-wife in California. No kids," Taylor said, her eyes shooting daggers. "Did your mother have a time in mind for rescheduling?"

"Perhaps this weekend. There's a limit to how long we can stay here. But, naturally, we're concerned about Little Junior's situation."

"Naturally," she said, using a mouse to scroll down her computer screen. "Weekends are busy for us. Right now, I have an opening at ten-thirty Saturday night. But that may not last long. It's possible we could also have a cancellation. Some people do get cold feet."

"If you don't mind my asking, how did you hear about Little Junior's arrest? From the police?"

"The police were back here this morning, but they didn't say anything about the arrest. I heard it from a friend," Taylor said. "You need to let me know as soon as possible about the rescheduling."

We were clearly being dismissed.

Di and I walked out the front door.

"That was quick thinking with the monogrammed hanky. I never knew you were such a smooth liar," I said, thinking how Di usually tended toward brutal honesty.

"Just one of my many talents—when the situation calls for it."

The VW was parked on the side in the shade. We walked over and climbed into our previous spots in the Beetle. Crystal was eating a candy bar.

"I get low blood sugar," she said as she licked melty chocolate off her fingertips.

"Crystal, Taylor said that Steve had an ex-wife in California. Besides her, can you think of anyone with a motive to kill him?" I asked.

"Just about anyone who knew him. He was a vain, self-centered womanizer."

"Is that what first attracted you to him?" Di asked with her deadpan charm.

"Obviously, he's good-looking, and he can be extremely charming. And he is talented. He seems like a catch until you get to know him."

"Do you know if he recently had any regular gigs, besides the chapel, or any regular women, besides Taylor?"

"I don't know that I'd describe Taylor as a regular. I think she was more a fallback between other women. I have caught sight of him a few times recently at the hotel."

"Was he gambling?"

"No, he was stepping into or out of the elevators that go up to the guest rooms. He had a part in the Ages of Elvis Show, playing the role of Elvis in his 1968 Comeback Special era. That show ended its run at the hotel a couple of months ago. But Steve could have hooked up with some woman who has a part in a current show or with someone who works at the hotel."

"You don't have any ideas who he might've been seeing?"

"No. I know I'm not flattering myself, seeing as I went out with him a few times. But honestly, it wouldn't surprise me if he was involved with any female as long as she's breathing."

In the rearview mirror, I spotted a woman walking to the back of the lot.

"Isn't that Taylor?" I said.

"I think so," Di said, eyeing the side mirror.

"You two duck down—quick," Crystal said.

Di put her face to her knees and I leaned over until my head was almost touching the gear shift.

"That's her, all right," Crystal said. "And she's getting into a black Cadillac."

"I wonder where she's off to," Di said.

"Crystal, let's follow her and see what she's up to. It's kind of early for lunch."

"Yeah, and that's not her car. It's one of the limos they use to pick up bridal parties. But I can't imagine Taylor working as a chauffeur."

Crystal fired up the bug and Di and I briefly ducked again as Taylor drove past on the other side of a line of cars.

"Will Taylor recognize your car?" Di asked.

"I don't know that she's ever seen my car, but I'll hang back a bit just to be safe."

She pulled out and fishtailed into her lane with just one car between us and Taylor.

I feared we were going to lose her when Taylor pushed a traffic light. Fortunately, the car between us ran the yellow light, too. Crystal stomped on the gas pedal and ran it on red.

Taylor pulled up to the front entrance at one of the larger hotels and stopped, apparently waiting for someone to come out. I began to fear she was just collecting a bride and groom to take to the chapel.

We pulled behind the line of taxis, which gave us a convenient spot to keep Taylor under surveillance. At least until one of the doormen spotted us or a taxi driver started honking for us to move. Fortunately, we didn't have to wait long.

An elegant man in an expensive-looking suit came out of the hotel and got into the front seat with Taylor.

"Look, they're leaving," I said.

Crystal pulled out and made a less than smooth maneuver around a shuttle bus, but managed not to lose Taylor as we merged back onto Las Vegas Boulevard. She made some dicey moves changing lanes, in my opinion, but managed to keep up and keep one or two cars' distance between us and our quarry. Pretty impressive, considering we had a Beetle matched against a big engine Cadillac.

"You two know who that is, don't you?" Crystal asked.

"No," we said almost in unison.

"That's Ben Bartoli. He owns the Burning Love Wedding Chapel and a limo service and a few other businesses in town."

"If he owns the chapel, would he have had anything to do with hiring Steve? And does he drop by the chapel very often?" I asked.

"I don't know how often he comes by. But I do know that the Elvis-impersonator ministers have to do an interview and audition for Bartoli, with Taylor and Gordy sitting in."

"Why Gordy?"

"He takes some photos to see if the guy is photogenic and will look good in people's wedding photos. That's what Little Junior told me," she said.

"Hmm. Why does Bartoli look so familiar to me?"

"You may have seen him on TV commercials or billboards. His picture gets around Vegas."

Taylor turned into another hotel-casino on the Strip. Crystal jerked the wheel and drove one tire over the curb after nearly missing the driveway. Taylor and the mystery man both got out of the car, and she passed off the keys to the valet.

"I have to go to work soon, so I'm just going to drop you here. Call me later if you find out anything interesting."

"Thanks, Crystal," I said.

Di and I jumped out of the car, hurrying to keep Taylor in sight.

Taylor and Bartoli slowly strolled, arm in arm. We followed them to a nice restaurant, where they appeared to have a reservation. We didn't have a reservation, and couldn't really trail them into the restaurant without being seen.

I fell in step with a group of students passing by and used them as cover to peer into the eatery, which had glassless windows facing out onto the colonnade. A waiter had seated Taylor and her guest next to a window. I saw the college group had split apart, avoiding me. I had lost sight of Di, but quickly slipped behind some greenery for a moment. I spied a wine bar with a view to the restaurant and grabbed a bistro chair on its patio. I was about to text Di, when she sat down in the chair next to me.

We ordered two glasses of Chardonnay and tried to keep a discreet eye on the couple. Taylor's back was to us, but we could see the man's face, which was illuminated by a skylight. I could also clearly see his left hand, which was devoid of a wedding band. That was just as well since he was gently brushing his fingers against Taylor's arm as he gazed at her attentively. After a moment of caressing, he clasped her hand, raised it to his lips, and kissed it.

"He's either her boyfriend or a creep," Di said.

"He could be both."

I desperately wished I could hear what they were saying. They appeared to be having a long, leisurely lunch.

"We'd better go. I think we'd be pushing our luck to follow them when they leave the restaurant, even if we could find a cab driver who would be willing to play the 'follow that car' game."

We caught a taxi back to our hotel.

"I'm starving. I didn't have breakfast and I'm guessing neither did you," I said as we walked in through the lobby.

"Yeah, let's hit the food court, or actually there's

a diner-style restaurant on the other side of the casino. We can grab a booth there. It might be quieter," Di offered.

We walked through the casino, our senses assaulted by the clanging, dinging, ringing of the slot machines, their musical excitement designed to lure people into stuffing money into them in hopes of a big payoff.

It was still a bit early for lunch, but the diner was already more than half full. But then, Las Vegas really is an open-twenty-four-hours kind of town. For some people who'd been up all night gambling, or working, this was their breakfast. The menu and style of the booths reminded me of Town Square Diner back in Dixie. But after one bite, I knew the food was no match for the down-home goodness of the restaurant situated just across the square from my office, where I frequently have lunch.

"Should you call and check on your mama and see what's up with your cousin?"

"If there was any real news about Little Junior, I'm sure Mama or Larry Joe would call me. And if I call Mama, she'll want a report on how our 'investigation' is going," I said, punctuating the word "investigation" with air quotes.

"We don't have anything to report at this point, do we?"

"Well, it seems Steve may have had some extra-curricular money-making activities that might not have been completely legal," I said.

"Gordy seems to think so. What about Taylor? Did she tell us anything new?"

"Not as much as I would have liked. We now know Steve has an ex-wife, but no kids. And Taylor knew about Little Junior's arrest, but she didn't hear it from the cops. She seems to be hiding something, but I don't know what."

"Just about everyone has *something* to hide," Di said,

"Yeah. So, what about Gordy? What do you think he's hiding? He has to be on the suspect list, since he was on-site around the time of the murder. What do you make of him? Do you think he was tossing dirt on Steve's grave to discourage us from digging up dirt on him?"

"He seems nice enough. But you're right. He's a suspect and we know nothing about him."

"I don't have any ideas about who could tell us more about Gordy, but I just had an idea about who might know something about Taylor," I said.

"Who's that?"

"My pal Jana."

"The one who hooked you up for the beefcake bachelorette dinner?"

"That's the one. As a wedding planner, Taylor may belong to the same local planners' association that Jana does. I think the conference is still going. I'll wander down to the meeting rooms and see if I can casually bump into Jana. If not, I can always text her. If Jana knows any gossip on Taylor, or anyone else for that matter, I have a feeling she'll be more than happy to dish. Do you want to come with me?"

"No, you'd probably have more luck with her if I don't tag along. Besides, we're in Las Vegas and I haven't even touched a slot machine. I think I'll stroll through the casino and see how Lady Luck treats me."

My phone dinged and I looked down to see I had a text from Holly.

Too many fat Elvises.

That was too intriguing not to follow up on, so I hit the call back button.

"I have to ask, what's up with the fat Elvises?"

"Oh, my heavens. You know we're having the Elvis and Priscilla look-alike contest before the dance."

"Right."

"Well, three or four men thought ahead and actually called and reserved costumes at the shop in Memphis. Most of them weren't planning to participate in the contest. Or if they were, they had bought some dime store Halloween Elvis costume. But now that they've arrived in Dixie and gotten a look at the sharp costumes some of the guys have rented or even purchased, a dozen beer-bellied men want high quality costumes—and they expect me to locate them. At the last minute. In their size. During Elvis Week in Memphis."

"Have you waved your magic wand?"

"No, but I'm about ready to wave a certain finger at some of these oversized, overbearing . . . gentlemen."

It's rare that Holly loses her cool. In fact, most of the time, she's practically Zen. I could tell she was being pushed to her limit.

"Do you want me to call some shops around the mid-South and see if we can locate some costumes and have them FedExed for this weekend?"

"No, thanks, darlin'. I've already done so. The guy at the Nashville shop, who has always been super helpful, as you know, offered to reach out and call in some favors. I'm waiting to hear back from him.

"I had the good fortune, if you want to call it that, of locating the largest size they make for a whale-sized man. After the costume was delivered yesterday, I had him come by Sweet Deal Realty to try it on. He took the costume into the restroom to change into it. The costume fit him like a sausage casing, which seemed appropriate—since he's a big wiener."

I'd been trying to fight back the laughter, but I was cracking up at this point. Despite her obvious frustration, Holly was giggling, too.

"That . . . hot dog had the nerve to tell me I'd have to get it altered for him. After I picked my jaw up off the floor, I told him the costume shop wouldn't allow us to do alterations, so he'd have to take it or leave it. He was mulling that over when Winette, God bless her, suggested he wear some spandex under it."

I tried to put that image out of my head.

"Liv, I'm sorry. I shouldn't have bothered you. It's really under control, or as under control as possible. I guess I just needed to vent."

"I'm glad you did. That's the best laugh I've had all day. And likely the last one."

"Oh, Winette told me about the wedding postponement. I'm so sorry."

"Things are worse than that," I said. "Since then, the police have arrested Little Junior for that Elvis minister's death."

"Oh, no. That's terrible. Your mother must be beside herself."

"She is. And Di and I are scouting around to find a replacement suspect for the police."

"Of course. Good luck—and be careful. I'll try not to bother you with minutiae, since you have important business to look after there."

"No, Holly, what you're doing in Dixie is important business, too—the stuff that pays the bills kind of business. Please keep me posted, or I'll worry."

Concern about the reunion situation back in Dixie, and guilt about leaving Holly to handle such a big event on her own, had kind of sucked the wind out of my sails. But I couldn't give in to my feelings. If we were ever going to get Mama married off and get out of Vegas, I needed to find a murderer—or at least a viable suspect—to get Little Junior out of trouble. I ambled down the hallway where I'd attended the session about Web sites. The halls were empty, but the meeting room doors were closed, so I hoped they were in session and people would come spilling out at any moment. In the meantime, I slipped into the restroom. I was putting on some lipstick when a few women started filing in. I didn't know how Lady Luck was treating Di, but she was smiling on me. One of the women who walked in was Jana.

"Hi, Jana. I don't think I ever thanked you properly for arranging such a"—I paused, searching my mind for the right word—"*fun* dinner the other night."

"It was my pleasure," she said with a devious grin. "So how was the wedding? Is your mama off on her honeymoon?"

"Not exactly. In fact, there's something I wanted to ask you about in that regard. Is there someplace we could talk more privately?"

"Of course. The sessions are breaking for lunch and I was about to run to my office to check in. Would you like to walk with me?"

I nodded and followed her out of the ladies' room. She was walking at a brisk pace and I fell in step with her. I asked her benign questions about the conference as we weaved through the crowded hallway. Once alone on the elevator, I told her about the Elvis minister dropping dead during the ceremony, before the "I dos."

"My cousin, also an aspiring Elvis tribute artist, just so happens to be in a relationship with a woman who had dated the deceased. And Steve—that's the dead guy's name—had a flask of whiskey stashed behind the flower arrangement in the chapel. My cousin was picking up the flowers for my mama and accidentally knocked the flask off the stand. He picked it up without thinking and when the cops dusted for fingerprints and found the only ones on the flask belonged to Steve and my cousin, it left Little Junior in a difficult position. He's been arrested, although we know he's completely innocent of the murder."

"Oh, my, that's terrible," Jana said as the elevator doors opened. She stepped off and began speed-walking again. I struggled to keep up. She pulled a key out of her purse and unlocked a door with her nameplate on it.

"I know how distressing this must be for your family. I'd be glad to give you the name of a good lawyer," she said, as she walked behind her desk and took a seat in a cushy leather swivel chair.

"Actually, my uncle has already engaged an attorney that came highly recommended. I was hoping you could give me a bit of information."

"Oh, about what?" Jana said. Her eyebrows involuntarily arched, briefly betraying her normally placid expression.

"The wedding coordinator at the Burning Love Wedding Chapel. It occurred to me that she might belong to the American Association of Event Planners. Her name is Taylor . . . something. I've got her card here somewhere," I said as I started digging through my purse.

"Kane. Taylor Kane. I know who she is," Jana said. "What about her?"

"Well, in just the couple of times we were at the chapel, we couldn't help but notice there seemed to be a relationship of a personal nature between Taylor and Steve, the deceased. I suppose someone could have slipped poison into Steve's flask earlier, but the most obvious suspects are the ones who were on-site when he died. . . ."

"Oh, I see. And you're playing Nancy Drew, trying to come up with a suspect that could divert the attention of the police away from your cousin."

"I don't know that I'd phrase it quite like that, but yes. Do you know anything about her that might cause the cops to take a closer look at her?"

"I honestly don't know her well. I did hear—just gossip, really—that she had been fired from her previous position with another wedding chapel in town. But I don't know why she was let go. Or if it's even true that she was let go."

"Could it be because she was helping herself to some of the business funds? I only ask because Gordy—that's the photographer at the chapel—mentioned that Steve seemed to be flush with cash lately, despite the fact he didn't have any other gigs at the moment. If they were romantically involved, it could be that Taylor and Steve had been dipping into the till. Or maybe he caught her with her hand in the cookie jar and was playing at blackmail. I'm just inventing scenarios here, but if you could find out anything about Taylor or why she left her last place of employment, it might be helpful. And I'd be much in your debt."

Jana seemed to be listening intently.

"Of course. I'm glad to help a fellow Tennessean any way that I can. I know a couple of people in the association who are friendly with Taylor. I'll see if I can get anything out of them—without being too obvious, of course. I'll let you know if I find out anything.

"But what about this photographer—what's his name? Gordy, is it?" she asked.

"Yeah, Gordy."

"How did he know the murder victim was flush with cash? Could it be he's involved somehow?"

"He said he saw Steve flashing a wad of cash at a bar and noticed that he had bought some expensive stuff lately. But you're right—he could be trying to draw attention away from himself. He's definitely on the suspect list, since he was there at the time of death."

"Well, I need to get some work done or my current employer may let *me* go," Jana said, standing up and giving me my cue to leave. "I'll ask around and let you know if I hear anything that might help your cousin."

I thanked Jana and left her office, hoping I could remember the way we came in.

I made my way to the casino and wandered around a bit looking for Di. I was just about to give up and text her when I spotted her and Dave standing beside a row of slot machines. They were having a conversation that at first looked friendly, then became less amicable. Di had a face like thunder as she stormed out. I hurried to catch up to her and stepped into the elevator just before the doors closed. There were other people in the elevator, so I didn't speak until we got off on our floor. No one else was around.

"Di, do you want to talk about what happened with Dave?"

"I don't want to talk to Dave, or about Dave, ever again."

Chapter Ten

When we reached Di's door, I asked if she wanted to be alone for a while.

"I don't have time to sulk. We need to find a killer. What do we need to do next?" Di asked.

I thought that over for a moment.

"I know just what you need. A pedicure, with a relaxing foot massage. What do you think?"

"I think there's something you're not telling me," Di said.

"Did you notice how Crystal said she had recently seen Steve going up to the guest rooms at our hotel? She acted like she just happened to see him. But what if she was keeping tabs on him? She seems to know more about Steve than she's telling us, and why is that, if things really are over between the two of them? As much as I want her to be innocent, for Little Junior's sake, I don't think we've been paying enough attention to Crystal as a suspect."

"Okay, how does that lead us to a foot massage?" Di said.

"Remember the hairdresser mentioning that she and Crystal go way back? I think that's a source we need to mine for information. We got a manicure there, so it would be perfectly logical for us to return for a pedicure."

"You may think I'm crazy for suggesting it, but I think we should take your mother along. I believe she might have more luck getting information out of . . . what's-her-name?"

"I think her name was Randi, and you may be right. Mama can play on her sympathy as the worried aunt. And I seem to remember Randi saying that she's fond of Little Junior. Besides, it would do Mama good to get out of the hotel for a bit."

I phoned Mama and, sure enough, she was in her room.

"Mama, put on your face. Di and I are coming up to get you. We're going out."

"Oh, hon. I don't feel much like getting out."

"You will when I tell you why. We're on a mission to help Little Junior and we may need your help. We'll see you in fifteen minutes."

"What are we going to do for the next fifteen minutes?"

"You can do whatever you like. I'm going to my room to freshen up and check in with Larry Joe."

Larry Joe wasn't in the room, so I called his cell. He and Earl were at the camper dealer checking into getting some accessories added to the already tricked-out Winnebago—a lighted, fogless shower mirror, among other things.

"Earl was getting restless, pacing the floor when I checked in on him this morning. I was able to get him out of the hotel, saying we needed to make sure the camper was equipped with everything they needed to hit the road. Liv, I think you need to try to get your mother out of the room. Right now, it seems like the only way to get her out would be to go see Little Junior. Dave said he's working on it."

"I'm already on it. Di and I are collecting her in fifteen minutes."

"I always knew you had secret super powers," he said.

"Nothing secret about it. I'm a party planner. I arrange activities that draw people in—or out. I'll check back with you later."

I put on some lipstick and changed into sandals, so my shoes wouldn't mess up my fresh pedicure, then walked to Di's room and tapped on the door. It opened a crack and I heard her say, "Come on in."

As I entered and closed the door, I saw her standing in front of the bathroom mirror, pulling her hair up into a ponytail.

"It's so hot, I thought I'd get my hair up off my neck. What's Larry Joe up to?"

"He and Earl are looking at getting the Winnebago pimped out."

"O . . . kay," she said doubtfully.

Di grabbed her purse and we proceeded to Mama's room.

Mama came to the door with a fresh coat of lipstick and a freshly powdered nose, which told me she planned to go with us. But she decided to put up a protest anyway.

"Liv, it's sweet of y'all to want to get me out and get my mind off Little Junior. But, I tell you, my heart's just not in it."

"We're not trying to get your mind off Little Junior. We want you to help us dig up some information on Crystal. We're going back to the salon for pedicures. Randi said she'd known Crystal a long time. She didn't have much to say about Crystal before. But we have more reason to press her now. Di and I figure she might have more compassion for a grieving aunt than a nosy cousin."

"So, you think Crystal had something to do with the Elvis minister's murder?"

"We don't know. But we have to consider her as a suspect, and right now we know diddly about her."

"All right. If you think it might help Little Junior, I guess I'm game." She let out a dramatic sigh and walked with weary steps to the hallway. But she had a spring to her step by the time we made it to the lobby. Mama was not one to sit happily on the sidelines and I knew she was secretly excited about getting to take part in a little sleuthing.

We took a taxi to the salon, and unlike Little Junior, the driver charged us full fare—and then some, I think. I had called ahead to see if Randi had openings this afternoon for the three of us to get pedicures. Randi had said she could work us in. Miss Betty had begged off. Truth be told, I think she had her own little investigation going on, secretly following my father-in-law to catch him cheating—on his diet.

I looked around the salon as we entered and felt certain she wouldn't have any trouble working us

in. We were the only customers in the place, besides
one woman with foil wraps all over her head, who
was getting a color job. Since the salon had been
nearly empty the one other time we'd been in, I
wondered about the financial health of the business. But I suspected their busiest times were on the
weekend and in the evenings, when most people
were off from work.

Mama, who has a penchant for drama and could
have pursued a career on the stage, or as a professional mourner—she can *boohoo* with the best—
wasted no time launching into her performance.

"Randi, you're a doll for fitting us in. I know it
may seem frivolous to be getting a pedicure when
my dear nephew is rotting in a filthy jail cell, falsely
accused of killing a man of the cloth."

Insert dramatic sigh here.

"But I let my daughter and her friend talk me
into drying my tears and leaving the hotel room
for a bit. I've been holed up, not even going out for
meals. I can hardly bear to be around people right
now. A comforting foot massage and a pedicure
might be just the thing to soothe my aching heart,
if only for a short while."

Insert another dramatic sigh, coupled with a tear
escaping from the corner of her eye. Mama's performance was masterful, but I decided to hold my
applause. Randi seemed truly moved.

Di and I aided her performance with small sup-
porting roles.

"Mama, don't upset yourself," I said, taking her
hand and leading her over to the pedicure station
at the back of the room.

Di pulled a tissue out of her purse and handed it to Mama, who dabbed tears from her eyes.

Randi turned on the whirlpool jets in the pedicure basin, before walking over and giving Mama a hug.

"Ms. Walford, you just sit down and put your feet in this warm water. I'm going to pamper you for a while."

Mama kicked off her sandals and climbed into the lounge chair and sank her feet into the warm, pulsating water. Randi turned on the chair's massage feature and questioned Mama about how the different types and levels of pulsing and undulating massage felt against her back until she had adjusted it to "just right."

Mama had the most downtrodden look on her face. I thought even I might start crying.

Randi took care of Mama personally, while another nail tech got Di set up at the pedicure station next to her. I sat next to Mama, eyeing her with a look of concern, ready to spring into action if Mama gave me a cue.

"I know it's been upsetting. But try not to worry about Little Junior. He's a really nice guy. And he's never been in any trouble with the cops before. I'm sure the police will get this cleared up," Randi said.

"I hope so. Sometimes it seems once they have someone in custody, they don't look very hard for the real killer. But as upsetting as this is for me, and Little Junior's daddy, I can only imagine how awful all this must be for Little Junior. I'm glad he has Crystal in his life. She seems really nice. I feel like maybe I should reach out to her, you know, as Little

Junior's family. But, of course, we had just met when all this happened. I do have one concern, if you don't mind me asking," Mama said. "I know Crystal had dated Steve at one time. . . ."

Randi suddenly had a wary expression.

"It just seems a little . . . unusual that Crystal has dated two different Elvis impersonators. Do you feel that Crystal and Little Junior are well suited, or is he just a particular type she's attracted to—you know, Elvisey types?"

Randi's expression relaxed, and she said, "Believe me, it's not the Elvis thing that Crystal's attracted to. In fact, I was completely surprised when I found out she was dating another Elvis impersonator. Not surprised she would happen upon more than one Elvis here in Vegas—we have more than our fair share per capita. Just after having such a bad experience with Steve, who was a liar and a cheat—not that I like to speak ill of the dead. It's also that . . . I don't know if I should tell you, because I don't think she'd ever want Little Junior to find out, but . . ."

Mama, Di, and I were all leaning slightly forward in tense anticipation, wondering what Randi was about to say.

"Crystal doesn't even like Elvis, can't stand his music. This was years ago, but once she even turned down a free trip to Graceland. So trust me when I say Crystal isn't in love with your nephew because of his Elvis impressions. Despite that, if anything. She's crazy about Little Junior because he's a funny, sweet little man who treats her like a queen."

Her admission of Crystal's aversion to Elvis

primed Randi's pump. She gushed out a stream of information about Crystal, none of it damaging—or particularly illuminating. She did give a couple of examples of Steve's womanizing ways, but that only confirmed what we'd already heard about him.

Mama went with the same pale lavender shade for her pedicure that she'd chosen for her fingernails. I went with the same shade of pink I'd selected for my manicure. Di decided to contrast the pale pink on her fingernails with a hot pink hue on her toes.

Riding back along the same route we'd traveled to the salon, in a strange taxi driven by someone other than Little Junior, was extremely depressing. All three of us sat slumped in our seats, staring straight ahead, wordless, all the way back to the hotel. When I paid the driver, he asked if we'd had a death in the family.

"Not yet," I replied.

Mama asked me to text Larry Joe, who was out with Earl and the other men at the Winnebago dealership. We arranged for our whole group to meet up for dinner at the hotel buffet in forty-five minutes.

Mama, Di, and I rode up in the elevator together. Mama said she was going to her room to rest until mealtime. We went to Di's room to hang out.

Di propped herself up on pillows against the headboard and I sat down at the foot of the bed.

"Earlier, when Dave came up to me in the casino," Di suddenly said without preface, "I thought maybe he was going to apologize for being such a rude . . ."

She bit her lip and waved her hand, but left the word she was thinking of unspoken.

"But instead, I find out he's busy trying to pin Steve's murder on Jimmy—just because Jimmy dropped me off at the chapel. Dave says that puts him at the scene of the murder. And Dave said Jimmy's the only one at the chapel around that time who has a criminal record. And Dave made sure to tell his cop friend about Jimmy. Even though the only crime Jimmy committed that night was being seen in a car with me."

Chapter Eleven

Mama called to tell me that Earl had inquired at the Italian restaurant in the hotel, just to see if they could accommodate a party of nine on short notice. It so happened they'd had a cancellation.

In a few minutes, Di and I knocked on Mama's door and the three of us went downstairs to meet the others. We were seated almost immediately, even though a couple of members of our party had not yet arrived.

We had already ordered drinks and appetizers when Uncle Junior and Dave came in. Uncle Junior had gotten in to see his son, and also had talked with Little Junior's attorney.

The case against Little Junior as my uncle understood it was that there was bad blood between Little Junior and the deceased. They had both dated the same woman, albeit at different times, but they had had a public altercation at the chapel just two days before the murder. He had been at the chapel at the time of Steve's death. And the police seemed to think it was significant that Little Junior had stopped by the chapel a couple of times in the past week inquiring about the status of his application for a job as an Elvis minister. The implication being, with Steve out of the way, he'd have a good chance at getting the job. Also the only fingerprints on the flask containing the poison, besides Steve's, were Little Junior's.

I had to interrupt at this point.

"Uncle Junior, the only reason Little Junior's prints were on that flask was because it fell off the pedestal when he moved the flowers and he reached down and picked it up without thinking. The cop who was there saw it. Does he really think Little Junior would have put his prints on the flask if he was the one who had put poison in it?"

Dave jumped in. "The police contend it's possible that Little Junior was trying to remove evidence when he went up to get the flowers. He could have accidentally knocked the flask off in the process. Or, he could have known his prints were on the flask and wanted a cop to see him have a plausible reason for picking up the flask—to cover his tracks."

"That's asinine," my father-in-law said.

"Wayne's right," Mama said. "The whole thing's ridiculous. They're railroading Little Junior without a speck of real evidence."

"Do they know what kind of poison it was? Is it something easy to get a hold of?" Di said, looking to Uncle Junior. But Dave responded.

"According to my buddy at the LVMPD, you can get anything you want in Vegas if you know who to ask. But they have determined the poison. It was sodium cyanide, which is present in a number of accessible products, including certain photo chemicals."

Di and I exchanged a brief glance, but neither of us said anything.

Dinner was delicious. I had the Alfredo and Larry Joe had the marinara with meatballs. And, feeling generally bummed out by the state of Little Junior's detainment, we ate dinner in relative quiet and finished off four bottles of red wine.

After dinner, as we were walking out, I said quietly to Di, "We need to take a closer look at Gordy tomorrow."

"I agree. But surely the cops are checking into him after what Dave said about the poison in photo chemicals."

"I don't know. They don't seem very motivated about looking at any suspects other than Little Junior."

After hearing the less than encouraging news at dinner about Little Junior's case, Larry Joe and I went straight upstairs. The siren call of the slot machines held no appeal as we walked past the casino. In our room, there was little conversation as we got ready for bed. Face washed, teeth brushed, and nightshirt on, I wearily climbed into bed next to my snoring husband.

I'm not sure exactly what time I drifted off, but I know exactly when I woke up. The landline on the nightstand rang, jolting me out of a deep sleep. I looked at the alarm clock. It was 2:37 a.m. when I answered the phone.

"Liv, your Uncle Junior is having chest pains,"

Earl said. "He called the front desk, before he called us. An ambulance just arrived and paramedics are loading him up now. Your mama and I are going to follow in a taxi. You two can meet us there in the emergency room. They said they're transporting him to Sunrise Hospital and Medical Center. We'll call you, of course, with any news."

"What's wrong?" Larry Joe said, looking at me bleary eyed.

"We've got to get up. Uncle Junior's on his way to the hospital with chest pains."

Larry Joe rolled out of bed and pulled on the pants he'd left lying across the armchair.

"Honey, I swear, my heart almost stopped when I heard Earl's voice on the phone. I just knew something had happened to Mama. But she had told us she was worried Uncle Junior's heart wouldn't be able to handle all this."

We both got dressed in a hurry, and as we were about to leave, Larry Joe asked, "Should we let Daddy and Mama know what's happening?"

"No, let's not wake them. They'll be up by about five anyway. We can call them then. With any luck, we'll be able to tell them Uncle Junior just had a bad case of indigestion."

In the elevator as we were descending to the lobby, Larry Joe asked, "Do you know the name of the hospital and the address?"

"Earl said it was Sunrise Hospital. The taxi driver should know where it is."

After a short ride, the taxi turned beside a sign that said TRAUMA EMERGENCY and pulled up to the entrance. Larry Joe handed him some cash and the driver told us he hoped everything turned out okay.

So did I.

The automatic doors slid open as we approached. The waiting room was furnished with rows of uncomfortable-looking chairs, more than half of them occupied. I spotted Mama pacing the tiled floor.

"Mama," I said, walking over and wrapping my arms around her. "Any news?"

"No, and they won't let me go back and be with him. I already tried to slip back there twice, but a burly nurse with an attitude stopped me—aided and abetted by Earl Daniels," she said, shooting Earl a peeved look.

Earl just shook his head.

"They're probably running tests, Mama. We'd just be in the way right now," I said. "Why don't you sit down?"

"I'm too dang antsy to sit."

"You getting swollen ankles isn't going to help Uncle Junior any."

"Liv's right, hon," Earl said.

She just shot him an indignant look.

"Earl, let's find the vending machine and get some coffee for all of us," Larry Joe said, getting up from his chair. Earl followed.

I tugged at Mama's hand and she reluctantly took a seat beside me.

"Earl's just trying to look after you."

"I know it. But what I need him to do is make those people at the desk *tell* us something."

"I know you're anxious. But there's probably nothing to tell just yet."

Mama sat quietly, which is unusual for her. Every minute or two I could see her cutting her eyes up and over to the clock on the wall.

The men returned and handed us disposable coffee cups, already sugared and creamed the way we liked them.

About thirty minutes later, a nurse came through the door and called, "Mrs. Walford."

Mama leapt to her feet and I followed her. The nurse led us down the hall to a curtained-off area.

"The doctor will be in in just a moment to talk to you," the nurse said before continuing down the hallway.

"Don't worry, Virginia. I'm going to be fine. I can't kick the bucket just when my boy needs me," Uncle Junior said with a faint smile.

"Don't try to talk right now, Junior," Mama said, grabbing hold of his hand.

He was hooked up to a heart monitor and an IV. A short, stocky doctor with a slight accent, Middle Eastern maybe, walked in holding a clipboard.

"Mr. Manning, is this your family?"

"Yes. My sister, Virginia, and niece, Liv."

The doctor introduced himself, stating a name I didn't quite catch, before giving us a report.

"We do not think you have had a heart attack. I believe it is angina, which can be a sign of an impending heart attack. Your pain has subsided, which is good, but doesn't necessarily indicate everything is okay. I'd like to keep you at least overnight and run some more tests in the morning."

"Is that really necessary? I'm here from Phoenix and I can check with my doc—"

"He'll stay overnight like you said, doctor," Mama said firmly.

"Very good. It may be a while before they have

a room to move him to. But one or two family members are welcome to sit with him here in the ER. I will see you in the morning, Mr. Manning."

The curtained-off cubby contained one chair and a rolling stool. I took a seat on the stool, leaving the chair for Mama.

"Don't sit down," she said. "You and Larry Joe get out of here and get some sleep. Earl and I will keep vigil here."

"Mama, I'd rather you and Earl go back to the hotel and get some rest. You can relieve us later this morning."

Mama waved me over and we stepped just outside the curtain.

"I don't want you taking shifts at the hospital. Betty and Wayne can relieve us later if needs be. I want you to get a little shut-eye and then get back to work clearing Little Junior's name. So, shoo," she said, pushing my shoulder blade and nudging me out into the hallway.

"Uncle Junior, we'll see you later. Try to get some rest."

He nodded as I waved.

The guys both stood when I walked back into the waiting room. A man sitting nearby had blood seeping through a towel wrapped around his hand. I hoped he didn't have to wait much longer to see a doctor.

"Larry Joe, we're leaving—Mama's orders. Earl, you can go back and sit with Mama. The doctor said it was okay for a couple of family members to stay with him. They don't think Uncle Junior had a heart attack but they're keeping him overnight and running more tests in the morning. We're just waiting for them to move him to a room. He and Mama are in a curtained-off area about halfway down that hall," I said. "I'm sure you'll hear Mama's voice."

I gave Earl a hug.

"Larry Joe's parents will come down later this morning. When they get here make Mama go back to the hotel and sleep for a bit."

"Will do."

Chapter Twelve

Friday morning, Larry Joe and I slept in. We'd both been exhausted when we got back from the hospital. We'd peeled off our clothes and fallen into bed. I was asleep within moments and woke up in the same position I'd fallen asleep in.

I gave Mama a quick call to see if there were any updates.

"Mama, what's going on with Uncle Junior?"

"His color was improved when we left. They were going to be running tests all morning, so Earl and I came back to the hotel. Betty's going to the hospital a little later this morning to sit with Junior."

"Okay, good. You two try to get some sleep."

"I will. I already caught a nap. But Earl slept half the night at the hospital already. How do men sleep sitting up in a straight-back chair?"

"I don't know. I'll check in with you later. Keep me posted," I said.

"Mama and Earl are back," I told Larry Joe. "Your mom's going over to the hospital in a bit to check on Uncle Junior. They're running tests on him now. So, what happened with the Winnebago? Did Earl decide to keep it, or return it?" I asked.

"Oh, he's keeping it," Larry Joe said. "I think he sees returning it as a sign that he's giving up on his and your mama's great honeymoon adventure. I know Earl has been quiet and focusing all the attention on your mama. But this is all taking a toll on him, too. Having the wedding postponed, maybe indefinitely, is hard on him, as well as your mama. And now, worrying over Uncle Junior."

"I know. I just hate it. I'm glad we slept in this morning. I needed the rest—we both did—after the past couple of days, and especially after our late-night sprint to the hospital. But Mama's right; I think it's time for me to get down to work on the investigation. I'm going to call Di to see if she's ready to make a game plan for the day.

"So where are you off to?"

"Oh, you know, just around," Larry Joe said, avoiding eye contact.

My husband is a bad liar, in the sense that I can usually tell when he's not being truthful.

"Honey, what are you not telling me?"

He hemmed and hawed for a moment.

"You know I won't let it go until I find out," I said.

"Yes. I do know that. I have a feeling you're not going to like it, but I've already told Dave I would."

"Would what?"

"He wants me to do a bit of surveillance on Jimmy Souther."

"I swear, Dave is like a dog with a bone—except there's no marrow in this bone. He may not like Jimmy, and for good reason. But we have absolutely no grounds to think Jimmy was involved in Steve's murder."

"Maybe we do," Larry Joe said. "When Jimmy dropped Di off at the chapel, Dave was standing inside the door waiting for her. She hurried past him without a word."

"Di said he glared at her."

"I wouldn't doubt it. But while she went on into the chapel, Dave lingered a moment to see where Jimmy went. And he didn't head straight out the driveway. He pulled around and parked."

"Meaning he could've entered the chapel, I suppose. But Di arrived just before the wedding started and Steve was already standing at the front of the aisle. And he'd already stashed the flask with the poisoned whiskey behind the flowers. Which means Jimmy couldn't have put the poison in the flask," I said.

"Even so, his hanging around the chapel after Di went in is suspicious. It could mean he has a connection to someone at the chapel."

"Like Taylor or Gordy?" I offered.

"Maybe. But even if he wasn't involved in killing Steve, if he's involved in something shady, shouldn't we try to find out what he's up to?"

"Di will be fit to be tied if she finds out Dave is trying to pin something on Jimmy and you're spying on him," I said. "And doing surveillance is more my style than yours."

"And you know I normally try to mind my own business. But I'm not convinced Di can think straight where this guy is concerned. Not after hearing all the stuff he's been arrested for. And, as Dave pointed out, I'm the only one who can spy on him up close without raising suspicion. He met you. And he certainly knows what Dave looks like. Jimmy had his back to me when Dave and I met up with you in the casino. Dave charged over to the bar, but you dragged me out before the fireworks began."

"I guess so. What's the plan?"

"Dave is on a stakeout at Jimmy's house right now. He was going to don sunglasses and a baseball cap and follow Jimmy using a car he borrowed from his cop friend. I'll take over once Jimmy goes to his job at the bar. I'm supposed to go in, hang out, see what I can find out about him from the regulars, eavesdrop on his conversations, and casually chat with him if I have the chance. Wish me luck." Larry Joe gave me a kiss and started for the door.

"Honey, be careful. You said yourself, Jimmy has a rap sheet as long as your arm. And he just spent the past six years or so in a Texas prison."

"Don't worry, Liv. Dave told me not to push for information, just pick up what I can. We don't want to make Jimmy suspicious.

"I'm grabbing some breakfast with Dad."

"Will this be your dad's second or third breakfast this morning?"

"I'm not asking."

Larry Joe gave me a smile and a quick smack on the lips before leaving.

I phoned Di, who said she had just gotten out of the shower. I pulled myself together while she got dressed and joined her in her room about twenty minutes later.

"I think we should have another chat with Gordy. See what he can tell us about Taylor and boss man

Ben Bartoli," Di said as soon as I walked through the door.

"Me too. After seeing him snacking on Taylor's hand during lunch yesterday, I'm wondering if he knew about her relationship with Steve, and what he thought about it if he did."

We were trying to figure out the best way to approach Gordy, but the fact was we didn't even know where to find him unless he was shooting a wedding at the chapel.

"I could call Taylor and tell her Gordy had been recommended to me as a wedding photographer and ask her how to contact him," I said.

"Something tells me unless you're booking the wedding at the Burning Love Wedding Chapel, she won't be very helpful."

"Oh, what if I say I'm planning a large charity gala and we'd like to engage Gordy, who comes highly recommended?" I said.

"Oh, wait a minute," Di said. "When Gordy was talking yesterday about his other jobs, didn't he say something about shooting beauty pageant contestants this morning at one of the hotels?"

"Yes. He sure did. At the Venetian."

"Okay, let's go crash a photo shoot," Di said.

We left through the front doors of our hotel and loitered at the curb. The doorman waved for a taxi to pull forward.

"Where to?" the driver asked.

"The Venetian."

He pulled out and merged into the heavy traffic on Las Vegas Boulevard. It was a short but rough ride, as he drove down the Strip, past shops and casinos and hotels, before turning into the Venetian and dropping us off at the entrance.

Riding in other taxis since Little Junior's arrest had caused me to realize what a good driver he was, expertly navigating the aggressive driving on the Strip, which included buses and taxis weaving in and out of lanes.

Since we didn't see Gordy shooting photos by the lake out front, we assumed he was taking pictures along the scenic indoor canals, lined with shops and restaurants with facades evoking the charm of an Italian village.

We headed in and started walking through the winding corridors along the canal. A gondola glided past, as a gondolier in a black-and-white striped shirt serenaded a starry-eyed couple. The crooner brought the boat to a stop and announced, "She said yes."

Pedestrians burst into applause and the newly engaged couple blushed appreciatively.

"This makes me think about your mama's odd-ball idea to have a gondola ferry her and Earl to that little island in the lake at Earl's farm for their wedding vows," Di said.

"I know. I was just thinking the same thing. It makes me sad their wedding's been put on hold."

"Let's see if we can't do something to remedy that. I see a bunch of pretty girls in short skirts lined up on that bridge over the canal just ahead," Di said.

As we approached, we got a better look at the setup.

The canal widened at the end where the boats turned around. Just above the turnaround was an upper level bordering a sunlit atrium, where Gordy was posing a group of beauties in front of two large, luminescent obelisks. Walkways to shops ran along each side, but large columns separating the shops from the upper atrium were cordoned off, with two beefy-looking security guys discouraging spectators from trying to slip through.

After Gordy finished taking some still shots, a videographer stepped in. Gordy walked to the edge of the atrium and took the lens off his camera. An assistant took the lens and handed him another one. A bevy of girls was standing just inside the roped off area between us and Gordy, with a woman who seemed to be explaining something to them. I gathered they were waiting their turn for photos.

"How are we going to get through to talk to Gordy?" Di asked.

"I have an idea. Wait here."

I dug around in my purse and pulled out a business card. I grasped the card so my name and Liv 4 Fun Party Planning was clearly displayed, while obscuring the Dixie, Tennessee, address with my thumb.

I put on my professional smile and walked over to the edge where the cordoned off area intersected with the railing above the canal below. I extended the hand holding the card across the rope as I edged past security, and cleared my throat to attract the attention of the woman directing the contestants.

She took a step in my direction.

"Hi, I'm Liv McKay. I'm a colleague of Jana Hively's and I'm coordinating an event with her this week."

She took a look at my business card. But as she reached for it, it tumbled out of my hand into the canal below.

"Oh, I'm sorry. How clumsy of me. Anyway, I've been unable to reach Gordy, the photographer, on his mobile, and I desperately need to confirm timelines for our event. Would it be possible for me to have a quick word with him?"

She gave me a half nod before hesitating, but before she could voice any opposition, I slipped under the rope.

"Oh, thank you. I promise I'll only be a minute."

I walked over to Gordy, who didn't even question my presence. I've found if you act like you have a right to be somewhere, most people assume you do.

"Hi, Gordy. If you have a moment before you start taking photos again, I thought of something we forgot to ask you when we spoke earlier."

"Shoot."

"First, did Steve get along with Ben Bartoli?"

"Yeah, but then most people get along with their boss—if they want to keep their job."

"I couldn't help but notice Taylor seemed to get along really well with Mr. Bartoli. Do you know just how close they are?"

"I honestly don't know what kind of arrangement Taylor and Bartoli have going. I have seen Taylor decorating his arm at events around town. But I've also seen him with plenty of other ladies, too. It could be Taylor is his date when he wants someone pretty, but respectable looking."

"He seemed pretty touchy-feely with Taylor when I saw them having lunch together."

"He's a touchy-feely kind of guy. And he's used to getting what he wants," Gordy said.

"Also, at the time of Steve's death, I didn't see anyone in the medium-sized chapel as I walked by. Do you know if there was another ceremony going on in the bigger chapel on the other side of the lobby? With another minister and photographer?"

"Yeah, actually there was."

"Do you know if that particular Elvis impersonator or photographer had had run-ins with Steve?" I asked.

"I don't know of anything specific, but if they knew Steve for more than five minutes chances are they had some kind of beef with him. He was just that kind of guy. Arrogant, full of himself. Had a tendency to rub people the wrong way."

"I see. But he seemed to rub some people the right way. Certain women, for instance."

"Yeah, he could charm the ladies for a while—at least until they got to know him. And some women, slow learners, for even longer."

"Would any of the women who stuck with Steve longer, the slow learners, include anyone I know?"

"Yes. It definitely would. My turn again," Gordy said, before walking toward a new group of beauty contestants gathering by the obelisks.

I mouthed "thank you" to the pageant coordinator as I slipped out.

"That was impressive," Di said, as we turned and started walking back to the parking garage. "I know you flashed your business card and dropped it in the water before she could look too closely. But what line did you give to the woman working with the contestants?"

"She appeared to be a pageant coordinator of some kind, so I had a feeling she knew, or at least had heard of, my pal Jana. So, I dropped her name and steamrolled my way through."

"Did you learn anything new from Gordy?"

"Maybe. He said there was another wedding happening in the chapel on the other side of the lobby when Steve died. That gives us at least two more people on the premises at the time of death—the minister and the photographer—who knew Steve and may have had reason to kill him. I'm sure the cops checked them out, so I'll ask Dave about them. But Gordy also hinted that there was one woman who seemed to be charmed by Steve even after she became acquainted with his flaws."

"Who?"

"Taylor."

We stepped out of the main entrance of the Venetian and asked the doorman to hail a cab for us. But just as he motioned to a driver, a police cruiser pulled up to the curb in front of the taxi line. The cop who had talked to us at the wedding chapel after Steve's death suddenly stepped around in front of us and flashed his badge.

"I'm Detective Bains, LVMPD, I need to ask you ladies some questions down at the station concerning an official murder investigation."

He opened the back door of the patrol car and motioned for us to get in.

"We'd be glad to sit down and talk to you in the coffee shop. Is it really necessary to drag us down to the police station?" Di asked.

"No point in arguing with the man," I interjected before Bains had a chance to speak.

I climbed into the cruiser and Di slid in beside me and gave me a puzzled look. Bains got into the front passenger seat and a uniformed officer drove. We traveled in silence to the Convention Center Area Command. I know that's what it was called because it said so in big letters on the side of the building.

I knew from experience that a cop wasn't going to change his mind and have a casual chat with us in the coffee shop after he'd already accosted us and told us he was taking us to the police station. And while I also knew from our little interrogations with Dave that it was highly unlikely the detective would slip up and divulge any information about the investigation, I clung to the faint hope that he might.

He made it obvious this wasn't going to be a friendly chat when he placed Di and me into separate interview rooms. Bains invited me to take a seat at the table, and then left the room for about thirty minutes. Every space I'd been inside in Las Vegas had been super chilled by air conditioning. Except this one. The interview room was on the uncomfortable side of warm.

When Bains returned he sat down across the table from me and stared.

"Am I a suspect?" I said, breaking the silence.

"It appears you think you're an investigator, Mrs. McKay, since everywhere I go you and your friend have been questioning witnesses."

He cast a stare at me again, but this time I didn't take the bait.

After a long, uncomfortable silence he said, "I

could arrest you for interfering in an official murder investigation."

Maybe he could, but we both knew he wasn't going to.

"Taylor Kane told me you'd been pumping her for information."

"I stopped by the chapel to ask Taylor about possibly rescheduling my mother's wedding—the one that was interrupted by Steve's death."

"You didn't ask her about matters pertaining to the deceased or possible suspects?"

"We chatted a bit. I don't recall exactly what was said, but naturally recent events would be on our minds."

"Okay, so you stopped by the chapel to inquire about scheduling a wedding. What purpose did you have in stalking that photographer to a photo shoot at the Venetian?"

"Taylor has been less than helpful. And the Burning Love Wedding Chapel holds some unpleasant memories for my mother. So we may hold the wedding elsewhere. If we do, we may want to engage Gordy as the photographer."

I was careful not to say we had asked Gordy about shooting the wedding, only that we "may."

As the detective narrowed his eyes, his trademark stare turned into a glare.

"Since I understand seeing a man die right in front of you at your mother's wedding must have been very stressful for you, I'm going to let you go, Mrs. McKay. But if I find you sticking your nose into this investigation, make no mistake, I will lock you up."

Di was waiting for me at the entrance to the police station.

"When the desk sergeant said you'd be out soon, I went ahead and called for a cab to pick us up. Seeing as they gave us a ride here but didn't offer to take us back to our hotel, it seemed like a good idea," Di said as I stepped up beside her. She was obviously piqued.

"Did you learn anything from your little chat with Detective Bains?" I asked.

"Just that the more I'm around lawmen lately, the less I like them," she said. "Oh, and that Taylor complained about us to the cops—no big surprise there."

Our taxi arrived.

"So what do we think of Gordy as a suspect now?" Di asked as we settled into the backseat.

"Taking pictures of pageant contestants seems like a prime opportunity to meet some pretty girls. It occurs to me that maybe Steve wasn't the only one with an eye for the ladies. And Gordy's not bad looking. Maybe he and Steve had set their sights on the same woman and there was bad blood between them."

"I know. Gordy puts on like he and Steve got along, but he never has a nice word to say about him. And Gordy seems to have a ready answer for everything. I don't trust him," Di said.

When the cab dropped us back at the hotel, my stomach was growling.

"What sounds good for lunch?" I asked.

We were still trying to come up with something

when my phone dinged, alerting me I had a text message.

Miss Betty had texted, **Meet me in the lobby by the elevators now. Thank you.**

I showed the phone screen to Di.

"What's that about?"

"I don't know. But since she never sends me texts like that—or sends me texts, period, I'm going to get down there and find out."

"Should I come with you, or do you think it's a personal, family kind of thing?"

"If it was a personal, family kind of thing I think she'd want to meet privately—not in the lobby. Let's go."

We walked to the elevators and I looked around for my mother-in-law. I spotted her giving me a coy wave from behind a potted plant. My first thought was that she had lost her mind.

"Sweetie, are you feeling okay?" I said as I put my hand on her shoulder and half whispered in her ear.

"I feel fine," she said with a quizzical expression. She waved for Di to join us. Di had been lingering on the other side of the bank of elevators. I assumed she didn't want to intrude on my mother-in-law's hideout.

Once Di joined us, she said, "Yesterday I thought I saw Crystal coming off one of the elevators that go up to the guest rooms, but I wasn't sure it was her. Just a few minutes ago I saw her get on the elevator, and this time I'm absolutely sure it was her. I couldn't think of any good reason she'd need to go up to the hotel guest rooms, so I decided to wait here until she comes down. But then I realized I didn't know what to do next. I don't have experience stalking people like you two do. Could her strange behavior have something to do with that man's death or Little Junior's troubles?"

Di and I looked at each other.

"Yes, it could, Miss Betty," I said. "Do you know which floor she got off on?"

"No. A bunch of people got on the elevator with her."

"So, how were things with Uncle Junior at the hospital this morning?" I asked.

"They were running tests, but he didn't seem to be in any pain."

"Good. I'm glad to hear it," I said.

About that time my father-in-law came lumbering toward us.

"You better go keep Daddy Wayne from asking what we're up to. We'll take it from here."

"Oh, nuts. Just when it was getting fun," she said, sounding like a kid whose balloon just got popped.

"Good work, spotting Crystal. This may be just the break we've been waiting for," Di said, giving my mother-in-law a pat on the back.

"Oh, and thanks for offering to sit with Uncle Junior at the hospital this morning so Mama could get some rest," I said.

"I'm going to go back to the hospital later to keep your mama company."

"Good. I know she'll appreciate it."

Miss Betty was beaming as she walked over and took my scowling father-in-law by the arm and led him in the direction of the food court.

"So what's the plan?"

I thought that over while keeping one eye on the elevators.

"If Crystal heads toward the door and leaves the building, we'll grab a taxi and try to follow her. See if she's going to meet someone."

"What if she goes toward the casino?" Di asked.

"Then, I say we confront her. Threaten to tell Little Junior the secret that Randi told us unless she explains what she's up to?"

After a few minutes, Di said, "Do you really think this plant is giving us any cover? We didn't have any trouble spotting your mother-in-law."

"Yeah, but we were looking for her. I think this shields us a bit. Tell you what—if we spot Crystal I'll take a step back and let you figure out which direction she's heading. She's more likely to notice us if we're shoulder to shoulder."

"Okay."

After what seemed like forever, but was probably more like twenty minutes, I spotted Crystal emerging from the elevators.

"Di, there she—"

"I see her."

I stepped behind Di and out of the sight line of the elevators.

"Come on. She's walking toward the center of the building, not the front exit," Di said.

We walked briskly trying to catch up to her. There was no reason to keep our distance since the plan now was to confront her, rather than clandestinely follow her.

As we closed in, Di and I parted and accosted Crystal on either side.

"We need to talk," I said, putting my hand to her elbow.

"I don't have time to talk to you," Crystal said, jerking her elbow away.

"Make time," Di said. "Or we'll just have to tell Little Junior your dirty little secret."

"I don't have any dirty little secrets," Crystal said.

"Is that so? We know that you don't like Elvis music," I said. "You wouldn't want me to tell Little Junior, would you?"

"He already knows," she said defiantly, as she kept walking.

"Okay, then. Come on, Di. Mama said we'd be able to visit with Little Junior at two."

Crystal didn't break stride and we started to walk away, hoping she'd call our bluff—since it was all we had.

One, two, three . . .

"Oh, wait," she said, stopping in her tracks.

I breathed a sigh of relief that I hoped Crystal didn't see.

"Let's go sit down in the food court area," I said, and the three of us turned in that direction. Crystal took a long look over her shoulder before she started moving.

After we were seated at a table without anyone nearby, Crystal said, "What is it you want to talk about?"

"About what you're up to. About why you keep slipping upstairs to the guest room area and who you're meeting there."

"I'm not meeting anyone there."

She seemed a little smug when she realized we didn't know much, so I pushed.

"Look, you're going to have to tell us exactly what's going on with you, or I *will* tell Little Junior about you know what. And we'll also tell our sheriff friend about what we've seen. And we'll follow you around like a hungry hound after a biscuit. My cousin's life is on the line here."

"He may be *your* cousin, but he's the love of *my* life. Do you really think you two are the only ones entitled to do a little snooping? Despite what you may believe, I'm trying to find information that will help clear his name, too."

"So have you found out anything?" Di said.

"I think so, but I'm not sure what it means."

"Well, talk it through with us. Maybe the three of us can figure it out," I said.

"Okay, I guess I have to trust someone. And I can't think of any reason your family would have had to kill Steve—especially before he finished your mother's wedding ceremony.

"I haven't been meeting anyone. I've been following Gordy. And you made me lose him as he made his way through the casino when you stopped me in the lobby."

"Wait. I didn't see Gordy," I said, not sure I was buying her story.

"He got off the elevator just ahead of me, wearing a baseball cap and sunglasses and casual clothes, not a suit like he wears when he shoots weddings. But it was him, all right."

"Why were you following him?" Di asked.

"I wanted to see who he was going to meet."

"What was he doing upstairs?" I asked.

"Okay . . . I had spotted him one day last week getting on the hotel elevator with his camera bag.

I thought that was odd, him taking pictures in the rooms. But I thought, maybe he was getting some pictures of the groom's father tying his bow tie, or the bride's mom fastening her daughter's necklace—you know, something like that. It also occurred to me that he might be shooting less innocent pictures. But that was before Little Junior got arrested, so I had no reason to care. And I know Gordy has a darkroom in his house where he prints what he calls 'art' photography.

"I tried to trail him yesterday, but I got on a different elevator and then I wasn't sure which floor he'd gotten off on. I wandered down the halls on a couple of floors before admitting I'd lost him. Today, I didn't lose him."

"Where did he go?"

"I followed him to the seventh floor. A lot of high rollers book on the seventh floor—they think it's good luck. I was in uniform and kept my head kind of turned away from him. The elevator was full and I don't think he even noticed me. When he got off on seven I acted like I was continuing up to a higher floor, but hit the door-open button and slipped off just after he'd walked away. I kept out of sight, but did see which room he went into. After about five minutes, I walked to the door he'd gone through and listened. I didn't hear anything from that room. But there was a real party going on in the room next door. A clothes optional kind of party, if you know what I mean."

I knew what she meant.

"I ducked into the stairwell and kept watch through the little glass panel in the door. When Gordy headed to the elevator, I ran down the stairs and got onto the elevator on the sixth floor, so he wouldn't know I'd been on his floor.

"Anyway, I thought maybe the party next door had hired him to film the action, but somebody got cold feet. Or maybe a second party was booked, but didn't show up."

"No, I'm thinking maybe he did film the party. Maybe through a two-way mirror?" I said.

"You mean blackmail? Oh, I don't think the suits would allow that. They've got a very 'what happens in Vegas, stays in Vegas' attitude about guests' privacy. And some of our guests are people you wouldn't want to mess with—especially on the seventh floor."

"What kind of people are you referring to? You mean organized crime types?"

"Sometimes. And the suits may have even arranged that little party I overheard. You know, to keep the big money customers happy."

"Maybe the suits set up the blackmail to nudge somebody who owes them money," Di said.

"Oh, they have much less subtle ways of dealing with people who owe them money," Crystal said.

"Maybe the suits don't know about this little blackmail operation. Would it be possible for someone in security or maintenance to install a two-way mirror without the powers that be knowing about it? And maybe that same person could alert Gordy when a blackmail target was in play," I said.

"I don't know. . . . Wait a minute. There might be a way. I know from someone who used to work in housekeeping that there are some rooms, and suites, that have a special security designation. Only certain maids and maintenance workers are allowed to go into those. So, it might be possible to work with someone in housekeeping or maintenance with security clearance, or at least pay them to look the other way. But that would be awfully risky. Makes me shaky just thinking about it. I hope the security cameras didn't zero in on me as I had my ear to the door."

Crystal looked really and truly frightened, which confirmed, for me at least, that she was telling the truth.

"I have a feeling security cameras may not be focused on those high security clearance rooms. Certain people might not want a record of everybody who comes and goes from their rooms," Di posited.

"*Hmm*, this is all pretty exciting. But I don't really see how Steve fits in to the picture," I said. "Was he in on the blackmail scheme? And if so, what part did he play? Gordy is filming the proceedings. And somebody is tipping him off on times, but that person has to be someone who works at the hotel, right?"

We all fell silent for a long moment.

"Wait," Di said. "What if Steve found out what Gordy was up to and started blackmailing him. He could have threatened to tell the hotel suits or one of the blackmail victims unless Gordy forked over a fat cut of the blackmail money."

"*Ooh*, that sounds promising," Crystal said.

"I had been working under the assumption that Steve got knocked off by a jilted girlfriend or a jealous boyfriend; it may be much more complicated than that," I said. "Or . . . maybe not. Crystal, remember you told us the day you drove us to the chapel that you had seen Steve going up to the rooms."

"Yeah. But now we know he was probably spying on, or meeting with, Gordy," Crystal said.

"Or he was hooking up with somebody's wife or girlfriend. Somebody who would take a very dim view of that kind of thing. Some *big* somebody—a high roller or maybe even someone with organized crime connections," I said.

"I'm confused," Crystal said. "Was Steve black-mailing Gordy or did Gordy video Steve in a compromising position?"

"We don't know yet," Di said. "Either way, it could've gotten Steve killed."

"Oh, wait. Crystal, didn't you say something about Gordy having a darkroom?" I asked.

"Yeah, I went to his house once when Steve and I were dating."

"We heard that the poison in the flask that killed Steve is something they use in photo chemicals. That could put Gordy squarely in the frame for murder," I said.

Chapter Thirteen

Crystal had to go work her shift. We agreed to meet with her later to discuss plans about what to do next for Operation: Free Little Junior.

"We were trying to figure out what we wanted for lunch an hour ago. Before Miss Betty texted. I'm starved," I said.

"Well, you can walk just a few steps from here and order pizza, Chinese food, or hot dogs. What do you want?" Di asked.

"I think I'll get a slice of pizza," I said, and Di decided to do the same.

We carried our pizza and beer back to one of the tables in the food court and continued to discuss various blackmail scenarios that could have led to Steve's death, and what role Gordy may have played.

"Liv, you know, something just occurred to me. Crystal was acting like Gordy wouldn't notice her on the elevator if she didn't make eye contact, like they're only passing acquaintances. Yet, she knew that Gordy has a darkroom, and even admitted that she'd been to his house."

"Good point. So what are you thinking?"

"I'm thinking her whole story about following Gordy to the seventh floor may be some hooey she made up for us. Maybe she was meeting Gordy. Maybe she even found out about some blackmail scheme and was trying to get in on the action. Maybe she was already in on blackmailing Steve and things got ugly."

"I don't know," I said. "She seems to genuinely care about Little Junior. Do you really think she'd let him take the fall for murder?"

"She may not have known about the murder. Or she may be trying to implicate Gordy to help Little Junior—or to help herself. Either way, I'm not convinced she's completely innocent in all this," Di said.

"I wish there was some way we could find out what's really been going on upstairs," I said.

"Well, if we could come up with any kind of evidence that Gordy, or Crystal, is involved in blackmail, or that Steve was involved somehow, the cops could probably get a warrant to look at hotel security footage."

We both mulled that over for a bit. I was about to suggest we go to the bar for some liquid inspiration when an idea popped into my head.

"Wait a minute . . ." I said, the wheels turning. "Maybe I have a connection that could get a peek at the surveillance video. I'm going to see if I can beg my pal Jana into helping us. I'll text you after I talk to Jana."

Di and I parted ways and I was making my way to

the conference area when my cell phone buzzed. It was Holly. "Hi, Holly."

"Liv, I swear and declare this reunion dinner is cursed," Holly said without even saying hello, which alerted me that something must be very wrong.

"What's wrong?"

"We have to change venues again—and truly at the eleventh hour. The toilet in the men's room at the Moose Lodge had backed up and overflowed. The head of the lodge got someone out to fix it right away. Sounds manageable, right? Except he brought in one of the lodge members who isn't really a plumber and had no idea what he was doing. So now we have a busted sewer pipe and raw sewage flooding into the kitchen! This is a monumental catastrophe."

Holly wasn't overstating the jam we were in. Finding a replacement venue a few days ago was a challenge. Finding one the day before the event would be nearly impossible.

"I've left messages at a couple of the churches and with people from the Elks Lodge and the VFW. But the two churches with halls big enough to accommodate the dinner are either stark or churchy looking. And our local VFW Post is very dated. Keep your fingers crossed that the Elks come through," Holly said.

"I'll say some prayers while you make a Hail Mary pass. Meanwhile, I'll see if I can come up with any other venues we might have missed."

I pushed the venue dilemma to the back of my mind for the moment. Partly because I knew Holly would leave no stone unturned. And mostly because

I needed to focus on getting Little Junior out of jail and Mama and Earl's wedding back on track.

After scouting the conference area with no sign of Jana, I decided to check her office. Just as I started walking to the elevator, my phone dinged. It was a text from Larry Joe.

In room. Need to talk. Pls bring ice cream.

Apparently it was my day to receive odd text messages from my family. If Larry Joe was asking me to bring ice cream instead of getting it for himself, I assumed he wasn't feeling well. So I returned to the food court and got him some mint chocolate chip in a cup.

I took the elevator up to our room. When I walked in the room I saw Larry Joe propped up on pillows against the headboard, holding an ice pack to his left eye.

I rushed over.

"Honey, are you okay? Did Jimmy Souther do this to you?"

I sat the ice-cream bowl down on the nightstand and gently pulled the hand with the ice pack away from his face, so I could get a look at that eye. It was swollen and already turning a painful shade of purple.

"It's not as bad as it looks. And Jimmy had nothing to do with it. I made the mistake of wading into the middle of a domestic dispute."

The ice wrapped inside a washcloth had begun to melt, leaving the cloth soggy.

"Here, give me that. I'll get you a fresh cloth and some more ice."

"Thanks, hon. There's ice in the bucket."

In a moment, I returned from the bathroom with a fresh ice pack. I sat down on the bed beside Larry Joe, who was lifting a spoonful of ice cream to his mouth. He flinched as I carefully placed the wrapped ice against his eye.

"Thanks for picking up the ice cream."

"You're welcome. Now, tell me what happened."

"This guy sitting at the end of the bar had been having words with his date. I wasn't really trying to listen to their conversation, so I'd only caught a few words here and there. But enough to know he wasn't treating her like a lady.

"She picked up her purse and slid off the bar stool. She took one step and he grabbed her arm and pulled her back, saying, 'You're not going anywhere.' She wrested her arm from his grasp and told him she was just going to the ladies' room. At that point, he grabbed her by the hair and pushed her against the wall, telling her again she wasn't going anywhere.

"You know I can't just stand by and watch some guy get rough with a woman. So I stepped in and told him to let her go. He swung around and clocked me. Pretty graceful move from a guy who'd been drinking all afternoon. At that point Jimmy and another guy stepped in and told him he had to leave. He said he wasn't leaving without his girlfriend. Jimmy told him it was up to her whether she stayed or went. But she said it was fine, and then left with the guy."

"Honey, you are a gentleman, and I'm proud of you," I said, leaning over and kissing my knight in slightly dented shining armor on the forehead. "Don't ever do that again, okay?

"Does Dave know about your black eye?"

"Yeah, he knows. We already conferred."

"Did he learn anything while he was watching Jimmy's house?"

"Yeah. Jimmy had two visitors and Dave had license plates run on both of them. The first was some woman named Cherita, who works at the bar with Jimmy. She stayed a couple of hours and Dave said their good-byes at the door were pretty friendly. So if Jimmy is trying to fan the flames of old embers with Di, she's not the only one he's setting fires with.

"The second visitor was a guy named Paul something. He only stayed about ten minutes. Don't know what they talked about, but he has a rap sheet as long as Jimmy's. In fact, hanging out with a known felon, like Paul, is likely a violation of Jimbo's parole."

He must have read the worried look on my face.

"Don't worry. Dave's not trying to get Jimmy in trouble with his parole officer for just talking to another felon. But if he finds evidence that suggests Jimmy's involved in any illegal activity, Dave will pass that information along to the Las Vegas cops."

"So what about you—did you learn anything of interest about Jimmy at the bar when you weren't getting into brawls?"

"Not much. Everybody seems to like him. He was talking up his new business venture, and I heard him inviting two different guys to invest in his photo booth scheme. But I don't guess that's illegal unless he takes their money and uses it for things other than the photo business.

"I did see him give a couple of free drinks to this one guy. The man had cash in his hand and slid it across the bar like he was paying. Jimmy pulled his hand across the bar like he was taking the cash— only he didn't. I saw the guy palm the money and slip it discreetly back into his pocket.

"I heard some people calling the guy 'Mac.' I didn't get a last name. But I did snap a picture of him. I texted it to Dave and he's going to see if the local cops know him."

My phone dinged again. It was a text from Di wanting to know if I had talked to Jana yet.

"Honey, are you going to be okay?" I asked Larry Joe. "I need to get back on the case."

"I'll be fine here with my ice pack and my ice cream. What are you up to?"

"I need to talk to Jana again to see if she can dig up some information for me. Wish me luck."

As I walked to the elevator, I texted Di back to let her know I'd gotten sidetracked but was on my way to talk to Jana now. I hit the elevator's down button and hoped I could remember my way through the maze of hallways leading to her office.

I tapped on the office door, and she said, "Enter," but her expression let me know she was surprised to see me.

"Liv, what are you doing here?"

She must've realized she had sounded abrupt, because she added, "Is there something I can help you with?"

"I really hope so. Jana, I need to ask you another favor. Let me start by saying I wouldn't ask if it weren't a life and death situation for my cousin. Nevada is a state that still has the death penalty—I Googled it."

"You know I'll help you if I can. What's the favor?"

"We need to look at some hotel surveillance videos."

"Now, that's something I can't do for you—even if I wanted to. The hotel executives take every measure possible to protect guests' privacy. They won't even let the police look at surveillance without a warrant."

"I understand, but we would only need to look at video from the seventh floor, covering rooms 7121 and 7123."

"That's really specific, but I still couldn't get access. . . ."

"Listen, we're pretty sure Gordy, the photographer at Burning Love Wedding Chapel, is involved in some kind of blackmail scheme using those rooms to get incriminating photos."

"I hear what you're saying, Liv. And I understand why this is so important to you. But looking at video footage in the hotel would be way above my pay grade. . . ."

"Oh, okay. I understand the heavy emphasis on privacy for the guest rooms. But what about in the casino? Security is always watching for gamblers who might be cheating or employees stealing, right? Would it be easier to get a look at casino footage? Say from today about eleven-thirty a.m.?"

"Let's say I could get a peek at casino surveillance

from such a specific time. What exactly would I be looking for?" Jana asked.

"Gordy. And more specifically, who Gordy may have met there."

"And this presumed blackmail business has something to do with that Elvis minister's death?"

"Yes. Steve was also seen going up to the guest rooms here recently. And the poison that they found in Steve's whiskey flask is one that's found in certain photo chemicals—chemicals that Gordy could have in his darkroom. And Gordy also would have known where Steve liked to stash his whiskey flask during weddings."

"So what do the police have to say about this? Do they believe Gordy is involved in the murder?"

"They won't listen to me. That's why I need some proof. Something concrete. Can you help me?"

"I can't get into surveillance of the guest rooms. But I might be able to get a look at the casino floor, especially for the short window of time you've specified. What time was that again?"

"Around eleven-thirty, give or take."

"It sounds like you could be right about Gordy. I mean, like you said, the killer had to be someone who had access to the poison—and to the victim's whiskey flask. Someone who knew he stashed his flask behind the roses in the chapel before weddings.

"Okay, I know you're worried about your cousin. I won't risk losing my job over this, but I might have a friendly connection in security who can get me a peek at the casino footage. I'll see what I can find out and get back to you."

"Thank you, Jana. I'll be forever in your debt."

Walking back from Jana's office, I felt dazed, trying to take it all in. What should I do next? What were we missing?

I made my way to the lobby level and sat down on a bench to think. I decided to call Holly and at least offer moral support, since I wasn't being much help to her otherwise.

"Hi, Holly . . ."

"Good news is the Elks Lodge is available, for a price. The bad news is the price they're asking is highway robbery."

"How much?"

"More than double what we were paying the restaurant or the Moose Lodge."

"That's ridiculous," I said.

"That's what I told the Exalted Ruler—that's what they call the head of the Benevolent and Protective Order of Elks. Benevolent, my eye. He's playing at extortion," Holly said.

Even when I'm nearly having a panic attack, Holly usually keeps her cool, exerting a calming influence on those around her, me especially. Even her genteel southern accent, her *r*'s polished smooth by a proper finishing school, has a calm, melodic cadence to it. At the moment, it sounded more like a growl. Obviously, the alpha Elk had gotten her dander up.

"Who is the Exalted Ruler—anybody I know?"

"Ronnie Mains. You know what an A-hole he can be."

I did. And, while Holly is gifted in the art of

persuasion, I knew Ronnie Mains wasn't a snake that would be easily charmed.

"Who are some of the other officers of the Elk Lodge? We need to do an end run around their Exalted Ruler," I said, knowing from experience that the man at the top of the roster wasn't necessarily the one in charge.

"Hang on. I'm pulling up their Web site. Here we go."

Holly ran down the list, from Esteemed Leading Knight and Esteemed Loyal Knight to Grand Inner Guard and Grand Trustees, telling who currently held each office. Two names leapt out at me.

"Holly, don't you worry about a thing. The reunion dinner *will* be held at the Elks Lodge. I'll take care of making that happen. You go take care of everything else—I know you have a million things to do, including the luau tonight. I'll check in with you later."

I took the elevator up to our floor and knocked on Di's door. After she let me in, I said, "Okay, I talked to Jana, but now you and I need to talk things through. There are so many bits and pieces, I feel like we're missing something. But first, would you mind going down and getting us some coffee. I can't get used to not having a coffeemaker in the room, but apparently that's the norm in Vegas. I think the caffeine hit might help me concentrate, and I have to make some phone calls to put out a few fires back in Dixie. I promised Holly I would handle some issues we're having with our problem-plagued reunion, and I haven't gotten around to it yet."

"Sure. I'd kind of like to stretch my legs anyway," Di said, grabbing her purse and heading out the door.

"Okay," I said aloud, trying to gather the thoughts I'd had on my ride up in the elevator about the problem of the Elks attempting to overcharge us on the hall rental.

There were two officers at the Elks Lodge I could reach out to, the chairman of the Elders at my church, Brother Scott Woods, and my landlord, Nathan Sweet. I could appeal to Brother Scott's sense of Christian charity about the Elks trying to gouge us with an exorbitant fee on the lodge rental. My landlord isn't so much the charitable type, but he wouldn't be happy if the Exalted Leader lost money for the lodge's coffers by refusing to offer us a reasonable rental fee.

I called Brother Scott first, just because he's more pleasant to talk to. But his cell phone went straight to voice mail. When I called his house, his wife said he was out on the golf course and always leaves his cell phone in his locker while he's playing. She would tell him to call me the minute he got home.

Since she wasn't sure when that would be, I had to move on to Nathan Sweet. He is the "Sweet" in Sweet Deal Realty and rents out the office above the real estate office to me for my party-planning business. To say he's eccentric would be an understatement— but he's also a shrewd businessman. Case in point, he has me paying rent on an office that doesn't even have a restroom. But, use of the facilities in Sweet Deal Realty is included in my rent. And all I have to do is go downstairs, out the front door, walk a few steps down the sidewalk and in through the front door of the real estate office. Not entirely convenient, but it gives my business the visibility of being on the town square—and the rent's cheap.

"Good mornin', Sweet Deal Realty, this is Winette. How may I help you?"

Winette is the only agent at Sweet Deal Realty, other than Mr. Sweet. Unlike her boss, she is charitable. In fact, she heads up Residential Rehab, a volunteer organization that provides house repairs for the disabled and elderly in our community.

"Hi, Winette, it's Liv."

"Well, hello. So have you gotten your mama married off?"

"Not yet, but that's a long story. Is Mr. Sweet around?"

"No. He's probably across the street in the barbershop talking to some other old men. What's up? Are your mother and Earl thinking about buying a new house?"

"No. The only way my mama will ever move out of her house is feet first. Besides, you know we'd hire you as the listing agent, not Mr. Sweet. I'm in a bind and I'm hoping Mr. Sweet can help me out."

"Girl, you are in a bind if you're depending on Nathan Sweet to help you out. Is there anything I can do?"

I gave Winette a quick rundown on what had become our traveling fiftieth high school class reunion dinner, which so far, had been evicted from the hotel restaurant *and* the Moose Lodge because of sewage issues.

"The Elks are being unreasonable about the rental fee. What do you think my chances are of getting Mr. Sweet to intervene on my behalf with the Exalted Leader? And do you think Ronnie Mains will listen to him?"

"Oh, he'll listen, all right. Being the big cheese at the Elks Lodge is the most exalted position Ronnie will ever hold. He's not going to risk messing that up by getting on Nathan Sweet's bad side. And you just leave Mr. Sweet to me. I can handle that old coot. Just tell me the rental fee you were paying elsewhere and I'll tell him that's how much his lodge is going to charge you. If he gives me any grief, I'll threaten to find you a new office space—one with a restroom," Winette said with inspiring confidence.

"Would you?" I said.

"Would I what?"

"Would you actually find me a new space with a bathroom?"

"I don't know. I've grown fond of our little chats when you come through to use the facilities or pilfer a cup of coffee. You wouldn't want to give all that up for a toilet, would you?"

"No, I really wouldn't," I said with complete honesty.

After I got off the phone, I heard what sounded like someone kicking the door, and realized Di probably had her hands full. I hurried over and opened the door for her.

She was holding two large coffees and a little bag containing sugars, creamers, and stir sticks.

"So were you able to put out some fires in Dixie?" Di asked.

"Winette volunteered to be my fire chief. She's going to tell Mr. Sweet what's what."

"If anyone can, it's her. Do we want to risk indigestion by talking about the murder suspects?"

"I've had a queasy feeling ever since Little Junior was arrested. And Uncle Junior having chest pains hasn't made things any better."

"Have you heard any more about your uncle's condition?"

"Not in a while. But Mama said she'd call as soon as they knew something."

"So what have we got?" she said.

"I'm not sure. But I feel we're getting close to something big."

"I hope you're right. First, we've got Steve dropping dead from poison that Gordy may have had lying around handy. And it sounds like Gordy has been playing at blackmail, which is a dangerous game at best," Di said.

"Right. And as much as I'd like to think otherwise, Crystal may not have been entirely honest with us. She could have been with Gordy upstairs, instead of keeping him under surveillance. And afraid of getting caught, she decided to throw him under the bus. Plus, she admitted she'd been to Gordy's house. She says it was only once, but for all we know they could be friends or even partners in crime. It's possible she even took the poison from Gordy's place."

"And Steve was up to something. Crystal saw him going up to the guest rooms on more than one occasion, when he wasn't performing in a show here," Di said.

"We only have Crystal's word for that."

"Yeah . . . Wait. What was it your mama overheard Steve and Taylor bickering about? Something about, 'they can't find out.'"

"Oh, right, let me check." I walked over to the desk and dug around in my purse for random notes I'd been taking about the investigation. I pulled out a couple of bank deposit slips I'd scribbled on.

"Here we go. Taylor said, 'We can't let *him* find out,' and Steve said, '*She* thinks she owns me, but she doesn't.'"

"If 'he' is Gordy, then is 'she' Crystal?" Di offered.

"Could be. But I think 'he' could be the owner of the wedding chapel. When I asked about Taylor, Jana said there were rumors—unconfirmed—that Taylor had been fired from her previous job for dipping into the till. Maybe she was up to her old tricks."

"Then who is 'she'?"

"That I don't know. But maybe their whispered conversation in the chapel wasn't about business. Maybe it was just a lover's quarrel. Maybe 'he' and 'she' were other romantic partners in their complicated affairs."

"I suppose," Di said.

We both sipped on our coffee while we mulled that over for a long moment.

"Steve was known for changing dance partners regularly. Next time I talk to her, I could ask Jana what the gossip is about Tay—"

I stopped before finishing my sentence, something nagging at me, just out of reach.

After a pause, Di asked, "What is it?"

"Seems like there was something Jana said. What was it?" I said. "Wait a minute. She said 'roses.' That's it."

Chapter Fourteen

Suddenly a lightbulb had lit up over my head.

"What?" Di asked, seeing my expression.

"Jana said 'roses.' She said Steve liked to stash his whiskey flask behind the *roses* in the chapel."

"Okay . . . so? He did, didn't he?"

"No, he didn't. The standard arrangements in the chapel are carnations and daisies. That's what Taylor told us. The only reason there were roses in the chapel was because Mama had upgraded the arrangements to roses for her wedding. And they were brought in fresh that afternoon. The florist's delivery van was in front of the chapel when Little Junior dropped us off at the door."

"Oh, I get it. The only way Jana could have known there were roses instead of carnations and daisies in the chapel when Steve died was if she was *there*. So, that means Jana is the murderer, right?"

"She either killed Steve or was working with whoever did," I said.

"But how do we know she even knew Steve?"

"We don't," I said, feeling deflated.

"Wait a minute. Gordy and Crystal both mentioned that Steve was in that Ages of Elvis show that ran here at the hotel. Jana could have met him then," Di offered.

"That's right. And Holly told me Jana's marriage broke up after she took up with some singer here in Las Vegas."

"Should we tell the cops?" Di asked.

"I doubt they're going to be as impressed with Jana's slip of the tongue as we are. Should we talk to Dave?"

"No. He's not even talking to me right now. And he's too busy trying to pin the murder on Jimmy to be bothered with another suspect—even if Jana is the real killer," Di said.

"I think we *have* to talk to Dave—he's the only one we know that the police might take seriously. Detective Bains certainly doesn't have fond feelings for us at the moment. But, you're right, I'm not sure Dave will listen to us either."

Di started chipping the polish off her recently manicured nails and I flopped back on a pillow. I shot up, suddenly sitting up straight in the bed.

"I know. I'm going to tell Larry Joe what we think and ask *him* to talk to Dave. If Larry Joe buys our conclusions about the real killer, I think our stubborn sheriff will listen to him."

I texted Larry Joe to see if he was still in the room. He replied that his mom and dad had just gotten back from visiting the hospital and, of course, his dad wanted to get something to eat.

I decided to just call him instead of composing a long text reply in my slow one-thumbed typing style.

"Hi, honey, could you let your mama put the feed bag on your dad. I need to talk to you—urgently. Can you come up to the room?"

"Sure, hon, I'll be right there."

"Larry Joe's on his way to our room. Would you call Crystal?" I asked Di. "It just occurred to me that, if we're right about Jana, she won't be trying to get a look at any security footage—especially if it implicates her. Tell Crystal what's going on and see if she knows anyone in security who could take a look at the footage from the casino this morning just after Gordy disappeared into the crowd."

"Okay, I will."

I started toward the door, and Di called out, "Wait, Liv. I don't have Crystal's phone number."

I texted her the number.

"Got it," she said. "And good luck with Larry Joe."

I went to our room, sat down on the edge of the bed, and tried to organize my thoughts. Larry Joe came in just a couple of minutes later.

"Honey, is your mama all right? Did something happen with Uncle Junior?" he said, walking over to me with a worried look.

"Oh, no. No medical emergencies—and nothing new on Uncle Junior." I stood up and gave him a hug. "There has been a major development in our murder investigation, though. Sit down and let me try to lay it all out for you."

He listened intently and didn't interrupt or roll his eyes even once, which I took as a good sign.

"So let me see if I have this straight," he began. "It seems Gordy is up to no good, maybe blackmail, and you believe Steve was involved as either a blackmailer or blackmail*ee*. The blackmail scheme on the seventh floor would've needed a connection from someone who works in the hotel, and you think that's probably Jana. And you know Jana was at the chapel around the time of Steve's murder because she slipped up and said the flask was behind the roses, when normally the flowers in the chapel are carnations and daisies."

It didn't sound like much when he played it back to me, but I was convinced we were right.

"Are you sure you didn't mention the word 'roses' to Jana and she just picked up on that?"

"I'm sure. I didn't even bring it up—she did. But the police should be able to check out at least the blackmail angle, if they can take a look at the security footage or set up their own quiet surveillance on the seventh floor."

"What does Dave think?"

"I was hoping you'd talk to Dave. He's not in a receptive mood to listen to Di or me—especially Di—at the moment. But if *you* think our take on things sounds plausible, he'll listen to you."

I looked at him with pleading eyes and was prepared to beg. But I didn't have to.

"I think you and Di are on to something. And Gordy's a photographer, so he would know how to get hold of the photo chemicals in the poison they found in the flask—and in Steve, by the way. Dave said the medical examiner confirmed the cause of death.

"I'll call and see where he is now."

Larry Joe dialed and put the phone to his ear.

"Dave, I need to talk to you. Where are you at? Great. I'll see you in ten minutes."

He dropped his phone back in his pocket.

"Dave's back in his room."

"So I have you to myself for ten whole minutes?"

"No. I have some other business to take care of," he said, going into the bathroom and closing the door.

I texted Di that Larry Joe thought we were on the right track and that he was going to tell Dave about it.

"Hold good thoughts," I said.

"Fingers crossed," she said. "Oh, and I talked to Crystal. She said she doesn't think she can get a look at surveillance video. But she has a friend in housekeeping she thinks might be able to get us into those rooms on the seventh floor for a quick look around. Does that help?"

"Ooh, it might."

Just then, Larry Joe came through the door.

"Put your shoes on, Liv. And if that's Di on the phone, tell her to meet us at the elevator. We're all going down to the police station."

"Di, did you hear that? Okay."

I ended my call with Di and asked Larry Joe, "So does Dave think the cops will listen to our story, or is he having us arrested for interfering in a police investigation?"

"He's thinking the former. But, the lead detective may have other ideas. We'll see."

Di came out of her hotel room just as Larry Joe and I stepped into the hallway. Dave was waiting for us by the elevator. We all got in and Larry Joe hit *L*.

"I think you two may have stumbled on something here," Dave said, staring straight ahead at the elevator doors.

I exchanged glances with Di. I could tell she shared my feeling that Dave was being condescending. But I think it bothered her more than me.

"Remember, this is Detective Bains's investigation," Dave continued. "Let him lead the questioning. Don't try to run the show and things will probably go more smoothly."

I couldn't help but wonder if Bains had clued Dave in on the conversation he had with Di and me at the station.

As we got off the elevator my phone dinged with a text message from Winette.

That man is putty in my hands. Called Holly with good news. Hug your mama for me.

I smiled and hoped things turned out as well down at the police station.

Larry Joe hailed a taxi. Dave sat in front with the driver and the three of us got in back, with me in the middle. *Why do I always end up in the middle?*

"Convention Center Area Command on Sierra Vista," Dave told the driver. Then Dave put his cell phone to his ear.

"Yeah, Bob. We're en route. Right. Gotcha."

Di was staring out the window. Dave tilted his head slightly toward us.

"Bains said Crystal will be joining us at the precinct as soon as she finishes her shift. Earlier it sounded like he was just going to chat with us informally. But he might take a more official approach and take Liv and Di into separate interview rooms," he said, apparently addressing Larry Joe.

Di and I shared a knowing look.

Few words were exchanged on the ride there. In about twenty minutes, the taxi dropped us off in front of the familiar precinct, a boxy white building across the street from an empty lot. Once inside, Dave spoke to someone at the counter and we waited until a uniformed officer came to fetch us.

Detective Bains did play things more "informally," as Dave had called it, by seating all of us around the table in one interview room. He talked to us for about forty-five minutes, rephrasing, but asking the same questions three or four times. I'd learned this was standard procedure from some of the less pleasant chats Di and I had had with Dave back in Dixie. More than once, he'd been less than gracious when we'd helped him out with a murder investigation.

The detective left the room. The blank walls and buzzing fluorescent light overhead felt like sensory deprivation after the past few days of neon overload. Bains returned about twenty minutes later and motioned for Dave to join him.

"The detective has on a poker face, like cops are wont to do," I said.

"I don't know. . . . Sheriff Davidson has been known to wear a scowl on more than a few occasions," Di said.

I decided it was better just to ignore the remark.

"Do either of you have a feeling about whether he's taking the information we've given him seriously?" I asked.

"Hon, I don't think he would have invested close to an hour questioning you if he thought it was a waste of time. He seems like a no-nonsense kind of guy," Larry Joe said, which sounded encouraging.

In a few minutes Dave and Detective Bains returned to the interview room, and Crystal was with them. The men sat down and the detective invited Crystal to be seated, as well.

Bains cleared his throat.

"With the information you've given us, along with some new information from Crystal Pryor, I believe there may be a way to wrap up this case. That is, if Mrs. McKay would feel comfortable assisting us with a suspect."

"*Mr.* McKay will have to feel comfortable with her assisting you before she agrees to anything," Larry Joe interjected, reaching over to grab my hand as he glared at the detective. "What exactly are you asking her to do?"

We spent the next twenty minutes or so listening to Bains lay out the plan, interrupted several times with questions from Larry Joe. After everything was explained and agreed to, I went down the hall with one of the uniformed officers to get prepared. A patrol car drove us all back to the hotel, except for Crystal, who had driven to the station in her own car.

Larry Joe, Di, and Dave and I went to the casino bar. The men ordered beers and Di and I opted for glasses of white wine. While we waited to hear from Detective Bains, I made a quick phone call to Earl.

"Hi, Earl. Are y'all still at the hospital?"

"Yeah, they're waiting on Junior's test results. They've got him hooked up to an IV and a heart monitor. To be honest, I'm more concerned about your mama. She's worrying herself sick over her brother and her nephew."

"Listen, Earl, I can't go into any details. But tell Mama we're on to something here, and if everything goes according to plan, Little Junior should be out of jail by tomorrow—if not sooner."

"I'll tell her. Can I also tell her not to worry about you doing anything dangerous?"

"Don't worry. I'll talk to you later."

"Any news on Uncle Junior," Larry Joe asked.

"No. They're still waiting on some test results."

I sipped on my wine and waited anxiously for the detective to call.

I jumped when Dave's phone buzzed.

In a moment, Dave nodded at me and said, "You're on."

I started to walk away. Larry Joe grabbed me by the hand, pulled me back, and wrapped his arms around me. He gave me a big kiss, one I wished I had more time to savor. But we'd have to save that for later.

I forced a smile and said, "Hey, I'm not going far, you know."

I walked across the lobby, past the elevators to a relatively quiet spot to make a phone call. Fortunately, Jana picked up. She started talking, making excuses, before I could even say anything.

"Jana, I understand you couldn't take a look at surveillance video in the casino for a specific time without raising questions. But I had an idea. Could you get your hands on the key card to room 7121 or 7123? There's bound to be a maid or maintenance guy who owes you a favor, or who would be willing to let you take a quick peek into the rooms in exchange for tickets to some new show. If we could look around and see if there really is a two-way mirror, that would be something we could take to the police. Tangible evidence and not just a theory."

Jana went quiet for a moment, then said, "That's an excellent idea, Liv. I can't believe I didn't think of it earlier. Could you meet me on the seventh floor in thirty minutes?"

I told her I'd be there. I wiped my sweaty palms against my pants leg, and walked down the hallways toward the meeting room area. The conference was over and the halls were mostly empty. I slipped into the ladies' room and made a pit stop. I washed my hands and stared at my reflection, taking a few deep breaths and steeling my courage. I tugged down on my shirt and turned to look at my back in the mirror, making sure everything was straight.

At the appointed time I took the elevator up to the seventh floor. Jana was waiting for me. We walked down the hall together, checking numbers until we arrived at room 7123. Jana inserted the key card and opened the door. She flipped on the light switch and I followed her to what appeared to be an ordinary mirror on the wall. She pulled her cell phone from her purse and told me to shut off the lights. Then she turned on her cell phone flashlight and held it very close to the mirror. I stepped over beside her and leaned forward, looking intently into the mirror. The bright illumination of the flashlight allowed us to peer dimly into the room next door. We could make out the shapes of the bed and nightstand.

"I read about this flashlight trick online," Jana said. "Apparently, blackmail victims could be viewed from the other side of a mirror. When the light's on in here and the light's out in there, someone could film the proceedings without being seen."

I was still peering curiously into the mirror. Jana turned around and flipped the lights on. When she turned back to face me, she was holding a gun, which she aimed directly at me.

"I turned the lights on because I want to see your face when I put a bullet in you. I give you credit, you're smarter than the average hick. You figured out the blackmail scheme.

"You were wrong about Steve blackmailing Gordy, though. Steve was actually stupid enough to black-mail *me*. So he had to go. Steve and I had enjoyed each other's company for a while, in a romantic way. He was even foolish enough to think I still had feelings for him, and that he was safe from any kind of reprisal. He was dead wrong."

"So you killed him and used the sodium cyanide in the photo chemicals to cast suspicion on Gordy. Only the cops weren't even smart enough to pick up on that."

"True. But when they arrested your dimwit cousin instead, that was fine. I didn't care who took the fall, as long as it wasn't me.

"Liv, I truly didn't want to have to kill you. If only you'd let go of the whole blackmail rooms on the seventh-floor thing. This is a lucrative little setup I have here. I wasn't going to let Steve mess it up— and I'm certainly not going to let you mess it up for me. I'm surprised none of the other threads you kept trying to unravel ever led you to me."

"Oh, but they did. I figured out earlier today that you were the one who killed Steve—when you told me maybe I was right about Gordy. That's when you slipped up."

"Really. Go ahead and prove to me how smart you are and how you had it all figured out. Right before I kill you."

"Okay. You said the flask was hidden behind the roses."

"What?"

"You said Steve's flask was tucked behind the roses. But the standard flowers in the chapel are carnations and daisies. Taylor had told us that. There were only roses there—which the florist delivered shortly before the ceremony—because my mama had upgraded the arrangement for her wedding. And you could only have known about the roses if you were there, in the chapel, around the time of Steve's death."

"Maybe it would have been smart of you to mention that tidbit to the police," she said as she raised the gun and aimed it straight at my heart.

"She did," a voice said through the microphone that usually recorded blackmail sessions. At the same instant, the light came on in the room on the other side of the two-way mirror. I dove down behind the king-size bed and Detective Bains along with a uniformed officer stormed in from the hall, with their weapons drawn.

Jana fired off a blind shot toward me as the uniformed officer grabbed her arm and seized the gun from her hand. The detective rushed over to me, and Dave spoke through the microphone in a panicked voice, "Liv, are you okay?"

I stood up tentatively, with help from the detective. Still shaking, I nodded and said, "Yeah, I'm fine."

I tugged on the Kevlar vest under my shirt, which had ridden up when I dived at the floor, and pulled off the recording device they had wired me with and handed it to Detective Bains. The officer hand-cuffed and escorted Jana out as she muttered curses, some of which I could understand. And Di and Crystal rushed in from the hall.

"Are you sure you're all right?" Crystal said, with a concerned expression.

"Yeah."

"Good. I'd hate for us to go to all this trouble and you mess it up by getting yourself killed," Di said with her trademark charm.

"I love you, too," I said, wrapping my arms around her waist and laying my head on her shoulder. Despite my best efforts to remain stalwart, I started to cry.

Di patted me on the back and said, "Liv, please don't cry. This blouse is dry-clean only."

The three of us started laughing. We joined Dave in the room next door, where the blackmailer's camera was usually set up. He talked to Bains and told him that he'd take me down to the station shortly so I could make a formal statement—and return the bullet-proof vest they had outfitted me with.

"You done good," Dave said, giving me a little shoulder hug. "Jana's confession should be enough to get your cousin sprung from jail within the next few hours."

Chapter Fifteen

After Jana had been taken away, we were standing around in the hallway recapping everything that had just happened, when Dave said, "There's somebody who's anxious to see you. Bains made Larry Joe stay downstairs with a uniformed cop keeping an eye on him. He was afraid Larry Joe's protective streak could prompt him to jump in to rescue you before we had everything we needed from Jana."

"It seems to me you could've jumped in a little sooner," I said, my heart palpitating at the thought of Jana pointing a gun squarely at me.

We rode the elevator one floor down to the hallway housing our block of rooms. Larry Joe was pacing the floor as a uniformed officer stood between him and the elevator. He looked up with an expression of great relief. I hurried over and threw my arms around his neck. He lifted me off the ground in a rib-cracking hug.

"Liv, are you okay?" he whispered, his lips against my ear. He pulled back a little and looked me in the eyes. "At one point I thought I heard a muffled gunshot, but the officer told me I was just jumpy."

"I'm fine. Everything went according to plan. I was never in any real danger," I said.

After giving us a moment, Di, Dave, and Crystal walked over to us.

"Dave, do you know if the cops have picked up Gordy yet?" I asked.

"Yeah, Bains said officers were standing by at Gordy's house waiting to pick him up as soon as we had Jana's confession here. When he realized she had used his photo chemicals to implicate him in Steve's murder, he came clean about the blackmail. He claims he knew nothing about the murder. The LVMPD detectives will have to sort out who knew what and when. The important thing is that Jana's behind bars and Little Junior will be released soon."

"Little Junior! Dave, we have to stop by the hospital on the way to the police station and tell Mama and Uncle Junior the good news. That'll be the best medicine for him right now."

"Agreed. We better get moving," Dave said.

"I'll see y'all later," Di said. "Something tells me there will be a celebration dinner tonight."

Larry Joe and Dave and I took a taxi to the hospital. Our transportation bill had gone up considerably since Little Junior's arrest.

We made our way through the hospital and took the elevator. I could hear Mama's booming voice from down the hall. We tapped on the half-open door to Uncle Junior's room. Upon entering, we saw that Uncle Junior was dressed and sitting in a chair.

Mama, who was perched on the side of the bed,

looked up, all smiles, when we walked in, with Dave behind me and Larry Joe behind him. Earl was standing at the foot of the bed.

"They're sending Junior home. We're just waiting on the dismissal papers," she said.

"They ran a bunch of tests and told me I don't have a heart," Uncle Junior said.

"I think they're kicking him out because he got fresh with a nurse. Said if he feels that perky it's time for him to leave," Mama said.

Larry Joe, who had been hanging back with his face slightly turned away, stepped forward into the room. Every head turned toward him, taking notice of his black eye.

"What happened, son?" Uncle Junior said. "Your wife catch you ogling some show girl?"

"No. I accidentally stepped in front of a drunk guy's fist. It's not as bad as it looks."

"I'm not sure I buy that story, but if Liv's satisfied with your explanation, I'm not going to interfere," Mama said doubtfully.

"Where's my mama?" Larry Joe asked, eager to change the subject.

"She left a little bit ago. She wanted to make sure Wayne didn't eat supper before we got there. We thought a little dinner to celebrate Junior getting a clean bill of health was in order. Although, he's not going to eat anything too heavy. Right, little brother?"

Uncle Junior nodded noncommittally.

"Uncle Junior getting out of the hospital is cause for celebration. But we have some other happy news. They're releasing Little Junior from jail this evening," I said.

"Glory be," Mama said as she jumped up and ran over to hug me.

After smothering me to her bosom, she said, "So, does this mean they caught the real killer?"

"Yes," Dave said. "And your daughter played a key role in bringing a murderer to justice."

"You didn't do something crazy, did you?" she said, eyeing me with suspicion.

"No, the cops were right there. But I wore a wire and they got the confession on tape," I said.

"You mean like on TV? Just wait until I tell the ladies in my Sunday School class. Sylvia's always going on about how her daughter once thwarted a shoplifter. All she did was squeal on some elderly woman in the lingerie department who was stuffing underwear into her purse. Sylvia's daughter yelled for the manager and held on to the lady's handbag until store security came running over."

When Mama stopped long enough to take a breath, Uncle Junior asked, "So who is the killer?"

"My money's on that snooty wedding coordinator, Taylor," Mama said.

"Nope. It's Jana Hively, the event coordinator at our hotel."

"And Liv knew her," Larry Joe interjected. "She used to be a member of the event-planning association in Memphis before she moved to Vegas."

"And she knew Steve, apparently in the biblical sense," I said.

"Did she kill him because he was two-timing her with Taylor?" Mama asked.

"No, it was more complicated than that. Jana and Gordy, the wedding photographer at the Burning Love Chapel, were running a blackmail scheme at the hotel. Gordy was taking compromising photos of people who didn't want to be compromised. Steve was either in on it or found out about it—I'm not quite clear on that point. Either way, he tried to blackmail Jana and she took him out of the picture," I said.

A nurse knocked on the open door as she entered.

"Mr. Manning, you're all set. We just need you to sign these papers."

She handed Uncle Junior the clipboard and a pen, and he scrawled his name at the bottom of the page.

Uncle Junior stood up and Earl grabbed his arm to steady him as he walked to the door. A nursing assistant was waiting in the hallway with a wheelchair.

"I can walk, thank you," Uncle Junior snapped.

"Mr. Manning, it's hospital rules. We'll roll you to the door. Do you have a ride waiting?"

"We should have," Mama said. "I called for a taxi thirty minutes ago. I'll call and check."

Just as Mama started pulling up the number, her phone buzzed.

"Yes. We're on our way down now with the patient. Thanks," she said. "We're good to go, Junior."

He groused a little as he sat down in the wheelchair.

"Don't be an old grouch. You're getting out of the hospital—and you'll get to see Little Junior in just a little while," she said, patting him on the shoulder.

"It just occurred to me, five of us plus the driver might be a little crowded for one cab," Mama said.

"We should've told our driver to wait," Larry Joe said. "Y'all go on back to the hotel. We'll call a taxi. We still need to go by the police precinct. Liv has to give a formal statement and turn in that Kevlar vest she's got on under her shirt."

"Wait a minute—why did Liv need a bulletproof vest?" Uncle Junior said.

"I'd like to hear the answer to that one myself," Mama said, looking displeased.

"It was purely a precaution," I said. "I told you the cops were right outside the door, listening the whole time."

We walked down with Mama, Earl, and Uncle Junior, who was being pushed in a wheelchair. We said our good-byes at the curb.

Dave called for a taxi and we waited about ten minutes for it to arrive before heading over to the police station. I turned in my bulletproof vest, hoping I'd never have need for one again, and filled out a statement.

"Why don't we call Crystal to pick us up? I'm sure she'd like to be here when they let Little Junior out," I said.

"That's not a bad idea, except Little Junior isn't here at the precinct. He's at the jail."

"Is that very far?" Larry Joe asked.

"No. It's not too far from the Neon Museum," Dave replied.

"Oh, I remember driving by that," I said.

We asked Bains if Jana was being cooperative.

"No. She's keeping her mouth shut. Waiting for her attorney," he said. "But she won't be getting out on bail."

Dave took Bains off to the side for a brief word

before we left. I had my suspicions he was asking
Bains to keep an eye on Jimmy Souther.

The three of us piled into yet another taxi. The
driver dropped Larry Joe and me at the hotel and
continued on to the Clark County Detention Center
with Dave in the backseat. I phoned Crystal and she
said she was meeting Dave at the jail. She would be
behind the wheel when Little Junior got sprung.
The hope was that the three of them would meet us
back at the hotel, if not in time for dinner, then at
least for dessert.

When we arrived, I called Mama to let her know
Larry Joe and I were back at the hotel, but we
didn't have an estimated time of arrival yet for
Little Junior. Dave said he would call when they
were in transit.

"All of your elders are in their hotel rooms, hon.
Junior wanted to take a quick shower. Said he had
gooey spots from where they stuck those electrodes
to him for the heart monitor. I wanted to put my
feet up for a bit, since I know you worry about my
swollen ankles. But we should be ready to head
down in thirty minutes, if that sounds good to you."

"That's fine. Head down to where? Have y'all decided where to have dinner?"

"At the buffet. It's not fancy, but we can push
tables together to seat our group. And since we
won't all be arriving at the same time, we don't have
to worry about placing orders. We'll meet y'all in
the lobby."

"Sounds like a plan to me. We'll see you shortly,"
I said.

"What are we doing?" Larry Joe asked, after I got
off the phone with command central.

"We're going to the buffet in thirty minutes. Just enough time for us to go upstairs and freshen up."

Sponging off before I put on fresh clothes, I noticed I had some "gooey spots" as Uncle Junior had called them, where they had taped the hidden recording wires to me. I came out of the bathroom and grabbed a clean blouse from the closet. I slipped it on, but before I could get it buttoned, Larry Joe had come over and pulled me close, wrapping his arms tightly around me.

"I was really scared today, knowing you were alone with a cold-blooded killer, trying to prod a confession out of her."

"I didn't have to prod anything out of Jana. She seemed to enjoy bragging to me about what she'd done."

"You're very brave, Liv McKay—and I'm proud of you," Larry Joe said, cupping my face with his hands and looking into my eyes. "But I don't want you to do anything like that ever again. I'm not brave enough to go through it."

He kissed me in the way that still makes me go weak in the knees, even after being married for a dozen years. When we came up for air, I glanced at the clock on the nightstand.

"We're going to be late for supper if we don't get moving," I said, giving him one more quick kiss for good measure.

The rest of our party was waiting when we came into the lobby. Without a word, Daddy Wayne turned and started walking toward the buffet.

"There are some tables along the wall. That might be a little quieter. I'm going to go over to reserve our tables," Mama said, before barreling across the expansive dining room that surrounded long runs of serving tables on three sides.

I trailed after Mama, who had plopped her purse in the middle of one table and sat down between two others, with a hand on each, signaling that these were taken. One of the tables had not been bussed yet, so Mama waved over a waitress.

"Hon, could you have someone clear this table as soon as you get a chance. We have a big group. And we're celebrating. My brother just got out of the hospital," Mama said with a big smile, turning on the charm. She didn't mention we also had a relative who was just getting out of jail. But that was a little harder to explain. The waitress returned in just a few moments with a gray plastic tub. She cleared and wiped down the table, then said she'd be back in a minute to take our drink orders.

"Hon, just make it iced teas all around. We have . . . Liv, how many people do we have?"

"We have nine here and three more joining us later."

The men had headed straight to the buffet lines. Earl came over first, carrying two plates, one with salad and one with rolls and butter pats.

"Virginia, I brought you some rolls in case you wanted something to nibble on before you go through the buffet."

Uncle Junior was walking just behind Earl with a sensible-looking salad on his plate.

Miss Betty and Di had sparse helpings of this and that, while Larry Joe had a plate with man-sized portions. Finally, Daddy Wayne came over to the tables carrying two plates piled high with everything fried they had on the buffet.

"Wayne McKay," Miss Betty said in a scolding tone.

"I had a light lunch," he shot back, not that anyone at the table believed him.

Mama started bragging about how I'd worn a wire to catch a killer, only in her version it sounded like I was wearing a cape, too. This gave me a little preview of the way I was sure she'd tell the story to her friends back in Dixie, not that any of them would believe her.

Everyone asked Uncle Junior how he was feeling and what the doctors had to say. No heart attack, he had angina—and on the first night maybe a touch of heartburn, as well. He said he'd be avoiding Italian food for a while, just in case. He finished off his salad and started to get up for another trip to the food bar, but Mama prevented him.

"Junior, you stay put. I'll go through the buffet and bring you back a healthy plate."

He didn't seem to like it much, but he didn't put up a fuss—until she returned with two plates, one plenteous and one meager, and handed the meager plate to him.

"Virginia, I'm supposed to be on a healthy diet, not a starvation diet," he protested.

"You should just be thankful you're not eating that hospital food. So, hush. If you behave you can have a small dessert," she said.

Dave called to let us know that he and Crystal and Little Junior were en route. There was an eruption of excitement when Larry Joe shared the news. I saw a tear fall from Uncle Junior's eye onto his small serving of steamed broccoli—no butter.

I had an idea, so I went to the dessert line and talked to the server. I told her we were having a little welcome home party for my cousin, who'd been . . . away. I returned to the table with a large slice of chocolate layer cake with a candle in it. I arranged for the waitress to come over and light the candle in a few minutes.

When we spotted Little Junior coming through the door with Crystal beside him and Dave right behind, we sprang to our feet with cheers and applause. Even Daddy Wayne took his head out of the feeding trough, briefly.

Earl rushed over, waving them in and telling the cashier he'd take care of their checks.

Little Junior stepped into a crush of hugs.

"Thanks. I have the best family in the whole world," Little Junior said, choking up a little. "And, Liv, Crystal and Dave told me what you did for me. I'll never be able to thank you."

After Mama finally released him from a smothering embrace, I stepped over and gave him a hug.

"No thanks necessary. We're family."

Chapter Sixteen

After everyone had enjoyed their fill, including cake, we started to break up the party. Di was the first to slip out, and I wondered if she was going to meet Jimmy. The look on Dave's face led me to believe he had the same thought. Crystal and Little Junior said their good nights. And Uncle Junior excused himself. He looked tired, but content.

Earl had escorted my uncle upstairs to make sure he was okay, and Larry Joe was walking just ahead of me with his parents. I was walking arm in arm with Mama, who was looking more relaxed than I'd seen her in days. I decided to broach the subject of the wedding.

"Mama, now that Little Junior is out of jail—and the real killer is behind bars—do you want me to call the Burning Love Wedding Chapel and see when we can schedule the wedding?"

"No, hon. That place holds bad memories for me."

"Of course. I can call around to the other chapels."

"I don't know that I want to get married in any Las Vegas chapel now."

Mama sighed and I had a sudden feeling of dread that she was going to say she wanted to go back to Dixie and the outrageous wedding plans Holly and I had begun work on before she opted for Vegas. Then I had a flash of genius, which was rare.

"Mama, what if we have an outdoor wedding like you originally wanted. Except, instead of beside Earl's pond, we have it beside Lake Mead. And we ask Little Junior to officiate."

Big tears started rolling down Mama's cheeks. She hugged me and smooshed my head against her bosom.

"Liv, that sounds perfect. What do we need to do?"

"You and Earl just start packing provisions into the Winnebago. I'll take care of arranging the wedding. Let's shoot for tomorrow evening."

I rallied the troops, calling or texting everyone in our group, including Little Junior and Crystal, and asked them to meet at the food court in thirty minutes. I hurried to my room and started making some phone calls to check on prices and availability. Then I pulled hotel stationery out of the drawer and started making my lists and timeline.

Everyone, except Di, showed up for muster, and I outlined the battle plan, starting with the officiant.

"Little Junior, Mama and Earl—well, all of us would love for you to perform the wedding ceremony. Are you free tomorrow evening?"

My cousin lit up like a Christmas tree on the town square, and said, "If I wasn't, I am now."

Everyone volunteered or was conscripted into duty. Actually, only my father-in-law had to be nudged. The rest of the gang was enthusiastic about making our rescheduled, hurried wedding plans special for Mama and Earl.

After the strategy meeting, Little Junior left to make other arrangements, while Crystal drove me to a bakery she said made the best-tasting cakes and cupcakes in town—and could do express orders. This being Vegas, they were open until midnight.

Di called as we were leaving the bakery. I told her the wedding was on, and she said she'd help out tomorrow with anything we needed.

Saturday morning I hit the ground running. Miss Betty was taking Mama shopping for a lightweight sundress and matching sandals. Her original dress was fine inside an air-conditioned chapel, but too heavy for outdoors. I sent Larry Joe and his dad shopping with a list I knew I could trust them with. Dave was running errands with Little Junior. And Di was on a shopping expedition with me for a variety of miscellany, both useful and decorative.

Mama phoned me and I texted that I was in a store and it was too noisy to talk. So she texted me. Fifteen times. I couldn't afford not to take Holly's calls with a huge event happening tonight in Dixie. But I didn't have time to talk to Mama because I was too busy getting things ready for a big event tonight in Vegas—her wedding.

After our shopping trip, Di and I stopped by Crystal's mother's house to pick up Crystal, then rendezvoused with Larry Joe and his dad at the wedding reception venue to get everything set up. Crystal stayed behind and waited for reinforcements while the rest of us went back to the hotel.

Evening was fast approaching. We went to our

respective hotel rooms to get cleaned up and make ourselves presentable.

At five o'clock, I called or texted everybody with a reminder to make sure we were ready for showtime. We all gathered in the hotel lobby. Promptly at 6:00 p.m. Little Junior, decked out in a blue rhinestone-studded jumpsuit, pulled up to the front door. This time, instead of a standard pink Cadillac, he was driving a pink Caddy stretch limousine. All nine of us piled in comfortably. Dave sat up front with Little Junior, while Di sat in back with us.

This ride wasn't a convertible, like the one we rode in when Mama and Earl almost got married. It was only a few minutes' drive to the chapel, but it would take about an hour to get to Lake Mead. The sun was slung low in the sky and I passed out Elvis-style aviator sunglasses to shield our eyes. Larry Joe, still self-conscious about his black eye, was the only one who left his shades on during the ceremony.

We left the Strip and headed into the desert, driving through wide swaths of sand and scrub between occasional buildings. After seeing nothing but desert, suddenly on the horizon an oasis of blue water known as Lake Mead, one of the largest man-made lakes in the world, came into view. Little Junior drove by the lake and up a winding incline. He turned off on a sand road and stopped. We got out of the car and walked toward a smiling man holding a camera and another man holding a guitar. Behind them was a white arched arbor with lit tiki torches on either side. I grabbed Mama's simple bouquet of white roses from the front seat and handed them to her as we approached the overlook. As we took our places around the arbor, an amazing view of Lake Mead opened up to us. Little Junior's friend, who worked as a photographer at another Vegas wedding chapel, began snapping pictures, and the other man began playing chords on his guitar.

Little Junior sang "Love Me Tender" as Mama and Earl held hands in front of the arch. He dispensed with the kitschy remarks like "Do you, Earl, promise to be Virginia's hunka, hunka burning love from now on?" Instead he performed a sweet and personal ceremony, with tears in his eyes as he pronounced them husband and wife. There wasn't a dry eye. Even my chronically grumpy father-in-law was sniffling.

Just after he told Earl, "You may kiss your bride," Little Junior began singing "And I Love You So." It was nearly seven-thirty, and as if on cue, the sun in shades of orange and purple began to sink into the lake. Earl took Mama's hand and they began to dance, gently swaying to the music. After the newly-weds had danced for a moment, Larry Joe wrapped his right arm around my waist, I clasped his left hand, and we started dancing, and so did my in-laws. Out of the corner of my eye, I saw Dave extend his hand to Di, and happily but somewhat surprisingly, she accepted and they joined the dance. Little Junior nodded to the guitarist and they repeated a verse and chorus.

When he finished the song, Little Junior waved to the musician, who played the guitar equivalent of a drum roll.

"Dear friends and family, I'd like to present to you Mr. and Mrs. Earl Daniels," Little Junior said.

Earl gave Mama another quick kiss and we all

burst into applause. The guitar player plucked a
reprise of "Love Me Tender." Earl and Mama held
hands and began walking toward the car, and the
rest of us fell in line behind them.

It was hot as blue blazes, but tears mingled with
sweat as we got to see these two dear people finally
say their "I dos." Moving on to the reception, we
drove the three miles or so from the wedding site to
the Lake Mead RV Village. Crystal had enlisted the
help of our hairdresser pal, Randi, and the two of
them were getting things ready for our arrival.

Mama lit up a broad smile and Earl's ears turned
red when we pulled up beside the campsite. The
newlyweds' Winnebago was parked and hooked up
to utilities. The awning on the side of the camper
was extended, and its underside was lined with
twinkling lights, and a JUST MARRIED banner adorned
the side of their honeymoon home.

Randi was cooking burgers and brats on a grill
on the concrete pad beside the camper. A table-
cloth, featuring images of Elvis Presley from the
movie *Blue Hawaii* against a blue background of
palm trees and orchids, covered a picnic table. A
film clapboard with "Wedding: Take Two" written
in chalk was propped beside a handsome framed
photo of Mama and Earl I had snapped of them
wearing their Sunday best after church one Sunday
back in Dixie. It was way too hot for them to wear a
suit and long-sleeved dress for the outdoor wedding.
August wasn't an ideal month, temperature-wise, for
an outdoor wedding in either Dixie or Las Vegas.
But since Mama had originally opted for an outdoor

wedding, I decided we'd go for it. We did our best to beat the heat with cold drinks and two box fans we had set up under the awning to at least stir a breeze.

The wedding dinner was rustic, but appropriate to a campsite. To accompany the burgers, the picnic table had platters of fixings and condiments, plus a big bowl of potato salad that Crystal's mom had made, and pitchers of iced tea and sangria. The center of the table featured a tray of cupcakes spelling out "Love Me Tender," with cupcakes decorated in hearts and musical notes circling the title. And, Crystal was right, the red velvet cupcakes tasted as good as they looked.

After Mama and Earl had surveyed the table, we sat them down in camp chairs under the awning and positioned between the two fans. Larry Joe and Dave quickly unfolded and set up lawn chairs that had been stashed at the back of the camper for the rest of us. Crystal and Di began taking drink orders.

Little Junior had to be melting inside that polyester jumpsuit, but he was a trouper. After he'd drunk a bottled water and everyone had helped their plates, he performed some Elvis standards accompanied by his guitar pal, whose name we learned, was Vinnie.

Little Junior launched into a leg-shaking, pelvis-swiveling rendition of "Hound Dog." We were all enjoying the show, including other campers who had begun to gather around. Our star attraction followed up with a slower number, "Can't Help Falling in Love." Larry Joe walked up behind me and slipped his arms around my waist. Di and Dave were sitting side by side on the picnic table bench, with her knee brushing up against his. Applause erupted when Little Junior finished the song. A neighboring camper rushed up with a bottle of wine and two champagne flutes in his hands. After glancing around the circle, he looked to Larry Joe and me and asked, "Are you the newlyweds?"

"No, *they* are," I said, pointing over to Mama and Earl.

He handed them the glasses, filled them with sparkling wine, and announced loudly, "Congratulations to the happy couple."

Those with beverages in hand joined the toast. Other neighbors hauled over an oversize ice chest and opened the lid, revealing a cooler filled with beers.

"We come bearing gifts. Is it okay if we join the party?"

Earl stood up and said, "The more the merrier. My sweet bride and I invite all of you to celebrate this special day with us."

People swarmed in, bringing offerings of chips, cookies, and whiskey, and some even brought their own hot dogs over and threw them on the grill over the white-hot coals.

Little Junior took an intermission to quench his parched throat with iced tea and eat a few nibbles. New friends—some of them adding their own lawn chairs to the circle, while others stood and mingled—introduced themselves. Our party now included people from Ontario to Oklahoma, from infants to elderly.

Mama was looking red faced. During the intermission, I encouraged her to go inside the air-conditioned camper for a few minutes. Earl felt duty bound, as host, to remain with the guests, but then he was used to cutting fields of hay in the summer heat. Mama was a bit more delicate.

It felt twenty degrees cooler inside the Winnebago. Mama plopped down on the banquette seat with her glass of iced tea, and I ripped several paper towels off a roll and handed them to her.

"Whew. Thanks, hon. I was getting a bit overheated out there. But everything, except maybe the weather, is absolutely perfect. You're good to your mama."

"I'm sorry the wedding at the chapel got ruined by a dead guy."

"Don't be, Liv. Truly. While I'm sorry a man got killed, this turned out so much better. It means the world to me, having Little Junior perform the ceremony. Nephew did a beautiful job, didn't he?"

"Yes, he did."

"And it was nice having my brother here for my wedding—even if it took a murder and an arrest to get him here. And where else could we have held a wedding reception where we'd make new friends from all over the country?"

I sat down next to her and gave her a hug. "As long as you're happy, Mama. That's all that matters."

We rejoined the party and Little Junior got the crowd on its feet, clapping and cheering with his performance of "All Shook Up."

I looked over at Crystal. She might not have liked Elvis music, but it was obvious from the look in her eyes she was smitten with a certain petite Elvis tribute artist.

Things wound down, neighboring campers started

returning to their mobile abodes, and Crystal, Di, and I started clearing up.

"Mama, the guys have loaded most of your belongings into the camper, and I put everything else left behind at the hotel into a suitcase for you. It's sitting on your bed inside the camper. I didn't know if you two would prefer to spend tonight here or back at the hotel. It's up to you."

"We might as well get settled into our little honeymoon shack," Mama said, looking over to Earl. "That okay with you?"

"Home is wherever you are, darlin'."

They were so cute. Larry Joe, sensing I was about to tear up again, leaned over and said, "Say your good-byes to your mama and try not to cry."

I wasn't making any promises, but I gave it my best.

"'Bye, Mama. You and Earl have a wonderful time—and take lots of pictures to show us when you get home."

I gave her a quick squeeze and stepped back so others could give her a hug, and so I had a shot at escaping without bawling.

Little Junior deposited us at the front door of the hotel. Since we were booked on midday flights tomorrow and planned to take the shuttle to the airport, we said our good-byes to Little Junior and Uncle Junior curbside.

I wrapped my arms around my cousin, still wearing his Elvis jumpsuit, and cried, hoping it wouldn't be as many years until our next visit as it had been since our last.

"Little Junior, let us hear from you. And you always have a place to stay in Tennessee, you know."

"I know. And I plan to come out and visit Aunt Virginia and Uncle Earl. Maybe next spring."

"Good. I'll throw you a party," I said.

Upstairs, I showered and packed our suitcases, except for toiletries and the clothes we planned to wear in the morning. Then I fell into bed after the busiest, most stressful, and exhausting vacation I'd ever had.

We made it to the airport in time for Daddy Wayne, Larry Joe, and Dave to plug a few dollars into the one-arm bandits before we boarded the plane. My mother-in-law sat in a padded seat at our gate, keeping an eye on everyone's carry-ons— something TSA would take a dim view of.

Di and I strolled over to the bank of windows, watching the runways as planes took off and landed.

"Dare I say there seemed to be a warming trend between you and the sheriff?" I ventured.

"You could say."

"Does that mean there's been a cooling trend with Jimmy? I gathered that you went to meet him after Little Junior's welcome home dinner."

"Yeah. I'm a complete idiot. Feel free to agree," she said.

"What happened?"

"What I should have seen coming. I went over to Jimmy's place to look over the plans for his new business and catch up on family news. What's going on with his mama and nieces. He has a roommate, but of course the roommate wasn't home."

"I don't like where this is going," I said.

"I liked it even less. Everything started out fine. We were fondly remembering old times—mostly with his family and not about us as a couple. One minute we were laughing and the next he was trying to romance me. Apparently, the first time I said no he didn't hear me clearly. The second time I made sure he heard loud and clear. He apologized and I was willing to let him off the hook, since we have a history in that department, and we *had* been taking a stroll down memory lane.

"Then he pulled something even more offensive."

I braced myself for what that might be.

"He hit me up for money for his new business enterprise. As if. I should've seen that coming since he'd been basically making a sales pitch ever since we ran into each other at the casino that first night.

"I started to leave and he offered to drive me back to the hotel, but I couldn't stand to be around him another minute—which felt more like old times. I called a taxi and waited on his front porch for it to arrive."

"Oh, Di, I'm so sorry."

"Don't be. Everyone but me could see I was playing the fool. Despite what Dave, or anybody else might think, it was never romantic. At least not on my part. I really just wanted to believe that the sweet, young kid I knew and fell in love with way back when had finally gotten his act together. But, now I know he'll never change. And I hate that, especially for his mama."

"Don't be too hard on yourself. It's not criminal to want to believe in people, even when they end up letting us down," I said. "At least it seems he is working, and trying to build a business."

"No, he isn't," Di said. "That's the part that hurts the most. He may have pipe dreams about this business. But he's really just running a scam, trying to get investors to give him money," she said, cupping air quotes around the word "investors."

"If he was really trying to save up his money, he wouldn't be driving around in a brand new car. It still had that new car smell. How did I not put that together sooner?"

"Because you wanted to give someone you used to care about the benefit of the doubt. You and his mother may be the only people in the world who were willing to do that. He blew it with you, so now it's just his mama. But that's entirely his fault—not yours."

"Thanks for saying so, anyway," she said, staring into the distance.

"Did you talk to Dave about any of this?"

"Some. Enough for him to know Jimmy is completely in my past. I hope Dave may still have some part to play in my future," she said.

"I'm glad."

We stood wordless until they announced our flight was boarding. I looked around to make sure our gamblers were ready to go home.

The men took the aisle seats to garner some extra leg room. After takeoff I gazed out the window with one last longing look at the shimmering desert oasis known as Las Vegas.

Chapter Seventeen

Gazing out over Dixie's town square from my office above Sweet Deal Realty, I couldn't help but smile. It felt good to be home. Last night, Larry Joe and I had celebrated our return after driving home from the Memphis airport by falling into bed and sleeping eleven hours straight.

I was checking e-mail and going over bills when my phone buzzed. It was Holly.

"Hi, Liv," she said. "I just wanted to check in with you. Do you want me to come into the office today so we can go over upcoming events?"

"I'm going to work for awhile today. But you should take some time off. You had so many fires to put out while I was gone, you should receive hazard pay. I owe you, big time, lady."

"Aw, it's *awlright*, darlin'. It's not like you were taking it easy—having to track down a killer to get your cousin out of jail and get your mama to the altar. You're the one who deserves a vacation. Besides, we have a pretty light load for the next couple of weeks."

"I know. That's why I'm planning to work on a special project," I said. "But it's not a paying gig."

"You're going to plan a welcome home party for your mama and Earl, aren't you? Count me in," Holly said, immediately reading my mind.

"You might want to hear what I have in mind before you sign on. It's a little crazy."

"Crazy is what we do best," Holly said. "Maybe we should make that our slogan."

"Oh, no," I said, laughing. "Crazy seems to find us easily enough. No need to advertise. Drop by the office after lunch, if you like. You still need to fill me in on how things turned out at the luau and the roving Class of 'Sixty-Eight dinner."

"Okay, but remember, truth is stranger than fiction," she said.

I had printed out planning sheets and started scribbling notes on them before Holly arrived at the office.

Holly swept in, wearing a tie-dye sundress with a very 1960s vibe, her hair pulled back in a short ponytail.

"Okay, I'm dying to know what your truth-is-stranger-than-fiction remark was all about," I said, as she sat in the chair across from my desk.

"Well, let me see. What would you like to hear about first—the semi-indecent exposure at the luau or the unladylike behavior at the Priscilla look-alike contest?"

"Ooh, I'll take door number one. I want to hear all about the semi-indecent exposure incident at the luau. Did someone get drunk and decide to skinny dip in the swimming pool?" I asked.

"If they'd been drunk I could have excused their behavior. Darlin', these women are just desperate. Do you know Malcolm Tate? His house is where we held the luau."

"Not really, but Mama was telling me about him. I know he's a widower. And Mama calls him 'Spock Ears.'"

"His ears are kind of pointy," Holly said, breaking down in giggles for a moment. "Anyway, a couple of the single women in the group have set their sights on him as husband material. And believe me when I say Malcolm, pointy ears or not, is the best either one of them could hope for in the romance department.

"They'd been practically elbowing each other out of the way every time he came around. During the cocktail hour before dinner, while everyone was mingling about with fruity cocktails topped with little umbrellas, a number of people, including Malcolm, went and sat by the pool. He was stretched out in a chaise longue and the two women raced to nab the chaise next to him. The one who won out was wearing a light blouse over a swimsuit top. Malcolm was politely chatting with everyone around him, and not paying any particular attention to her, even though she had shed the blouse and was sitting there in a somewhat skimpy swimsuit top. So then, she reclined the chair all the way flat, rolled over on her stomach, and unhooked her bikini top to sunbathe, presumably."

"Oh, my word," I said, my mouth agape.

"It gets better," Holly said, taunting me. "The other

contender for Spock Ears was so desperate to attract his attention, she jumped into the pool and then pulled herself up the side, looking like a contestant in a wet T-shirt contest."

"Who won?"

"He did. He got up and coolly walked away from the pool area, saying he really should check on the other guests."

"Good for him," I said. "Now, what about the Godzilla Priscillas? Did they get into a hair-pulling fight?"

"There was no hair pulling, but there was some nasty name calling and bad sportsmanship. They behaved until the winners were named, and the first runner-up took exception to not taking the blue suede ribbon. She started yelling about how the winner was too fat for a Priscilla look-alike and that she looked more like Elvis in his bloated later years."

"How did it end?"

"The loser's husband dragged her off the stage. Honestly, none of her classmates looked all that surprised. Apparently, she was a pill even back in high school."

"Oh, Holly," I said, wiping tears from laughing so hard. "You deserve the blue ribbon for putting up with this group. Thank you from the bottom of my heart."

"All in a day's work," she said. "So what are you planning for your mama and Earl's homecoming? Ooh, how about an ice-cream sundae buffet? I know how much your mother loves ice cream," Holly asked.

"Nope. Are you ready for this? We're going to throw Mama a belated reception based on some of her outrageous wedding ideas. You know, the one we were planning before she and Earl decided to just go to Vegas instead."

Holly furrowed her brow doubtfully for a moment before a broad smile crept across her pleasant face.

"That's brilliant, Liv. We already have some of the plans in place—and we know your mama will like it."

"My thoughts exactly. We're going to scale things back a bit. The guest list is getting trimmed considerably, for one thing. But it still won't be easy. We don't have a lot of time to pull it all together."

"Trust me, after the Class of 'Sixty-Eight reunion, this will be a piece of cake. At least we have the venue. Earl's farm, right?"

"Right. And I already checked with Billy Tucker, and his Grills on Wheels barbecue catering is available for the evening. And he's giving us the friends and family discount—after Nell told him he'd better."

"As I recall, your mama wanted a Viking-style gondola to ferry her and Earl out to the little island in the middle of the pond. And some swans swimming around for ambience? Are you dropping those elements since we're just doing a reception, sans the ceremony?"

"Not completely, but I'm going to take the original idea and mix it up a bit. Leave that part to me," I said.

"Gladly. What do you want me to do?"

"We'll go with a DJ if we have to, but I'd love to have a live band. Two-stepping and line dance music. But it's short notice . . ."

"You leave *that* to me," Holly said resolutely.

"Great. I'll take care of the table and chair rentals and make sure Kenny and Harold are available to set up the stage and string lights in the barn. Larry Joe and I will go out to tidy up and sweep out the space."

"*Awlright,* darlin'. What else do we need to do?"

"Pray it doesn't rain," I said with all seriousness. Those things that were beyond my control—like the weather for an outdoor event—were the bane of every party planner's existence.

I didn't say so to Holly, but even more unpredictable than the weather would be whether or not I could persuade my little sister to come for the party.

Tuesday afternoon, after having performed a half dozen minor miracles getting details worked out for Mama and Earl's party on short notice, I decided to tackle the truly difficult chore of calling my sister. I knew the best wedding gift Mama could receive would be Emma's acceptance of her marriage to Earl. I also knew it was going to be a hard sell.

"Hey, little sister. We got back from Vegas day before yesterday. I think we've just about recovered. Hadn't talked to you in a while. So how are my favorite niece and nephew?"

"Lulu is four going on fourteen. That child already rolls her eyes at me. I swear, she's so stubborn I don't know what we're going to do with her."

I resisted the temptation to say she took after her mom.

"And Trey is into everything. He's cruising the furniture and I believe he's going to start walking any day now."

"Be sure to shoot video—and take lots of pictures—for Aunt Liv. I do wish we lived closer."

While I truly wished I could see my sister and the kids more often, the geographic distance of her living in North Carolina was also a blessing in some ways. I may be the oldest, but she's the bossy one. And she doesn't just want to run my life, but Mama's, too. After catching me up on the kids and making some pleasant chitchat, Emma finally addressed the elephant in the room.

"So tell me about Las Vegas . . . and the wedding," she said haltingly.

I decided to start with Little Junior's troubles, which led to us reminiscing about our cousin growing up, and about how Mama used to make Uncle Junior show everybody the hole in his leg left from a snakebite he got as a kid.

I moved on to talking about how upset Mama had been about Little Junior's arrest, and made a point of mentioning how Earl had been so good to Mama when she needed emotional support. My sister had gone quiet, but hadn't launched into a tirade against Earl, which I mistakenly took as a positive sign.

"Emma, Larry Joe and I are putting together a surprise welcome home party for Mama and Earl and I know it would mean a lot to Mama if you and Hobie and the kids were there—"

"You can stop right there, Liv. I'll do my best to hold my tongue when I talk to Mama. I won't say anything to her against that man, now that she's gone ahead and married him. But I will not pretend to celebrate or give my blessing to their union.

And I will *not* have my children calling some man Granddaddy who is *not* my daddy."

"Emma," I said, trying to talk over her and interject some sanity. "The kids don't have to call him Granddaddy, any more than you have to call him Daddy. And nobody's asking for your blessing. . . ."

Click.

She hung up on me, which was exactly what she'd done after she first found out that Mama and Earl were engaged. Sometimes I wished we had a brother. For some reason, I fantasized Emma would listen to him. At the very least, I'd have someone to talk to when she hung up on me. Unless he took her side and they ganged up against me. Maybe one sibling was enough. It was certainly all I could deal with at the moment.

Larry Joe had already left for work when I shuffled into the kitchen Wednesday morning around seven. As I waited for the coffee to brew, I peered blearily out the window. I spotted my pesky neighbor, Edna Cleats, stepping out her front door in a terrycloth robe and slippers, with her prized Persian cat cradled in one arm. Mr. Winky was the reason I was bleary eyed this morning. He had set off the Newsoms' car alarm again in the middle of the night, a far too frequent occurrence in the neighborhood—although Mrs. Cleats refuses to believe Mr. Winky is capable of such mischief.

I watched as Mrs. Cleats padded down to the end of the driveway to retrieve her newspaper. It's childish of me, I know, but I secretly hoped someone had stolen this week's grocery coupons out of her newspaper.

I actually got to the office by about five after eight, which is early for me. I needed to check with vendors and caterers for a couple of upcoming events. And I wanted to research a lead I had on a wedding gift for Mama.

Mid-afternoon, Holly called to fill me in on her progress and see how things were coming along on my end.

"I've had a productive day, including going to see a man about a swan," I said.

"I'm intrigued," Holly said.

"I tracked down what I think is the perfect wedding gift for Mama and Earl. But even though I got a good deal on it, it's still a pretty expensive present. And one I haven't told Larry Joe about yet."

"With all the minor miracles you've pulled off lately, I'm sure you can handle convincing one mild-mannered husband that you got the deal of the century on one expensive little gift," Holly said.

"I hope you're right."

Chapter Eighteen

When I got home, I checked the answering machine. Since my sister has a habit of calling our landline instead of my cell, I was hoping for a message, or at least a missed call from her. Even if she wasn't willing to accept Earl or swallow her pride and come to Mama's welcome home party, I thought she might feel guilty about hanging up on me and offer an apology. But, apparently, little sister wasn't contemplating any of the above.

The next morning, I was at the office going over my lists for Mama and Earl's party when I realized I had hired the caterer, and rented the chairs and tables, etc. And I had "cake" on my list, but I hadn't ordered the cake yet, or even talked to the bakery. I called Holly because I wanted her input on the cake design.

"Hey, I almost forgot to order a wedding cake for the newlyweds," I said. "So what kind of design do we want? Something that says Vegas to connect with their wedding? Or something simple and elegant?

Something with purple, since it's Mama's favorite color?"

"Since it's an intimate guest list, you're going with a smallish cake, right?" Holly said.

"Right."

"Then I think we should keep it simple, add a few touches of purple—a few scattered flowers, perhaps. And go with a bold topper of some kind. Any ideas on that?"

After a quiet moment, we both said in unison, "Swans!"

"Yes, with their necks forming a heart. It'll go perfectly with their wedding gift," I said. "Thanks, Holly. By the way, have you confirmed with the band yet?"

"About that . . ."

"Uh-oh. I sense bad news," I said.

"More like mixed news. We have the band, but the lead singer is in the hospital. Nothing serious, but enough to put him out of the picture for our party. They assure me they can get someone else, but . . . I'd feel better if it were someone I've heard perform. I was thinking about reaching out to the Elvis tribute artist we had for the reunion. He was wonderful. And since your mama and Earl had an Elvis theme for the wedding, it would be appropriate. And I'm sure he could do a few non-Elvis tunes, as well. And the band could throw in some instrumental pieces—"

"Holly, you're a genius," I said, interrupting her.

"Hold off on calling Elvis. I'll get back to you."

I was so excited I was pacing the floor. After a quick phone call to the bakery, I got on the computer to start researching flights.

With the cake and topper squared away I could move on to a much more complicated—and expensive—project. I started to go into Sweet Deal Realty and ask Winette for advice, but decided my mother-in-law would be the best counsel on this one. So I called her.

"Miss Betty, I wanted to come by and talk to you. How 'bout I pick up lunch for the two of us and head on over?"

She told me she had some fresh from the garden tomatoes and lettuce, some sourdough bread—and peaches.

"Hon, just come on over. I'll make us some BLTs."

"I'm on my way."

The aroma and sound of bacon sizzling in a frying pan greeted me as I stepped into my mother-in-law's kitchen, tapping on the unlocked door as I entered.

"*Mmm*, that bacon is making my mouth water."

I retrieved glasses from the cupboard and ice from the fridge. A pitcher of fresh-brewed sweet tea was sitting on the kitchen table, along with plates bearing tomato slices. "I wanted to ask your advice about Larry Joe."

She looked worried. While my mother-in-law and I were pretty close, I don't talk to her about any squabbles Larry Joe and I may have. Although she'd be just as likely, or more, to take my side as his.

"Don't worry; it's not marital problems. It's just I've already spent a good bit of money on a kind of expensive gift for Mama and Earl, in addition to the party. And now, I have another idea that will also cost a good bit. It's not a gift per se, but if it works out, it will mean the world to Mama. The biggest problem is, really, that I'm spending all this money in the same week. And I haven't given Larry Joe any ballpark figures on what all this is costing. How do you think I should broach the subject?"

"Oh, I am relieved. I thought you were going to ask me a hard question. First off, don't try to soft soap Larry Joe. He's a lot like his dad and he always sees right through that. So just be up front. And secondly, your mama and Earl just paid our airfare, hotel, and most of our meals to go to Las Vegas. I realize it didn't turn out to be a vacation, entirely. But it was still very generous. And I'll be more than happy to point that out to my son if you need me to."

"Thanks, and you're right. Larry Joe tends to get more worried about what he thinks I'm not telling him, so I should just tell him the truth."

"And, hon, I have a little savings account of my own, and I'd be glad to help with a special gift for your mama. Virginia is one of my dearest friends. Well, more than that, obviously. She's family."

"Aw, thank you, Miss Betty. You're a sweetie. But I don't need your money. It's not like Larry Joe and I can't afford this. It's just . . . we generally try to budget ahead for more expensive things."

"Would it be nosy of me to ask about this kind of expensive gift for your mama that's not exactly a gift?"

"No. In fact I'm dying to share it with somebody. And you know all the parties involved, so you tell me if this is a harebrained idea.

"I phoned Emma after we got back, but haven't had any luck getting her to come to the welcome home party. But she did get all excited when I told her about Little Junior's budding career as an

Elvis tribute artist, and started waxing nostalgic about memories of Little Junior when we were growing up.

"And today Holly told me the lead singer of the band we've hired for the party is out of commission and she was thinking about trying to engage the Elvis tribute artist who performed at the Class of 'Sixty-Eight Comeback Special—"

"And you thought you could hire Little Junior to perform instead," she said, nearly springing out of her chair with excitement. "Liv, I think that's an absolutely brilliant idea. It might be an enticement for Emma to come—and bring the grandkids. But even if she doesn't come, I think your mama would be absolutely delighted to have Little Junior perform here. And it might be really nice for Little Junior, too, to get away for a few days after his recent troubles."

"But I'm sure he'll only be able to come if I pay his airfare, and it may be hard to find a good price on such short notice."

"Don't worry about any of that. We'll chip in for his flight. And don't call Emma back. Get Larry Joe to call Hobie. It's not just about Emma coming; it would mean the world to your mama to see the grandchildren. Maybe if Hobie tells Emma he's going to come to the reception and bring the kids with or without her, she'll straighten up.

"Anyway, I'm so excited I can't stand it. You need to get to work making it happen. Wayne and I are completely onboard, whether that old geezer knows it or not."

I went to the office and got busy. First order of business was to call my recently exonerated cousin to see if he would come to Dixie.

"Hey, Little Junior. Your cousin Liv, here."

"Hi, Liv. Have you heard from your mama?" he asked with sincere interest.

"No. But then she and Earl are honeymooning under big skies and away from cell towers. They're supposed to arrive back in Dixie on Saturday, and Larry Joe and I are throwing a surprise welcome home party and wedding reception of sorts for them. That's why I'm calling. I'd like to hire you to perform at the reception. I can only pay you two hundred dollars, plus airfare. But it would be a wonderful surprise for Mama—and it would be a real treat for family and friends who weren't at the wedding to see you perform. What do you say?"

"I don't know what to say."

"Say yes. Please."

"I should really talk to Crystal about it."

"Of course. And, while I can only afford *your* airfare, Crystal is certainly welcome to come."

"Thanks, Liv. Let me get back to you after I talk to Crystal."

"Okay. But I really need to know today. I have a live band booked, but if you can't make it I'll have to get another singer."

I didn't expect to hear an answer from Little Junior for a few hours. But he called back in less than thirty minutes and yes, he was coming to Dixie.

"But I won't accept the two-hundred-dollar payment. Covering my airfare is more than generous of you," he said. I told him I'd text him with the details as soon as I'd booked his flight.

I called Holly and told her about my grand scheme to get little sister to come to the party, and that she no longer needed to worry about finding a replacement singer.

"You don't think the band will have an issue about working with my cousin the Elvis singer, do you?"

"Don't worry, you just leave them to me," Holly said with confidence.

"Do you have time to track down our best deal on airfare?"

"Consider it done. Good luck with getting Emma to the party. That's one chore I wouldn't even know how to attempt."

"That makes two of us. But we'll see what happens."

I went back to the office and created e-mail invitations to send out. After tying up a few other loose ends, I went to the grocery store. I was going to tell Larry Joe the truth, straight up, but I thought he might digest it better on a full stomach.

I bought the ingredients to make meat loaf, one of my husband's favorites.

Supper was just about ready when Larry Joe got home.

"*Mmm,* smells good, hon. And it's meat loaf, my favorite," he said with a Cheshire cat smile.

"What are you grinning about?"

"You don't have to butter me up. Mama called. She told me to just pony up the money. And reminded me how lucky I am to have a wife like you, and that it's not as if you're spending the money on yourself. And that your mama and Earl have been good to us. And . . ."

"And . . . what else?"

"She's absolutely right. I'm lucky to have you. And you're pretty low maintenance—most of the time," he said, taking a step forward, wrapping one arm around me, and pulling me close. Then, with the other arm, he reached past me and snitched a bite of meat loaf off the stove. I smacked his hand.

"And I thought I might have to use my feminine wiles on you. All these years, and I never knew all I had to do was talk to your mama."

Larry Joe grabbed a beer from the fridge and I set our plates on the table and poured myself a glass of wine.

"It would still be okay with me if you wanted to unleash your feminine wiles on me after supper."

"We'll see. Did your mama also tell you that you're supposed to call Hobie about coming to the party? Do you think that might help?"

"She did—and it couldn't hurt. I think Mama's right about it being easier to make headway with Hobie than with Emma. So I'll give him a call tomorrow."

"Great, and thanks, honey."

"Liv, you know even with Little Junior coming and even if Hobie's on board, your sister may not come around about your mama's marriage to Earl, at least not for a few years. She's stubborn."

"I know, but I feel like we have to try. It would mean so much to Mama."

"When are the great travelers supposed to get home?"

"Saturday. And I hate to admit it, but despite the fact she drives me crazy a lot of times, I've actually missed Mama. I can't wait to hear her tales about the open road."

"They're not getting back until Saturday? Aren't

you cutting it close having the party the same day they get home?"

"Yes, I am. But if they're home for a whole day there's no way we can pull off a surprise. You know *somebody* in town would tell them about it."

"Has your mama called?" Larry Joe asked.

"No, I didn't really expect her to."

"You should probably check in and make sure they don't decide to extend their trip by a day or two. It would be a shame if the guests of honor didn't show up for their party."

"Oh, no. That thought hadn't entered my mind. I'll go call her right now. I won't be able to sleep until I know they're making their way toward Tennessee."

As I suspected, Earl was keeping to a strict schedule, and Mama said she couldn't wait to get home to her own bed and her own kitchen.

Chapter Nineteen

On Saturday, we were working frantically to get everything ready for the party. Last we'd heard, Hobie was driving in with the kids, but he told Larry Joe that Emma was being pouty and noncommittal about coming. I didn't have time to worry about her, but I was holding out hope.

Holly was making phone calls, double-checking on everything. My go-to guys, Harold and Kenny, were out at the farm, stringing lights and setting up the stage and sound system in the barn. I was running out to the farm to check on things between running other errands. And saying silent prayers that Mama and Earl didn't get held up with engine trouble or a big accident on the highway somewhere.

Larry Joe was helping with hauling heavy things out to the barn in his truck, so Di had volunteered to drive to the Memphis airport to pick up my uncle and cousin. We stowed them and their suitcases at Earl's farmhouse.

Di came out to the barn, where I was supervising

setup to see if there was anything else she could do to help.

"No, I think we're in good shape," I said. "But if things start looking desperate I'll send out an SOS."

"Good deal," she said. "What should I wear tonight?"

"Anything except that new green sundress," I said, thinking how it might stir up old jealousies for Dave if he saw her in the same dress she'd been wearing when she got out of Jimmy's car at the chapel that fateful night.

She gave me a quizzical look.

"I just mean I think most everyone will be dressed more casual tonight for the barn dance. Jeans and a tank top would be just fine," I said.

Since the Winnebago wouldn't fit in Mama's driveway, Larry Joe had phoned Earl and arranged for us to meet them at the farm with Mama's car. That way they could park the camper and drive back to Mama's house. We had an ETA, but Earl said they would give us a call when they reached Memphis. This gave us the perfect opportunity to get them out to the farm without arousing their suspicions.

I had followed Larry Joe in my car. When the newlyweds pulled up to Earl's farmhouse, Larry Joe and I were sitting in the front porch swing with the front porch light on. The barn doors were closed, the back porch light was off, and the guests had parked their cars out of sight, behind the barn.

"Hi, Mama," I said, standing to embrace her as she reached the top step. "It's so good to see you two."

"We had a wonderful trip, but it's sure good to be home," she said, giving me a big hug.

"I want to take a quick look around the house while we're here," Earl said.

He and Larry Joe shook hands, then Earl unlocked the front door, and held it open for all of us to enter.

"Mama, since you're here, Larry Joe and I have a wedding gift for you and Earl—and I just can't wait to give it to you. It's oversized, so we'll have to go out on the back porch."

As soon as Earl and Mama had stepped onto the back porch, I hit "send" on a text alerting Holly we were ready. At her signal Harold and Kenny slid open the barn doors and switched on the lights that were strung across the rafters to illuminate the barn and the huge WELCOME HOME banner hanging above the guests' heads. Mama squealed with delight and started granny waving to family and friends. The band began to play as we walked to the barn. The guest list of twenty-five friends and family had expanded to about thirty-five, and they were lined up to form a reverse receiving line as Earl and Mama made their way through the crowd.

At the back of the line, my niece, Lulu, broke free from her daddy's arms and ran toward Mama, calling out, "Grandma!" Mama leaned down to gather her into a hug, and my sister, Emma, walked up behind Lulu, holding baby Trey in her arms. Mama flung her arms around both of them and showered them with kisses, while Lulu clung to her legs.

Earl smiled, keeping a respectful distance for the little family reunion. He looked over and gave me a wink.

Larry Joe stepped onto the stage and took the mike. "Liv and I would like to thank all of you for joining us to welcome home the newlyweds. And, I hope y'all are hungry because Grills on Wheels is serving up enough barbecue to feed an army. Please help yourselves. The buffet table is loaded."

Naturally, Daddy Wayne was the first in line and others queued up behind him. Iced tea and lemonade were set up on a table beside the pulled pork barbecue, slaw, beans, and chips. A bar serving beer and wine was set up on the back porch.

As people went through the serving line, Mama and Earl walked over to me. She wrapped me in one of her oversized hugs and said, "Liv, the party is wonderful . . . and I can't even imagine how you talked your baby sister into coming. But this is the best gift you could ever have given me," she said with watery eyes.

"Oh, speaking of your wedding gift—come with me, please."

Both of them followed me to the pond and I used a remote control in my pocket that Harold, the electrician, had rigged somehow. It activated the battery-operated lights on a swan-shaped paddleboat, along with a lantern sitting on the little island in the middle of the pond.

"Mama, this is my and Larry Joe's wedding gift to you and Earl."

"What in the world?" Mama said, with a surprised but pleased look on her face. "Earl, did you ever?"

"Liv, you've already done so much, with the party—" Earl said before I interrupted.

"We wanted you to have something you could keep. Mama, in the original plans you wanted a gondola to ferry you out to the island for your wedding, and swans swimming in the pond. You two may not have exchanged vows on this island, but now y'all can pedal out to it anytime you want—without the help of a gondolier."

Mama hugged me and Earl wrapped his long arms around both of us.

"You two better get back to the party. You *are* the guests of honor, after all."

"That barbecue is smelling awful good to me," Earl said.

About forty minutes later most people had finished eating dinner. Harold dimmed the barn lights a bit, and from the hayloft aimed a spotlight at the center of the stage.

The band started playing "Teddy Bear," and Little Junior, wearing the same jumpsuit he'd worn at the wedding, emerged from the shadows and leapt onto the stage. Mama clasped her hands together and shook her head in joyous disbelief.

Lulu rushed to the front of the stage and started doing the bounce-up-and-down dance of a preschooler, while brother Trey clapped his hands in approval. Friends joined the dance, and so did Mama, twisting and swaying with her baby grandson in her arms. Uncle Junior walked over and her eyes flew wide open in surprise. He gave Mama a peck on the cheek and then kissed his great nephew on the top of the head.

After a couple of upbeat numbers, the band slowed things down a bit, and Little Junior started singing "And I Love You So," as he had at the wedding.

Mama walked over and sat baby Trey down on my lap and grabbed Earl by the hand. They danced just as they had as the sun set on Lake Mead, nuzzling nose to nose like newlyweds do. I noticed my sister looking away. She took Lulu by the hand and quietly slipped out of the barn, walking toward the house. In a moment, I handed Trey off to Miss Betty and hurried to catch up to Emma.

"Hey, does Lulu need a trip to the little girl's room?"

"Yeah. Sometimes she doesn't think about it when there's a lot going on. I figured I should make a preemptive potty stop."

"I could use a pit stop myself," I said, falling in step beside her.

Lulu slipped between us and skipped along, holding both our hands. I looked down and smiled.

"I really wish I could see you and the kids more often," I said. "I can't believe how much they've grown."

"I know, me too," Emma said, before going quiet.

I decided to let a comfortable silence hang between us as we walked to the house. I directed Emma to the powder room. When they came back, Emma sat down in the rocker by the fire. Lulu sat on her lap, her head nodding forward, with heavy eyelids.

"Would you like to lay Lulu down on the sofa or in the guest bedroom? Or would you like me to hold her so you can rejoin the party? I'd hate for you to miss Little Junior's second act."

"When we were growing up I never would have imagined Little Junior performing—especially as an Elvis impersonator. But he's really good."

"I know. And I'm just as proud of the fact he has a good heart. He was really good to Mama while we were in Vegas—well, to all of us. And he treats his girlfriend, Crystal, like a queen."

"What's she like, his girlfriend?"

"She's really sweet and seems crazy about him. She's also taller than him, and I'm guessing, about twenty years older."

"Wow. I guess love is a strange and wonderful thing," she said. "Sometimes more strange than wonderful. Listen, Liv, you don't have to worry about me being unkind to Earl. I know he's good to Mama. And I understand she's been lonely since Daddy died. Mama's a social person. She's not one of those people who can be truly happy on her own. Hobie helped me see that. But I don't know that I'll ever be able to be close to Earl the way you and Larry Joe are. Can you understand that?"

"Yeah, Emma, I think so. And it's fine. But you made Mama very happy just by being here tonight— and bringing the grandkids."

"I owed her that much. I haven't come back to Dixie to visit as often as I should. Hobie helped me see that, too."

"I never realized Hobie was such a wise and sensitive man," I said.

"He has his moments. And then he has moments when I could kill him, too."

"You just described married life," I said.

"I guess so. I really hope Earl gives Mama more of those Mr. Wonderful moments."

"I can tell you that he has so far. And let's face it, anyone who can put up with our mama has to be at least a minor saint."

Emma laughed. It was the first time I'd heard her laugh since she'd arrived. Lulu roused.

"Why you laughing, Mommy?"

"Because life is funny sometimes, sweet girl."

Emma, Lulu, and I started walking back to the barn, and we could hear Little Junior wowing the crowd with a hip-swiveling performance of "All Shook Up."

We rejoined the party and I sat down beside Di.

I looked up to see Dave in the doorway of the barn. He took off his hat and ran his hand through a crop of thick, wavy hair as he walked over to Di.

"Sorry I'm so late. Had an accident out on the highway."

"Oh, no. Was anyone hurt?" she said.

"No, it just bottled up traffic until we could get the vehicles towed away."

After "All Shook Up," the band slowed the tempo down again. Di rose from her chair as Dave took her hand. They walked to the center of the barn, where they began dancing very slow and very close.

Epilogue

The Grills on Wheels crew were bagging up the trash and loading up gear. I walked over to their van, parked beside the barn, to thank Billy and the guys for a great job with the barbecue dinner.

I saw Mama standing by the pond, gazing dreamily at the water and thinking about either her new husband, or admiring her new swan paddleboat. I was leaning toward the boat. Either way, it made me smile.

Suddenly, Mama screamed and shook her leg wildly while waving her arms over her head. It took me a moment to decipher the source of the distress. But by the dim illumination of the boat lights, I could see the movement of a striped snake winding itself around her lower leg. Emma and I ran over and started screaming, too.

The guys came out of the barn and rushed toward Mama. Everyone gathered at the front of the barn to see what was going on. With quick strides, Earl walked calmly over and firmly grabbed the snake just below its head and yanked a couple of times. The snake unfurled and danced at the end of Earl's extended arm. He walked out beyond the barn and tossed the still wriggling snake into a field.

As he walked back toward the pond, Mama hurried over and embraced him, throwing her arms around his neck. Then she jumped back.

"Earl Daniels," she said in her thunderous voice. "That was a foolish thing to do. You could've been snake bit," she said, before wrapping her arms around his waist and burying her head against his chest, her shoulders shuddering.

"Now, Virginia," he said, hugging her tightly. "Calm down, hon. It wasn't poisonous. It was just a garter snake."

They started walking back to the barn and Emma and I fell in step behind them.

"Everything's fine, nothing to worry about," Earl called out to the partygoers standing shoulder to shoulder in the barn entrance.

"Don't tell me snakes are nothing to worry about," Mama said. "Have y'all ever seen the hole in Junior's leg from when he got snake bit as a child. Junior, roll up your pants leg."

He complied and people gathered around to gawk.

"I've been terrified of snakes ever since it happened," Mama said.

It had been quite a few years since we'd been treated to a viewing of Uncle Junior's snakebite hole.

"Is Uncle Junior married right now?" Emma asked.

"No. Divorced."

"How many wives is he up to now?"

"Four. But he's only had one at a time—as far as we know," I said.

Uncle Junior bared his leg and stood there silently, while Mama explained in great detail exactly how it had happened.

"Do you think he impresses the ladies by showing them the hole in his leg?" Emma said.

"We'll see. Wife number five could be standing right here in the barn."

Emma slipped her arm around my waist and we both laughed until it hurt.

Party Tips and Recipes

Tips for a Backyard Luau

Not everyone can manage a true pit barbecue—roasting a whole hog in the ground, like they did at the Dixie reunion luau in the book. But anyone can throw a fabulous backyard luau on a modest budget.

Invites

Send out invitations with borders or covers featuring flip-flops or colorful tropical flowers or fun tiki images. Encourage guests to wear tropical print sundresses or Hawaiian shirts and shorts. Cool and casual. And welcome guests with leis as they arrive.

Suggested Menu

BBQ Pulled Pork (from restaurant or pit roasted) OR
Grilled Chicken with Teriyaki Sauce OR
Skewered Chicken and Pineapple Chunk Kabobs
with Hawaiian Sauce
Tropical Fruit Salad
Cabbage Slaw
Pineapple-Coconut Rice

For Dessert:
Cupcakes!

Pineapple-Coconut Rice

1½ cups uncooked long grain rice, rinsed
    until water runs clear
1 20-oz. can crushed pineapple in
    pineapple juice
1 3.5-oz. can unsweetened coconut milk
3 tablespoons sweetened coconut flakes
1 teaspoon red curry paste
1 clove garlic, minced
½ teaspoon onion powder
1 teaspoon grated ginger
salt and pepper to taste

GARNISH

Fresh squeezed lime juice to taste
½ cup salted roasted cashews

DIRECTIONS

Drain can of crushed pineapple. Measure ½ cup
pineapple juice. Add 2½ cups coconut milk.
Pour liquids into saucepan and bring to a simmer.

Stir in crushed pineapple and remaining ingredients
(except garnish).

Bring to a boil, cover, lower heat, and simmer
about 20 minutes, until liquid is absorbed and rice
is cooked.

Take off heat and leave covered for 5 minutes.
Fluff rice with fork, garnish, and serve.

Yields: 6 to 8 servings

Kahlúa and Chocolate Cupcakes

1¾ cups all-purpose flour
1¾ cups sugar
¾ cup cocoa powder
1 teaspoon baking powder
2 teaspoons baking soda
½ teaspoon salt
2 eggs, lightly beaten
1 cup milk
⅔ cup strong coffee
¼ cup Kahlúa
¼ cup vegetable oil
¼ teaspoon vanilla extract

FROSTING

¾ cup unsweetened cocoa powder
2 tablespoons Kahlúa
6 tablespoons hot water
4 tablespoons softened butter
4 cups powdered sugar

DIRECTIONS

Preheat oven to 350 degrees and line pans with paper cupcake liners.

Stir together flour, sugar, cocoa powder, baking powder, baking soda, and salt in large bowl. Add eggs, milk, coffee, Kahlúa, oil, and vanilla extract. Beat on medium speed for a few minutes.

Divide batter evenly among cupcake liners.

Bake 18 minutes or until toothpick comes out clean. Let cupcakes cool at least 15 minutes before transferring to cooling rack.

FROSTING

Add cocoa powder to a large mixing bowl and pour in Kahlúa and hot water.

Stir until smooth.

Add butter and blend with mixer on low speed until mixture is well-combined.

Add powdered sugar one cup at a time and beat on low speed until sugar is incorporated.

Turn up to medium speed until frosting is light and fluffy.

Let cupcakes cool completely before frosting.

Yields: 24 cupcakes

Beverages

Serve fruity cocktails—and don't forget the little paper umbrellas, which add a lot of fun for very little cost. And be sure to have bottled water and other nonalcoholic beverages on hand to keep guests hydrated, especially in warm weather.

Decorations

Have fun with festive colored table coverings and napkins. Trim edges of tables with "grass skirt" fringe. Strategically place tiki torches and hang some paper lanterns. Make a table centerpiece or runner, featuring whole pineapples surrounded by paper tropical flowers, and coconut-inspired candle holders.

Activities

Play some Hawaiian music to inspire guests to get on their hula moves. Pass out hula hoops to those who have trouble getting their hips to swivel.

And—limbo!

Tips for a
Movie Night Under the Stars

Pick Your Flick

Choose a film that fits your audience. Sticking with classics is the safest bet. And, if neighbors can see into your backyard, be considerate. Don't show loud action movie explosions after most people have gone to bed. And keep it clean and family friendly, especially if youngsters live next door!

(Tip: Encourage guests to dress as characters from the film—from gangsters to zombies!)

Get a Projector

Buy or rent a movie projector. There are good deals to be found for not entirely new equipment on Web sites like eBay and Craigslist. Rentals may be available in your area from audio-video equipment stores. You may be able to borrow a projector from a local church, with a security deposit. And some libraries even have projectors available to check out.

(NOTE: For outdoor viewing, find a projector with an output of at least two thousand lumens. A higher output of lumens (three thousand or more) means you'll be able to start your movie shortly after the sun sets instead of waiting for the darkness of nightfall.)

Get a Screen

Screens are also available used and for a good price. But your least expensive option is a sheet or drop cloth. Painter's drop cloths, available in white at hardware stores, are heavier than sheets and less likely to be blown around by the wind. And after movie night, you can use it when you paint your living room!

Snacks

Popcorn, of course! Pop in batches earlier in the day and fill up a galvanized tub. Have guests scoop popcorn into bowls or cardboard popcorn boxes from the party store. You could also offer a selection of flavored popcorns, such as buttered, cheesy, and caramel.

And don't forget the candy! Set up a concession stand with a "candy bar." Include traditional movie house favorites, like M & M's, Milk Duds, Raisinets, and Goobers.

Dinner and a Movie?

You may want to include a cookout before the movie, with burgers and brats on the grill—or fancier fare, if you like.

Table decor can match the theme of your film. (*Elvis* or *Viva Las Vegas*, for instance.) Or stick with a movie theater theme. Among the plates and serving dishes and beverages, place a chalk clapboard with the name and show time for your movie. And maybe you could score a cool-looking, but non-working, projector at a thrift store, just for decoration. And string some large-bulb, white Christmas lights from trees to provide some low-light, movie house ambience.

Get Comfy

Ask guests to bring along pillows and blankets, unless you have a huge inventory. (Be sure you have some extras on hand for those guests who forget to bring theirs.) Inexpensive inflatable pool floats make for comfortable padding under blankets. Beach chairs and lawn chairs provide off-the-ground seating for those who may prefer it.

Bonus Tip

Five things you should know if you ever decide to go to Memphis during Elvis Week (held annually the week of August 16, the anniversary of Elvis's death):

1. It's hot. Really hot. Temperatures in mid-August will be in the mid- to upper nineties, with high humidity. Use sunscreen, stay hydrated, find shade—or better yet, air-conditioning.

2. There will be crowds! Tens of thousands of people descend on Memphis every year during Elvis Week, including fans from abroad. And they will be everywhere—Beale Street, Sun Studio, Memphis Zoo, favorite restaurants—at all the local attractions, not just at Graceland. But it's a great chance to meet and chat with people from around the world. (Don't tell anyone if you're not an Elvis fan; keep that your little secret!)

3. There will be some people dressed as Elvis, at every age and stage of his career, walking the streets and dining in restaurants.

4. Hotels fill up. Make reservations early.

5. The biggest event of Elvis Week (sometimes referred to as "Death Week" by locals) is the Candlelight Vigil. On the night of August 15 each year, after an opening ceremony, hosted by Priscilla or Lisa Marie Presley at the gates of Graceland, fans walk up the drive and file past Elvis's grave in the Meditation Garden. An estimated seventy-five thousand people have taken part in this event in recent years. Fans begin lining up early in the day for the procession, where people carry candles and place wreaths near the gravesite as they pay their respects.

If you enjoyed *Til Death Do Us Party*,
be sure not to miss any of
Vickie Fee's Liv and Di in Dixie Mystery series,
including

ONE FETE IN THE GRAVE

Party planner Liv McKay has outdone herself this
time. She's put together an unforgettable
Fourth of July celebration for the town of
Dixie, Tennessee—including breathtaking
fireworks and an exciting Miss Dixie Beauty
Pageant. Maybe a little too exciting.

As the party is winding down, Liv's sense of
triumph fizzles when the body of town
councilman Bubba Rowland is discovered
on the festival grounds. And now the prime
suspect in his murder is Liv's mother's fiancé,
Earl, who had a flare-up recently with Bubba.
To clear Earl's name, Liv and her best friend Di
burst into action to smoke out the real killer
before another life is extinguished . . .

Keep reading for a special excerpt.

A Kensington mass-market paperback and eBook
on sale now!

There were a series of deafening explosions. Babies were crying. A dog was howling. And out of the corner of my eye, I could see the outline of a man, no doubt intoxicated, relieving himself in the bushes.

It was the annual Fourth of July fireworks celebration in Dixie, Tennessee, capping off a daylong festival.

I was lying on a blanket next to my husband, watching the pyrotechnic display. The fireworks were being ignited in a field just the other side of Tiptoe Creek, which runs through Centennial Park. Balls of fire raced through the night sky directly overhead looking as if they would fall on us and set the crowd ablaze.

Larry Joe reached into the ice chest, pulled out an unlabeled brown bottle, and popped it open. If anyone asked, he'd say it was root beer. It wasn't root beer. But alcoholic beverages were technically illegal in the public park. On holidays, the law turned a blind eye to such infractions, as long as people made an effort to be discreet.

He tilted the bottle toward me in a gesture that asked, "Want one?" I shook my head. Words would be useless at this point competing with the ear-piercing explosions, now being accompanied by the high school band playing a John Philip Sousa tune. The fireworks show had started tentatively with lapses between the colorful explosions and crescendoed to rapid-fire bursts stacked one upon another like a deck of cards.

An impressive multicolor firework erupted as the band reached a rousing conclusion. Everyone clapped and cheered. A moment later, an even more impressive display lit up the velvet sky. The crowd remained silent for a few seconds to see if this truly was the finale before bursting once again into cheers and applause.

Eventgoers started streaming toward the exits. The row of bouncy houses that had earlier been buoyant with the energy and laughter of children was now in various stages of deflation. The aroma of fried foods, from funnel cakes to pronto pups and catfish, clung to the humid air even as vendors packed it in and shuttered their walk-up service windows.

Larry Joe and I stood up and started gathering our blanket, ice chest, and other supplies: sunscreen, sunglasses, mosquito repellent.

Suddenly, a woman's scream pierced through the noise of the crowd. The clapping tapered off as the hysterical screaming persisted. Everyone looked around for the source. I could see Sheriff Eulyse

"Dave" Davidson and Deputy Ted Horton making their way to a row of porta potties beyond the vendor booths.

Helen Maples was standing outside one of the portable outhouses screaming her head off. I assumed she had entered the facilities and had an unfortunately intimate encounter with a snake or some such thing. But I was wrong.

The sheriff opened the door and there sat town councilman Bubba Rowland, with his pants around his ankles and a large red circle staining the front of his shirt.

This wasn't the first time Bubba had been caught with his pants down. But it certainly looked like it would be his last.

Deputy Ted closed the door on Bubba and started cordoning off the area around bathroom row. The sheriff spoke with some of the security volunteers and reserve deputies before making his way to the stage microphone. Dozens of people had clearly seen Bubba through the open door, and that information had spread like wildfire within moments, so Sheriff Dave didn't skirt the issue.

"We're investigating the death of Councilman Bubba Rowland," he said into the microphone. "Anyone who talked with Mr. Rowland, and, of course, anyone who noticed *anything* that seemed suspicious, make your way to the stage area so we can take your statements. Everyone else may leave in an orderly fashion, but please give your name and phone number to one of the volunteers who will be standing at the exits with clipboards to take your information. Thank you."

Dave came down the stage steps and made a beeline to where I was standing. He nodded to Larry Joe before turning his attention to me.

"Liv McKay, you're up first on the interview list."

"Why me?"

"Because every time a dead body shows up in this town you're within spitting distance of it. And for once I'd like to ask you some questions before you launch your own little investigation."

I opened my mouth to protest that accusation, but he cut me off.

"And . . . since you were the events coordinator for the festival, you're probably in the best position to fill me in on any incidents or unpleasantness that went down today. I'm especially interested in anything that involved Bubba Rowland, as you might expect."

Larry Joe started to walk away, but Dave stopped him.

"Larry Joe, just a couple of quick questions while I've got you here."

"Okay, shoot."

"Have you been around the festival much today? Did you help out in any particular area?"

"No, this was Liv's baby. I was at work most of the day. I did stop by and eat lunch here on the grounds with Liv and I came back shortly before the fireworks show tonight. I was here at the park for a while last night helping them set up the stage."

"Did you have any conversations with Bubba Rowland today?"

"No. He waved at me as I walked through from the

parking lot this evening and I returned the favor," Larry Joe said.

"All right, thanks. I think we're good."

Larry Joe wandered off to start picking up litter on the festival grounds.

"Okay, Mrs. McKay, follow me."

Generally, Dave calls me "Mrs. McKay" only when he's interrogating me. I'm not sure why he calls my husband "Larry Joe" during questioning, but I'm always "Mrs. McKay" when someone drops dead in my vicinity.

I fished a Diet Coke out of the ice chest at my feet, trailed Dave to the stage area, and took a seat in one of the folding chairs.

"That big bloodstain on Bubba's shirt makes natural causes seem unlikely," I said. "Is it too much to hope it was suicide?"

"Not unless Bubba managed to shoot himself in the back," Dave said. "There's a bullet hole through the back of the porta john. My best guess is someone with a rifle positioned themself in that strip of woods," Dave said, motioning toward a stand of trees and underbrush.

"You've been here pretty much all day, right?" Dave asked.

I nodded before adding, "Feels longer."

"So tell me every time you remember seeing Bubba today and who was with him at the time."

"We started things off with the 5K run. I'm pretty sure Bubba wasn't here for that," I said, envisioning the overweight councilman with a limp, who kept putting off knee-replacement surgery.

I related to Dave what I remembered about an

altercation between Bubba and the man who was
running against him for his seat on the town council
in the upcoming election. Webster Flack is a staunch
conservationist who represents a passionate group
of protesters with ecological concerns about a pro-
posed residential/commercial development. Bubba
had strongly advocated for the development, in
which—not coincidentally—he was one of the major
investors. Flack and his placard-toting followers had
recently picketed in front of Bubba's building supply
company and were strongly suspected of leaving
behind some unflattering graffiti on the side of the
building.

Flack had rented a booth at the festival, as had
other candidates running for the council. Difference being, instead of just passing out pamphlets
that touted his stellar attributes and qualifications,
Flack had additional literature, signs, and posters
pointing out Bubba's many moral shortcomings.
Bubba naturally took issue with this and the two
men had had a loud and ugly name-calling con-
frontation, followed by some chest-thumping.

"Your deputy broke it up before any punches
were thrown," I said. "I overheard bits and pieces,
but Ted could give you more details."

"All right," Dave said, scribbling something on
his notepad. "Who else did you see talk to Bubba?"

"Bubba spoke to half the people at the festival at
some point," I said incredulously. "He was in full-on
campaign mode, shaking hands and kissing babies."
After pausing to think for a moment, I said, "Oh,
there was some unpleasantness with Bubba over the
Miss Dixie Beauty Pageant results."

"I heard some people thought Cassie Latham

should have won," Dave said. "What did Bubba have to do with it?"

"I heard part of a conversation Pageant Director Rosemary Dell had with Bubba," I said. "She started out talking in a hushed tone, but she looked livid. As I walked past, she was giving him a piece of her mind in a very loud stage whisper. Apparently she overheard part of a conversation Bubba had with one of the judges and accused him of trying to influence the outcome of the pageant in favor of his niece, Jennifer Rowland—who ended up winning, as you know."

"When was this?" Dave asked.

"Shortly before the pageant started."

"And where were they?"

"Standing near the contestants' tent."

"What's your take on the accusation? You think there's anything to it?"

"I don't know if Bubba interfered with the judging or not. I do know that I felt certain Cassie would be the hands-down winner after the talent portion. I think most other people did, too. Did you hear her performance?"

"No, I can't say that I did."

"Jennifer Rowland played a number on the piano that any third-year piano student could have managed. Cassie, on the other hand, sang a song she wrote herself that I believe could land her a recording contract in Nashville if the right person heard it."

Dave made another entry in his notepad.

"Do you know if Cassie or her family has lodged a formal complaint? Did you hear anybody else take issue with the pageant results publicly?"

"I don't know about anything official, but later, after the pageant, Lynn Latham, Cassie's mother, had a tearful encounter with Bubba. She walked past me crying, and obviously drunk. I didn't hear much of what she said to Bubba except, 'Why?' Bubba, talking loud enough that I could hear him from a distance, was acting solicitous and told her he understood she was disappointed, but she should be proud that her daughter was named first runner-up.

"I think someone must have gone and found Lynn's mama and alerted her to the situation, because in a minute Nonie Jones came over and said something to Lynn before putting her arm around her and leading her daughter away."

"When and where was this?"

"This was maybe an hour or so after the pageant results were announced," I said. "Lynn came up to Bubba. He was standing by the Coca-Cola stand with a bunch of other men, sipping Cokes spiked with whiskey from under the counter."

I sat back and massaged my temples. I had a throbbing headache.

"I can't really think of anything else at the moment. It's been a long day," I said.

"Okay. Thank you, Mrs. McKay," Dave said. "Go home and get some sleep. But come by the office sometime tomorrow afternoon, so we can continue our little chat."

Apparently, Sunday was not going to be a day of rest for me.

"You're too good to me," I said, before turning to walk back to where we'd left the ice chest, blanket, and other items on the grass.

I scanned the park and waved to Larry Joe to signal I was ready to leave. Since we had driven separate vehicles, I assumed Larry Joe had hung around only to see if I needed help with anything. He came over and took charge of the ice chest, while I gathered up the blanket and other small items. I'd have to come back tomorrow to make sure everything was cleaned up and hauled away, but I was more than ready to call it a day.

When Mayor Virgil Haynes had asked me to take on the job of event coordinator for this year's Fourth of July festival my gut instinct was to say "no." I should have listened to my gut. I honestly tried to say no, in a roundabout way. I quoted a price for my services as a professional planner that I believed the town council would never go for. They approved it without batting an eye. That should have been a warning.

I was serenaded by cicadas as I walked to my car. Past ten-thirty, the air was still thick with humidity and my SUV, which had been parked in the sun all afternoon, was stuffy and hot when I opened the door and climbed in. I started the engine and cranked up the air-conditioning. In the enclosed car, I was overwhelmed by the scent of mosquito repellent I had liberally doused on myself. Summer in Dixie—and all across the South— means heat, humidity and mosquitoes. With two reported cases of West Nile virus and one case of Zika virus in western Tennessee so far this season, local stores were selling a lot of DEET.

Once I made it past the traffic leaving the festival area, the streets were dark and quiet as I drove the short distance to our house on Elm Street.

I was dead on my feet by the time I made it home. But my shoulders were aching and my head was throbbing. I took some aspirin and told Larry Joe, who had made it home just ahead of me, that I was going to take a quick shower.

I pinned up my cocker spaniel blond hair, as my mama has dubbed my dishwater blond locks, because I didn't think I could stay awake long enough to blow-dry it. I stripped and stepped into the downstairs shower—the only working shower in the slightly dilapidated Victorian we call home, which is in the midst of never-ending renovations.

The hot water from the massage showerhead pelted against my neck and shoulders, smoothing out the kinks. The aspirin had helped my headache, as well. I slipped on a nightshirt that was hanging on the hook and slowly ascended the stairs to the bedroom. I crawled into bed with Larry Joe, who woke up just long enough to lean over to kiss me before rolling over and snoring like a bear. I was too tired for the snoring to bother me. I was asleep almost as soon as I closed my eyes. During the night I awoke in a sweat when the image of Bubba Rowland's blood-soaked shirt invaded my dreams.

Follow P.I. Savannah Reid
with
G.A. McKevett